Summer Escapes on the Scottish Isle

Lilac Mills lives on a Welsh mountain with her very patient husband and incredibly sweet dog, where she grows veggies (if the slugs don't get them), bakes (badly) and loves making things out of glitter and glue (a mess, usually). She's been an avid reader ever since she got her hands on a copy of *Noddy Goes to Toytown* when she was five, and she once tried to read everything in her local library starting with A and working her way through the alphabet. She loves long, hot summer days and cold winter ones snuggled in front of the fire, but whatever the weather she's usually writing or thinking about writing, with heartwarming romance and happy-ever-afters always on her mind.

Also by Lilac Mills

Summer on the Turquoise Coast
Love in the City by the Sea
The Cosy Travelling Christmas Shop

Tanglewood Village series

The Tanglewood Tea Shop
The Tanglewood Flower Shop
The Tanglewood Wedding Shop
The Tanglewood Bookshop

Island Romance

Sunrise on the Coast
Holiday in the Hills
Sunset on the Square

Applewell Village

Waste Not, Want Not in Applewell
Make Do and Mend in Applewell
A Stitch in Time in Applewell

Foxmore Village

The Corner Shop on Foxmore Green
The Christmas Fayre on Holly Field
The Allotment on Willow Tree Lane

Coorie Castle Crafts

Surprises on the Scottish Isle
Summer Escapes on the Scottish Isle

LILAC MILLS

Summer Escapes ON THE Scottish Isle

CANELO

First published in the United Kingdom in 2025 by

Canelo, an imprint of
Canelo Digital Publishing Limited,
20 Vauxhall Bridge Road,
London SW1V 2SA
United Kingdom

A Penguin Random House Company

The authorised representative in the EEA is Dorling Kindersley Verlag
GmbH. Arnulfstr. 124, 80636 Munich, Germany

Copyright © Lilac Mills 2025

The moral right of Lilac Mills to be identified as the creator of this work has
been asserted in accordance with the Copyright, Designs and Patents Act,
1988.

All rights reserved. No part of this publication may be reproduced or
transmitted in any form or by any means, electronic or mechanical,
including photocopy, recording, or any information storage and retrieval
system, without permission in writing from the publisher.

No part of this book may be used or reproduced in any manner for the
purpose of training artificial intelligence technologies or systems. In
accordance with Article 4(3) of the DSM Directive 2019/790, Canelo
expressly reserves this work from the text and data mining exception.

A CIP catalogue record for this book is available from the British Library.

Print ISBN 978 1 80032 890 7
Ebook ISBN 978 1 80032 889 1

This book is a work of fiction. Names, characters, businesses, organizations,
places and events are either the product of the author's imagination or are
used fictitiously. Any resemblance to actual persons, living or dead, events
or locales is entirely coincidental.

Cover design by Head Design

Printed and bound in Great Britain by Clays Ltd, Elcograf S.p.A.

Look for more great books at
www.canelo.co
www.dk.com

Prologue

Freya Sinclair watched the wind snatch the ashes, sucking them greedily into the air, and she prayed that her mother's soul flew with them. Most landed in the loch, lying on the water's rippling surface like a shroud, but some drifted upwards, and it was these last few fragments which held Freya's anguished gaze.

It was hard to see clearly through her tears. They welled and fell in a steady trickling stream she feared might never end. She seemed to have been crying forever.

Her father stood resolute and grim by her side, holding the now empty urn in his hands. A private moment: they were the only two to witness the scattering of Sandra Sinclair's ashes. They were the only two who mattered. Freya's mother would have loved the turnout for the brief service in the kirk, but she would have loved this intimate goodbye even more.

Her wishes had been explicit and simple: *When I'm done with this world, give me to the loch.*

Already the fine film of ashes on the surface of the water was dispersing, the last vestiges being carried out to sea by the retreating tide. Soon they would be gone, and Freya didn't know what she was going to do or how she would cope now that her mother was no more.

She wanted to wait until every speck had disappeared, but her father drew her away with an arm around her shoulders.

'It's done, hen. It's over.' His voice broke and she bit back a sob.

It didn't feel over. To Freya, it felt as though it was beginning. She would have to live in a world without her mother. How could such a thing be possible?

She put her head on her father's shoulder and, arms around each other, they made their way along the rocky shoreline.

Once, she lifted her head and looked back. She didn't know what she was hoping to see – a sign that her mum wasn't truly gone, perhaps? But there was only the swell of the waves and the call of a wheeling gull.

All that was left was the memory of her mother... *Promise me...*

And Freya *had* promised, because what else could she do?

'Have you got everything?'

'Yes, Dad.'

'Are you sure?'

'They do have shops in London, you know.'

'I don't want you to have to buy anything if you can take it with you.'

Freya was fairly sure she wouldn't need the spanner set he'd tried to foist on her, or the spirit level. She was going to college to study ceramics, not construction. And if there was any DIY to be done in the halls of residence, she was sure the uni would have maintenance staff for that.

'I can't fit anything else in the car,' she said.

'I wish you could fit *me* in it,' her dad grumbled. 'I don't like the thought of you driving all that way on your own. You're not used to motorways.'

'Neither are you.' Skye was motorway-free, and her father rarely left the island. By road, that is: he left it most days by water because he had a trawler just up the way on Muirporth Quay. Thankfully, he fished the loch and not the open sea beyond, but her mum nevertheless worried every time he went out.

Had worried.

Freya swallowed, the ever-present grief threatening to erupt into tears.

'I'm going out for a bit,' she said.

This was her last day in Duncoorie; she would leave in the morning. With everything packed, apart from the clothes she would be wearing for the journey and a few toiletries, there was nothing left to do. She couldn't breathe in the house. Every nook and cranny reminded her of Mum. Everywhere she looked, everything she touched was awash with memories of her, and suddenly Freya had to escape. But not to the loch. She hadn't been down to the water's edge since...

She didn't want to speak to anyone or see anyone, and the hillside was the best place to avoid people. There was only so much sympathy and pity she could take. Besides, she'd said goodbye to everyone, apart from her father. The hardest goodbye had been the most final and had broken her heart. It was a goodbye she'd had to say, because there was no arguing with death. Every other parting paled in comparison.

The path was steep, the gradient making her thighs cry out for mercy as she stomped upwards, breathing hard. With the need to escape her grief driving her onwards and upwards, Freya pushed herself to her limit. Her misery was making the climb more brutal, but she had to reach the top one last time.

She would be able to see more clearly up there.

Maybe she'd be able to see her future, because right now a future without her mother in it was a dark and frightening place. But she'd made a promise, and she intended to keep it.

Fly, little one, promise me you'll fly. They were her mother's last words, before the pain meds had stolen her voice and before death had silenced her for eternity.

Gasping, Freya battled on, almost bent double, her hands on her thighs helping to push her legs up the path. She didn't stop to catch her breath, she didn't pause to take in the view, and her attention didn't veer from the narrow trail through the heather and tussocky grasses as she focused on the next step and the next.

Finally, she reached the top and only then did she allow herself to stop.

Collapsing on a boulder, her chest heaving, her legs weak and aching, she sat on the sun-warmed rock and gazed down at the home she would be leaving behind.

Coorie Castle, with its white walls shimmering in the late-afternoon sunlight, was the most prominent feature. Built on a rocky outcrop some eight hundred years ago, it gave the village of Duncoorie its name.

Beyond it lay the loch, its waters a deep unfathomable indigo with ribbons of navy, cobalt and sapphire. And near the shore, where the sea was shallower, the water swirled in swathes of turquoise and green.

The mountains on the opposite shore were purpled with heather and looked almost dove-grey in the distance. Overhead, wisps of white cirrus clouds feathered the sky.

Freya felt so small up here, insignificant in the face of the vastness of nature, yet Duncoorie was an anchor she was about to set herself adrift from.

It was both terrifying and exhilarating.

As her eyes roamed over the village, her gaze was caught by the old stone kirk with its spire and vaulted windows, and she remembered the sombre tones of the vicar as he asked the congregation to pray for her mother's soul.

'Oh, Mum…' she whispered. It was a familiar refrain. Since her mother's death, she'd found herself saying it often, the rest of the sentence always choked by grief and regret.

Freya was keeping her promise.

Against the odds, she'd obtained a place at one of the best art colleges in the world. She was going to follow her dreams and make a name for herself.

She had also promised her mum that she wouldn't mourn her, that she would move beyond grief, but how could she do that when everything here reminded her of her loss?

London was a new beginning, a new life. And in that city where no one knew her, she hoped she would be able to keep that promise, too.

Chapter 1

15 years later

'Fantastic turnout, Freya,' a man she didn't recognise said.

'Congratulations. Your best work yet!' A woman placed a hand on Freya's shoulder as she eased through the crowded art gallery, and Freya smiled politely.

'Give me a call and we'll chat about commissioning some pieces, yeah?' someone else told her, and Freya barely had time to register who they were before they'd gone.

'Here.' Sean Pickles, the vice chancellor of the prestigious London art college where Freya taught ceramics, handed her a half-filled fluted glass of pale liquid.

Freya sipped it gratefully, the bubbles of the sparkling wine tickling the back of her throat. 'Thanks, I needed this.'

Sean gazed around the gallery with a satisfied smile. After all, having one of his staff be the draw for a successful exhibition would help enormously with the profile of the college.

He said, 'It was a good idea of yours to combine three strands with the same theme. It makes for a cohesive message. The punters seem to like it.'

'The punters' were her peers and colleagues in the art world, as well as a carefully curated selection of the press, businesspeople, critics, and patrons of the college. So far, the exhibition appeared to be a roaring success, with each of the three artists showcased (Freya being the most well-known) receiving enthusiastic praise.

The title of the event was *Colour in Motion*, and the three strands of artwork complemented each other. Several large and striking oil-on-canvas paintings adorned the gallery's plain white walls, and fabrics created by an up-and-coming textile designer were draped and folded to show off their jewelled colours. Freya's ceramic pieces were placed at strategic points in between to bring the elements together.

A man caught her eye as he approached, and she recognised him by his purple goatee as the renowned critic Gustav Horn.

'Freya, my darling, so lovely to meet you at last,' he gushed. 'I've been a fan of your work for some time.' He held out a hand, and she shook it.

'Nice to meet you, Mr Horn,' she replied.

He offered her a humble smile, as though surprised she knew his name, even though he expected everyone at the exhibition to have heard of him.

'Call me Gustav.' He scanned the room, before his gaze returned to her. 'How does it feel to be called the *new Betty Woodman*?'

'An honour I don't deserve,' she replied honestly.

'Come now, you're being modest.'

She actually wasn't. Betty Woodman was one of the most important ceramicists in post-war America, her work inspiring a whole generation of potters due to her innovative and original use of colour and form. Freya's work didn't come close.

The critic was scrutinising her. 'You *mean* it,' he declared, sounding surprised. 'How very refreshing.'

'Freya isn't one to blow her own trumpet,' the vice chancellor said.

Gustav Horn blinked, as though he had only just noticed him. 'And you are…?' He shook his head and wafted a hand in the air. 'Never mind. It was a pleasure to meet you, Freya.'

'You too, Gustav,' she said. Freya watched him work his way through the crowd, bemused.

An arm encircled her waist as Hadrian, her significant other, appeared at her side. 'Was that Gustav Horn?'

'It was.'

'What did he say? Did he like the exhibition?'

Sean offered Hadrian his hand. 'Hadrian, how are you? Gustav was most complimentary.'

Hadrian smiled. 'So he should be. Freya's work is outstanding.' He leant in and kissed her hair, just above her ear. Only she could hear him whisper, 'You look gorgeous.'

She inclined her head. 'Thank you, kind sir.'

'I can't wait to get you out of that dress,' he murmured, his breath tickling her skin.

She edged away, knowing she wasn't going to be in the mood for bedtime antics when all this was done.

Hadrian snagged another glass of bubbly. It was the fourth one she'd seen him drink, but he may well have had more. If he carried on at this rate, even if he did manage to get her out of the dress, he wouldn't be capable of doing anything.

Freya couldn't wait to take the dress off either, but for a different reason. Although she scrubbed up well enough when she had to, cocktail dresses and heels weren't her preferred attire. Freya was happiest in dungarees and Doc Martens, with an apron on top to protect her old, worn clothes. She'd dressed up this evening because it was expected, but she didn't feel comfortable.

Her boyfriend, however, did. He was clad in an expensive navy suit, loafers and a crisp white shirt which was open at the neck. Designer stubble, carefully tended, graced his chin, and his dark brown hair curled artfully over his forehead.

'Look at you!' someone cried, and Freya turned to see Wanda, the chancellor's PA, walking towards her.

Wanda held out both hands and Freya grasped them with a smile. She was touched and humbled that so many of her college colleagues had shown up this evening, considering today was the last day of the academic year and the summer break would start tomorrow.

'Congratulations,' Wanda said. 'I've heard nothing but good things. You must be so proud.'

Freya was. She'd put her heart and soul into it. Her best items were on display and even though this was only the opening night, she was delighted to see quite a few sold stickers on her work, as well as that of the other two artists.

But she was also so done with it. The exhibition was the culmination of months of work, and she was ready for a new challenge. What form that challenge would take, Freya had yet to determine.

It seemed greedy to want more, though. After all, she had not one, but *two* dream jobs. She held a professorship at one of the top universities in the world, and she also made a decent living from doing what she loved: pottery. Not only that, she lived in an airy apartment in a converted warehouse and had a seriously handsome boyfriend.

Hadrian had wandered off, probably to do some networking. He was ambitious and hungry for success, and sometimes (very occasionally) Freya got the impression he was envious of her. He needn't be, because he certainly had talent. His speciality was abstract expressionism, and his paintings were in the style of Jackson Pollock. But what he lacked, Freya thought, was the passion and determination to succeed. If Freya could, she would spend every second of every hour in her studio. Hadrian, although dedicated to his art, wasn't driven in the way she was, and she suspected he preferred the hype that went with being an artist to knuckling down to the task of producing said art. She'd once heard someone unkindly call him an 'art groupie', and while she hated the term, it did have a ring of truth to it.

As she strolled around the series of interconnecting rooms, Freya couldn't understand why she felt so restless this evening. She'd worked so hard and for so long on the pieces for this exhibition, that she'd have thought she would be ecstatic that it was the opening night. But she felt oddly flat.

Was it because she needed a new challenge, a new creative direction? Or was it simply the result of being so intensely focused over these past few months that now the exhibition was up and running, such intense focus was no longer needed?

She became aware of a woman staring intently at her and smiled uncertainly, wondering whether she'd seen her before.

The woman approached and when she was close enough, she asked in an American accent, 'Freya Sinclair?'

'That's me,' Freya replied.

The woman said, 'I love your work. It's so innovative – the shape and form, and those colours.' She fanned herself and fluttered her lashes. 'It makes me giddy with excitement.'

Freya blinked in surprise. She didn't think her ceramics had ever made anyone *giddy* before, but she was happy to accept the compliment. She took great delight in making a pot, a bowl, a vase, a platter – whatever the size and shape – and contorting it. The inspiration came from her native Scotland (the Isle of Skye, to be exact) and the swirling colours emphasised the flowing lines of her ceramics. It was what she was renowned for.

'Can I give you this?' The woman pressed a business card into Freya's hand.

Freya glanced at it and her eyes widened. 'Jocasta Black? That's *you*?' Gosh! No wonder she'd thought the woman looked familiar. Jocasta Black was the founder of the Black and White Art Academy in New York, which was considered *the* top place in the world to study ceramics.

Freya looked up from the card to examine the woman properly. She'd seen photos of her, but Jocasta was less flamboyant in real life: a toned-down version who wasn't wearing one of her signature scarves.

'It's lovely to meet you,' Freya said weakly, glancing around to check Hadrian's whereabouts. He was nowhere to be seen, and she felt relieved, although she couldn't pinpoint why. It was something to unpick later. Right now, she needed her wits about her if she wasn't to make a fool of herself.

Jocasta's eyes were boring into hers, and Freya shifted uncomfortably; such intense scrutiny was making her self-conscious.

Jocasta nodded as though agreeing with an unspoken statement. Then she said, 'I've got a proposition for you.'

Not many people would understand why, when given the opportunity to purchase the top-floor apartment of a converted warehouse in Fulham, Freya had opted for the ground floor, especially since the ground-floor flat had been only marginally less expensive.

Another potter would, though. Her kiln was heavy and dangerous, and needed adequate ventilation.

The ground floor of the former warehouse had an exterior brick building which was large enough to house her studio, and Freya had paid over the odds to purchase it along with the flat. To her, it had been worth every penny, especially since she'd been able to knock a doorway through to it, connecting the two together. The two areas often became blurred. Several times Hadrian had quipped that Freya's apartment could be better described as a pottery studio with a bed in it, rather than a flat with a separate studio. She didn't think he had been joking. If it wasn't for the invasive clay dust, which could get everywhere if she wasn't scrupulous about cleanliness, she had a suspicion she may well have set up her bed next to the kiln. As it was, her open-plan living space was littered with photos, sketches and paintings: the 2D ideas behind her 3D creations.

Many of the completed pieces found their way from her studio to her flat, where they were photographed and packed, although it was rare that she sold directly from her website. Most of her work was sold through galleries and upmarket shops. Increasingly, she did commissioned pieces, but she often found it too restricting. Freya had to make what was in her heart, not what was in someone else's head.

Right now, her heart was in turmoil and it had nothing to do with Hadrian.

After being approached by Jocasta Black, Freya had found it difficult to enjoy the remainder of the opening night and had decided to leave. She hadn't left with Hadrian, though. Despite having told her that he couldn't wait to take her dress off, he hadn't appeared to be too put out when she'd informed him that she was tired and just wanted to crash out.

He hadn't seemed put out *at all*, in fact. When she'd found him, he'd been deep in conversation with a journalist who was known for his scathing reviews.

Freya had briefly kissed Hadrian, then silently wished him luck as she made her way to the door. She'd learnt early on in her career that sucking up to journalists and critics rarely did any good. Friendly and polite, with the same degree of wariness that you'd reserve for a wasp, was Freya's preferred method of dealing with them.

She was stripping off almost before she'd got through the door to her flat. By the time she'd reached her bedroom, her shoes had been kicked off and her dress was a puddle of emerald silk in the sitting room.

Thirty seconds later she had pulled a T-shirt over her head, had donned a faded pair of dungarees and had shoved her feet into a pair of Crocs. The only remnant of the evening was the make-up she still wore, as she scooped up her bright chestnut hair and tied it on top of her head with a pink bandana.

Working with clay always soothed her, and tonight she needed to be soothed. Freya's mind was racing, her thoughts all over the place, and she needed the serenity of her studio to calm her. The repetition of familiar movements as she unwrapped the lump of clay and tore off a piece had an instant effect, and she let out a slow breath as she began to focus.

But no sooner had she slapped the clay on the wheel, her hands wet, her foot on the pedal, than Jocasta Black's words slipped into her head – *'I've got a proposition for you...'*

New York. Was this the new challenge she had been hankering after? Or was it a step too far? She loved her job at the college, and she adored her flat and studio.

And what about Hadrian? How would she feel about leaving him behind?

As she dug her thumb into the spinning ball of clay and gently pulled, drawing the material up, she let out a muted snort as she realised that she'd put him third on the list of things she would miss if she moved to New York.

Thankfully, she didn't have to decide just yet. She had a couple of weeks. She'd give it time to cure, time for the offer of working as a course director in the New York academy to sink in, time to think about it rationally – because right now her heart was screaming yes.

When Freya sliced through the base of the final vase and lifted the piece off the wheel, it was light outside. She'd worked through the night, and she was utterly exhausted.

After scrupulously cleaning her equipment and the area around the wheel (she would never, ever leave her space in a mess), she closed the door on the studio and dug something out of the freezer to reheat, eating it slumped over the table, barely able to keep her eyes open.

She desperately needed sleep. A shower first, though.

With a face scrubbed clean of make-up and her hair damp at the neck, Freya climbed into bed and fell into a dreamless sleep, only to be woken several hours later by a phone call.

The news wasn't good.

Chapter 2

Freya was lucky to have found a parking space, and she drove the rental car into an empty bay just seconds ahead of another driver, who had spotted it at the same time as she had. In no mood for the sour look the driver gave her, she switched off the engine and leant her head against the back of the seat.

She was exhausted and close to tears. A fall, the hospital had said. Being transferred to Raigmore Hospital in Inverness, they'd said. He needed an operation, they'd said.

It's what they *hadn't* said that concerned Freya. Skye's Broadford Hospital had an Accident and Emergency department which was perfectly adequate for minor injuries. But her father had been taken to the hospital in Inverness instead, which told her that his fall was definitely something to worry about, so she had thrown some clothes and toiletries into a suitcase and dashed to the airport. Flying was the fastest way to get to Inverness from London.

She had repeatedly phoned her dad on his mobile but hadn't been able to get an answer. While she'd waited for her flight to be called, she'd paced up and down, hoping to be connected to someone in Raigmore Hospital who could tell her what was going on, but all they'd been prepared to say was that he was out of surgery and was comfortable.

Gathering herself, Freya climbed out of the car and headed for the main entrance, and as she walked through the doors, she was hit with the same feeling of dread and grief that she'd had the first time she'd visited her mother in hospital. That feeling had never gone away, and just the sight of those clinical corridors was enough to make her stomach churn and her heart race.

Taking a deep, calming breath, she went in search of the lifts. *He'll be OK, he'll be OK*, she chanted silently.

She'd been saying the same thing over and over, all the way from London, but she hadn't managed to convince herself yet. The only way she would be convinced was by seeing him.

It took her a while to locate the correct ward, and when she did, she found her dad in a bed near the window. His eyes were closed, and she took a moment to compose herself. He looked grey and drawn, his hair whiter than the last time she'd seen him, his cheeks more lined. He had a drip in his left hand.

She would find someone to give her an update of his condition, then she'd sit with him until they threw her out.

'Are you a relative?' a nurse enquired when Freya asked for information.

'I'm his daughter. Broadford rang me this morning to say he'd had a fall and was being transferred here because he needed an operation. They told me he'd broken his hip.' Dad was seventy-four, and she was aware that fractured hips were more common the older you got. But surely he wasn't *that* old? 'How did it happen, do you know?' she asked.

'I'm not sure.' The nurse touched her lightly on the arm. 'He's doing OK; try not to worry. I expect you've got loads of questions, but it's best to ask the doctor when she does her rounds in the morning. You should be able to catch her between nine and ten o'clock.'

'Right. Thanks. I'll… um…' Freya pointed to the ward, smiled uncertainly, then went back to sit with her sleeping father.

'I told them not to bother you.'

Freya jerked up at the sound of her father's creaky voice, wincing when her neck went into a spasm at the sudden movement. Scrambling to her feet, she leant over him.

'Dad,' she murmured, relieved to see him awake and looking more like his old self. Some of the colour had returned to his face and his cheeks didn't look as sunken. 'I'm glad they did.'

'What day is it?'

It took Freya a moment to remember. Was it only yesterday evening that she'd been feted at her own exhibition? It seemed like weeks ago. 'Thursday.'

He licked his lips, his eyes drifting shut once more, and she wondered whether she should call anyone. 'Wait there, Dad. I'll go find someone.'

He opened an eye. 'Hen, I'm not going anywhere. Did they tell you I've fractured my hip? What a silly billy, eh?'

She shook her head. 'How did it happen?'

'Och, you know. Lost my balance.' He swallowed. 'Is there any water?'

There was a plastic jug on a table next to the bed and as Freya picked it up, he grasped her hand and she was alarmed at how weak his grip was.

'And painkillers,' he said, discomfort etched on his face.

When she returned to tell him that a nurse would be along shortly with some tablets, he appeared to be asleep, but he opened his eyes when she touched his arm.

After the nurse had given him his pills, Freya sat with him for a while, watching him sleep, but when he stirred, she said, 'I've got to go. I'll be back in the morning. I want to be here when the doctor does her rounds.'

Panic flared in his eyes and she guessed the reason. 'I can't stay much longer,' she told him. 'I've got to find a bed for the night.' Hoping to lighten his mood, she added, 'It's all right for you, you've got somewhere to sleep.'

To her dismay, his eyes filled with tears and guilt engulfed her. This wasn't the time for levity. Her poor dad had been through an ordeal, and all she could do was *joke* about it?

'I'm sorry, Dad, that was insensitive.' She rubbed the back of her hand across her forehead, holding back tears.

'I'm the one who should be sorry, hen. I didn't want to drag you all this way. I asked them not to bother you.'

'They were right to phone me,' Freya said once again. She narrowed her eyes. 'When exactly did you fall?'

'Tuesday night. I got up and went downstairs because I couldn't sleep, and tripped over my own feet. Rhona heard me calling when she let her cat out in the morning. She phoned for an ambulance, and they took me to Broadford.'

'Why didn't you ring me straight away or ask Rhona to?' she demanded, appalled to think that he'd been lying on the floor for hours and he'd had to pray that his next-door neighbour heard his calls for help. It broke her heart to think how much pain he'd been in, and how scared he must have been.

'I was hoping it wasn't too bad, but they did an X-ray and told me I needed to go to Raigmore because they couldn't do the surgery at Broadford.'

'But why didn't you ring me?' she persisted.

'My mobile's in the house, by my bed. I haven't got it with me.'

'Dad, that's no excuse. Thank God someone had the sense to call me.'

Her father's eyes were downcast, and she abruptly realised that the reason he hadn't wanted to 'bother her' was because he hadn't wanted to spoil the opening night of the exhibition. It pained her that he'd felt he wasn't able to call on her. It made her feel like the worst daughter in the world.

It didn't help that she lived so far away. It wasn't as though she could pop in every week to check on him. She relied on him to tell her how he was, in between visits.

Now wasn't the best time to have this out with him, but they'd definitely be having a wee chat once he was back on his feet again.

Freya sighed with exasperation. She could seriously do without a cross-examination from Hadrian.

'I don't know,' she replied. 'I've only just got here. Days, probably.'

'Days?'

'He's fractured his hip,' she repeated. Had her boyfriend not listened to a word she'd said?

She knew what was wrong with him – he was sulking because they were supposed to be going out to dinner tomorrow evening with someone Hadrian wanted to impress. What did he expect her to do? Hightail it back to London tonight?

'Yes, but *days*?' he repeated.

She huffed out an irritated breath. 'It could be longer.' Freya wouldn't know until she'd spoken with the doctor and found out how long her dad's recovery might take. 'Hang on, I'm putting you on speakerphone,' she said, and sat on the edge of the bed to undo the laces on her Doc Martens.

'Where are you exactly?' he asked.

'Inverness. I've just booked into a hotel for the night.'

'What are you doing in *Inverness*?'

Freya kicked her boots off. One of them flew across the room and landed with a thud. 'That's where my dad is.'

'I thought he lived on Skye?'

'He does.' She took pity on him and explained, 'Inverness is the nearest hospital to Skye that can perform hip operations.'

'But that's like a hundred miles away,' he protested, and she guessed he was looking it up as they spoke.

'The Highlands isn't like London. Look, I've got to go. I haven't eaten a thing all day and I need a shower.'

'I wish I could join you in it, babe.' He chuckled.

Freya rolled her eyes. 'Good night, Hadrian. I'll speak to you tomorrow.'

She ended the call and flopped back onto the bed. She was too worn out to move, but she knew she'd have to eat, and she would definitely feel better after a shower.

Thankfully, the hotel had room service. She'd have a quick shower, order some food, then settle down in bed and scour the internet. After all, forewarned is forearmed, and she wanted to find out as much as she could about fractured hips before she spoke with the doctor tomorrow.

Freya laid out the pyjamas and toiletries she'd bought for her dad, placing each one on his bed, hoping he'd approve.

'You shouldn't have,' he kept saying as she pulled each item out of the bag.

Thank goodness she'd found a supermarket nearby and had been able to drop in on the way to the hospital this morning. She'd noticed that he didn't have anything with him and, since he would probably be in hospital for a few days, she'd taken it upon herself to buy him some bits and bobs.

He touched the hem of the pyjama bottoms, and she noticed a tremor in his hand. The fall and subsequent operation had badly shaken him, she realised, her heart aching at how frail he seemed.

'I've arranged for a bouquet to be sent to Rhona,' she told him.

'That's nice. She'll like that. I'll thank her myself when I see her. I might even buy that cat of hers a little treat.' He closed his eyes, and Freya watched the rise and fall of his chest, wondering whether he had drifted off to sleep.

If he had, he soon came awake again when a nurse bustled in, wheeling some kind of contraption.

She smiled at Freya, then said, 'Right, Vinnie, let's take your vitals, shall we?' She picked up his hand, the one with the needle in the vein, and popped a peg on his index finger. 'Blood sats,' she explained, noticing Freya's concern. 'Oxygen levels.' She made a note of the results, then took his temperature and blood pressure.

'Is everything OK?' Freya asked anxiously.

'He's fine,' the nurse replied.

Freya was about to question her further when a small woman in a white coat walked onto the ward, trailing three people in her wake.

'Hello, Vincent,' she said. 'I'm Magda Poole, your consultant. We met yesterday, but don't worry if you can't remember – you were a bit out of it. I performed the surgery on your hip. Do you mind if I check your wound?'

Freya looked away until the consultant had finished her examination, not wanting to embarrass him.

Mrs Poole said, 'That's looking good. I'm pleased to say that the surgery went well.'

Thank goodness, Freya thought, breathing a sigh of relief. Her dad had a way to go before he was back on his feet again, but with some TLC from her, he should make a full recovery.

As the consultant was about to leave, her dad asked, 'How soon can I go home?'

Freya wanted to know the answer to that as well.

The consultant said, 'You do understand that a fractured hip is a serious injury, and although the procedure to repair it is a routine one, it's still a major operation. Recovery is likely to take several months. Your muscles, bones and ligaments need time to heal.' She pursed her lips. 'I expect you'll be here for ten to fourteen days, under the circumstances.'

Freya was dismayed. She'd hoped she could have taken him home in a couple of days. She could see the disappointment on his face, too.

The consultant hadn't finished. 'The physiotherapist will be along later to help you get out of bed, and we'll see how you progress from there. I want you to be able to get around with a walker before we discuss discharging you.'

Freya was horrified. 'You intend to get him out of bed *today*?'

'That's right. It'll help reduce the risk of chest infection and blood clots. The more mobile he is, the better.' She turned back to Freya's dad and said, 'An occupational therapist will speak to you about your home situation and will want to discuss your ability to manage. A broken hip is a serious injury, so you may well need extra help at home for some considerable time.'

After the consultant left, Freya knew she should have asked how long the 'considerable time' might be – but she was too scared of the answer.

Chapter 3

Mackenzie Burns ran a practised critical eye over the deck of the *Sea Serpent*. Whenever his boat was put to sea, he insisted on it being given a thorough hosing-down with fresh water as soon as it returned. Not only that, the head (or the loo, as customers called it) was scrubbed, any rubbish was removed, the cockpit was wiped down, and all the gauges were checked to ensure they were working and the engine was running smoothly.

Mack had already given the hull his customary once-over, scanning it for signs of wear and tear. To others, it might seem excessive to check it after every trip, but he liked being ahead of the game, hoping to spot minor problems quickly so they didn't become big, expensive issues further down the line.

After checking the oil, he asked Angus, one of his crew, to flush the engine with fresh water (salt water was incredibly corrosive), while he examined the anchor, the dock lines, and every other line and rope on board. His final task was to inspect the life jackets and buoys.

Mack was fanatical about the safety of his passengers and crew. Although it might be a pain in the backside after a long day out on the loch to then do all this cleaning and perform all these checks, it had to be done. He could go home, happy that the *Sea Serpent* would be ready to set sail tomorrow, when he had three more whale and dolphin trips lined up, all fully booked.

'See you tomorrow, Skip,' Angus said, giving him a mock salute as he leapt onto the quay.

Mack saluted him back, feeling faintly ridiculous. Anyone would think they were in the Navy! And if any of his crew (he had three people working for him on and off, depending on the time of year and the weather) said, 'Aye, aye, Cap'n,' he might just make them walk the plank. They were a good bunch, though, and he would struggle to run his business without them. If he saw them in the pub later, he'd do what he always did and buy them a pint or two.

Satisfied that he'd done everything that needed to be done, Mack ensured the boat was secure, then sauntered towards his truck and climbed in. He was looking forward to a shower, followed by some home-cooked food, courtesy of his mum. As far as he was concerned, nothing could beat his mum's cooking. He dropped in every Friday for his tea, and sometimes during the week as well.

He wondered what was on the menu tonight. Gossip, certainly, because his mum loved nothing better than to keep abreast of everything that went on in Duncoorie. His brother would probably get a couple of mentions too, usually in the form of nagging Mack as to, 'When are you going to find yourself a nice girl like Jinny?' Jinny was his brother's wife, and his mum loved her to bits.

Mack couldn't understand this drive to see him settle down that everyone seemed to have. It pained him that Cal, one of his best mates, had also joined the ranks of happy coupledom, and now was extolling its virtues and trying to get Mack all loved-up.

Mack wasn't having any of it. He was having too much fun being footloose and fancy-free. Besides, he'd done the serious relationship bit, and it hadn't ended well. There was no way he was going to risk being hurt a second time.

Forty minutes later, he was striding past a row of five terraced whitewashed cottages. His mother lived in the middle one. She'd moved in a few years back, after Mack had bought his own place, saying that the three-bed family home was too big for her and the wrap-around garden too much to cope with.

He had to admit that this cottage was rather cute. The two bedrooms were built into the loft, and although small, they were light and airy due to the skylights set into both sides of the grey slate roof. With a kitchen on one side of the little vestibule and a sitting room on the other, it was the perfect size for her.

When he entered the kitchen, his nose began working overtime as he sniffed the delicious aroma of frying sausages. His mum was at the stove, her face red from the heat, and she beamed when she saw him.

'What are we having?' he asked, giving her cheek a quick peck as he peered into a bubbling saucepan.

'Sausage and neeps.'

'And onion gravy?'

'You and your gravy.' Jean rolled her eyes. 'I'm mashing carrots in with the neeps.'

'Why?'

'Because you don't eat enough veg,' she said.

'Neeps is veg.'

'Swede only counts as *one* of your five a day.'

'Potatoes don't?' he teased, and she waved a spatula at him.

'Go lay the table, else I'll feed your sausages to the dog.'

Mack laughed out loud. 'We haven't got a dog.'

'The cat, then.'

'We don't have a cat either,' he pointed out, then hastily glanced around the kitchen in case his mother had suddenly acquired one.

'Rhona has, although it spends enough time in my house that it may as well be mine,' she replied.

Mack took some knives and forks out of the drawer and placed them on the table, while his mum drained the pan containing the swede, potatoes and carrots.

'Have you heard?' she asked.

Mack grinned. *Here we go*, he thought, *gossip time*. He supposed it was inevitable in a small place like Duncoorie, where everyone knew everyone else – unless they were tourists, of course. The village, along with the rest of Skye, had a fair number of those. And very glad he was too; tourists wanting to go whale and dolphin watching were what kept a roof over his head.

'Heard what?' he asked.

'Vinnie's had a fall.'

Mack pulled a sympathetic face. Vinnie Sinclair owned the end cottage two doors down. An elderly chap, he lived alone, his wife having passed away many years ago. He used to have a trawler operating out of the same quay where Mack moored his boat, but that was before Mack had started his whale-watching business.

'Is he OK?' he asked, pouring two glasses of water.

'Broken hip, Rhona reckons. She was the one who found him. Poor man had been lying on the kitchen floor for most of the night. She only heard him because that cat of hers was nagging to go out, otherwise he could still be there. She says they've transferred him to Inverness.'

Mack's heart went out to the old fella. It was awful what old age did to a person, and he thanked God that his mum was fit and healthy.

'Shall I mash the neeps?' he asked, selecting a masher from the rack of utensils on the wall.

'You're a good wee laddie.'

'*Wee?*' He laughed. He towered over his mother by about a foot.

'I'm just wondering how poor Vinnie will cope. He'll never manage on his own.' She reached up to pat him on the cheek. 'If anything happened to me, at least I've got you and Carter to look after me.'

Vinnie's daughter lived in London and had done so for years. She'd gone to university there and hadn't come back – not to live, anyway. Mack was aware that she visited her dad now and again, but he hadn't seen her since school.

As he tucked into his delicious tea, his thoughts lingered on Freya Sinclair and he idly wondered what she was doing now.

Mack supped the pint of dark ale and smacked his lips. He'd had a good day on the loch and a lovely meal that he hadn't had to cook himself (*Thanks, Mum*), and he was now enjoying a pint with his mates. Even though he had work tomorrow, Friday night down the pub was a symbolic start to his non-existent weekend.

The place was buzzing, full of locals and tourists alike, and he made his way towards a group in the corner, careful to ensure no one jogged his elbow.

He was pleased to see a good turnout, as not everyone could make it every Friday. His brother, Carter, was there with Jinny. So was his mate Cal along with his better half, Tara, plus a few of the people who worked at Coorie Castle.

Among them was Giselle, and as Mack approached the table, he gave her a speculative look. Would it be worth asking her out again?

'We've saved you a seat,' his sister-in-law said, removing her handbag from a chair as she noticed him.

'*Jinny* saved you a seat,' Carter said. 'If it was up to me, I wouldn't have bothered.' He smirked as Mack sat down.

'You're just jealous because Mum loves *me* best,' Mack shot back.

'You're mistaking love for pity, bro. She feels sorry for you.'

'You're not funny, you know.'

'My wife thinks I am.' Carter patted Jinny's knee.

'I really don't think she does,' Mack argued. 'She's just humouring you for an easy life.'

Jinny rolled her eyes and said, 'Don't involve me in your childishness.' She turned to the others. 'These two are worse than the kids. Speaking of kids... Calan, I thought this was your weekend to have Bonnie?'

Cal had a daughter who he looked after every other weekend. She was a sweet kid.

He shook his head. 'I had her two weekends on the trot because Yvaine and Lenn went to Liverpool for a city break.'

Jinny said, 'Katie will be disappointed; she was hoping to see her.'

Katie (Carter and Jinny's daughter) was another sweet kid. Mack quite enjoyed being an uncle, and he often took her and her younger brother out on the boat. Ted, especially, loved being on the loch, and Mack always found something his nephew could do so he felt 'part of the crew'.

As the conversation swirled around him, Mack caught Giselle's eye.

She smiled shyly, and he hoped it meant she was more receptive to his advances than she'd been the last time he'd asked her out.

'How's business?' he asked.

Giselle's reply was practically a whisper. 'Steady.'

Nevertheless, Jinny overheard. '*Steady?* She's being modest. Giselle's stuff flies out the door.'

Mack supposed Jinny ought to know, considering she managed the gift shop up at the castle. Giselle was one of the talented artists who rented a studio in the castle's craft centre. She made the most amazing pictures out of sea glass and other bits and pieces, such as shells, pebbles and driftwood. He had one of her creations on the wall of his sitting room.

Giselle dropped her gaze and a light blush spread across her alabaster cheeks. She reminded Mack of the mist that crept over the loch in the early mornings: ethereal and beautiful, and not something you could hold in your hands. Dreamy – that was another way to describe her, as well as reserved. She'd had a studio at the castle for a couple of years and lived in the village, yet he knew next to nothing about her.

Would he like to?

Actually, Mack wasn't certain he would. He had a feeling Giselle was an all-or-nothing kind of woman, and Mack didn't want a steady relationship and definitely wasn't looking to settle down, so maybe he should leave her be. Anyway, he would probably have more luck with a tourist.

There was a group of women who had taken up residence near the bar, and from their laughter he guessed they were having a good time.

Finishing his pint, he got to his feet. 'Refill, anyone?' he asked and after some of his mates had taken him up on the offer, he sauntered casually up to the bar and placed the order.

While he waited for the drinks to be poured, he leant back against the counter and pretended to casually glance around.

One of the women smiled at him and Mack smiled back. She held up her glass, and he noticed it was almost empty. But as he was debating whether to buy her a drink, he felt a tap on his elbow.

'You'll have as much luck with that lot as you'll have with Giselle,' Cal said. 'I noticed you eyeing her up. If you upset one of my crafters…' He wagged a finger.

'*Mhairi's* crafters. She rules the roost.'

Cal narrowed his eyes in mock irritation and reminded him, 'Mhairi employs me to manage the castle.'

'And you do it brilliantly.' Mack chuckled.

'It won't be so brilliant if you upset Giselle. Don't worry, there's someone out there who'll make an honest man of you. Just not Giselle.'

Mack was used to the ribbing. 'An honest man? No chance! I'm not the settling-down type.'

'You know what your problem is?' Cal observed. 'You've not found the right woman yet.'

'I've found lots of women.' Mack fished his wallet out of his pocket to pay for the drinks, caught the woman's eye again and smiled.

Cal followed his gaze. 'One of these days someone will give you a taste of your own medicine,' he warned.

This was also a familiar refrain. Mack couldn't help it if women found him attractive. He found them attractive, too. He just didn't want to be tied down, and as long as both parties understood this, he couldn't see the harm in it.

Chapter 4

When Freya unlocked the door to her father's house, she felt utterly drained. This past week had been exhausting, worrying and frustrating. Her dad wasn't the easiest of patients, she'd discovered, and she dreaded the time when he would be allowed to go home and she would be the one responsible for his care. She pitied the poor nurses for having to put up with his surliness. He resented having to be cared for, and she got the feeling he would resent it even more when he was in his own house.

Hopefully, his mood would improve once his mobility started to return, but as both the physio and the occupational therapist had warned, it could be a long journey before he was completely mobile again and able to cope on his own. It didn't help that Freya had read that three-quarters of people who'd suffered hip fractures were unable to do their own shopping after a year and, more worryingly, over half were still unable to feed or dress themselves.

She hadn't shared that little nugget with her dad, of course, not wanting to upset him more than he was already. However, if determination was any indicator of recovery, he would be fighting fit in a matter of weeks.

He was still in hospital in Inverness, but Freya had fought tooth and nail to have him transferred to Broadford on Skye, and she'd been informed that they'd be moving him in the morning, which was the main reason she had travelled to Duncoorie today. The other reason was that her dad had been fretting about his cottage, and she hoped to be able to put his mind at rest when she visited him tomorrow. Also, after spending several nights in a hotel, Freya was more than ready to live in a proper house again.

However, he had no idea that she intended to move back in with him for a while. Bless him, he was convinced he'd be able to manage on his own, with a bit of help with his shopping every few days.

She was dreading having *that* conversation with him and had been putting it off, but it was clear he would struggle on his own for a while, so he didn't have any choice.

Her dad being so helpless and so dependent on others had been distressing for both of them, and she was shocked to discover that her strong, dependable father had grown old, almost overnight. She could see in his eyes that he was aware of how frail he'd become, and he was railing against it with all his might.

As she heaved her case out of the hire car and dragged it into the tiny hall, kicking the door shut behind her, Freya shook her head ruefully. If anyone could beat the odds and make a full recovery, it was her dad.

The house felt chilled and damp, despite the afternoon warmth, and the air smelt stale and musty. It was gloomy too, with the curtains in the sitting room still drawn, and she hurried to open them. Then wished she hadn't, as she saw the state of it.

'Oh, Dad,' she murmured, tears springing to her eyes. Not only did everything look older and more careworn since the last time she was here (which was only three months ago), but there were also little piles of what her mum used to refer to as 'messes' everywhere. Used plates, old flyers and leaflets, clothes... And she hadn't ventured into the kitchen yet.

Her mother would have been horrified. She used to be so house-proud, and had always ensured everything was just so. What had happened for her dad to let standards slide so much?

Freya took in the dresser, with the ornaments she knew so well now covered in a layer of dust thick enough to draw her name in, and her heart ached. If she closed her eyes, she could imagine Mum flicking a duster over them. Her most treasured, and the one that brought tears to Freya's eyes every time she saw it, was the little pot she'd made in high school. Her mum had been so proud of it. Even then, she used to tell people that her daughter was destined to be a potter.

Freya swallowed hard, the memories threatening to swamp her. They made coming back to Duncoorie and to this house difficult, and she didn't know how she was going to cope with living here for the next few weeks. But she would have to put her grief to one side for her father's sake, no matter how hard she might find it.

The house was an end-of-terrace; a simple farm-worker's dwelling, it had originally had two downstairs rooms and a small bathroom, but at some point a staircase had been put in and the attic had been converted into two bedrooms.

As Freya looked at the stairs, she knew her dad wasn't going to be able to negotiate them for a while, so she would need to bring his bed downstairs. At least he'd be within easy reach of the bathroom, she thought, but she guessed he wouldn't consider it much of a consolation.

However, before that could happen, the place needed a damn good clean and tidy, and Freya couldn't escape the feeling that she was invading her dad's personal space as she set to.

Starting with the kitchen, she pulled a face at the sour smell from the sink, which was half-full of greasy grey water. The bin wasn't much better, and she held her breath as she emptied it.

Wishing she had a pair of rubber gloves, she ran the hot water tap, then squirted in a generous dollop of washing-up liquid. Deciding that she may as well make a proper job of it, she emptied each cupboard, one at a time, before wiping them thoroughly and putting everything back. Once that was done, she turned her attention to the cooker and the fridge.

In all, it took her nearly two hours to make the kitchen sparkle, and she was knackered after she'd finished, but she also felt weirdly satisfied at a job well done.

She couldn't face cleaning the rest of the house right now, though. She needed food and a bath (she would have preferred a shower, but her father only had a bath), and she didn't care which order they occurred in. Remembering that there wasn't a great deal in the fridge, she decided to order a take-away and have her bath while she waited for it to arrive. However, that plan was soon scuppered when she discovered that delivery wasn't an option in Duncoorie. She would have to go out and forage.

Bath first, then (although she ended up giving the bathroom a quick once-over while she was in there), and afterwards she got dressed and hurried out the door.

By now her stomach was loudly informing her that it needed to be fed, and she was beginning to feel quite drained. No wonder, after the week she'd had, she thought, as she locked the door, but hopefully a meal in Duncoorie's pub would sort her out.

The pub was more crowded than Freya expected, and she berated herself for forgetting how busy Duncoorie could get during the summer months. But there was a lot about Duncoorie that she'd forgotten, the memories buried deep.

As she searched for a free table, she almost turned tail and left, but the delicious aroma of food enticed her to stay, and she eventually found a small unoccupied table tucked away in a corner near the door leading to the loos.

After perusing the menu, she realised that she had to order at the bar, so she left her denim jacket draped over the back of the chair and placed her bag on the table. Taking out her keys, purse and phone (she hoped her bag wouldn't get stolen, but she wasn't taking any chances with her valuables), she walked up to the bar.

As she waited to catch the attention of a staff member, Freya gazed around curiously. It was many years since she'd had a drink in here but the place hadn't changed much. The layout was the same: the fireplace with its wood-burning stove was still there, although as it was the beginning of summer, it was currently unlit, and the pub still had the old-world charm she remembered.

She placed her order, then took her drink back to the table, thankful that her bag and jacket were still there. Then as she waited for her food to arrive, she pretended to look at her phone when what she was actually doing was people-watching.

Trying not to be obvious about it, Freya scrutinised each face, wondering whether she knew them. Her dad had kept her abreast of some of what went on in the village, but he rarely mentioned anyone in her age group; he was more interested in the goings-on of his cronies and his neighbours, so her old friends hadn't concerned him.

Her eyes alighted on a large group of people on the other side of the room, and Freya was sure that the tall woman with the dark, curly hair was Jinny Rothwell. Hadn't Dad told her that she'd married Jean Burns's son Carter? Jean lived a couple of doors down from her dad, which was probably why he'd mentioned it. Carter was five years older than Freya; she'd hardly known him, but his brother, Mackenzie, had been in the year above her at school.

Talk of the devil...

The man himself was standing at the bar and he hadn't changed a bit. Well, he *had* – he'd grown even more handsome. His hair was longer than she remembered, and his previously dirty-blond locks were now several shades lighter. He'd grown a beard too, and the combination was reminiscent of a Viking or a surfer dude.

She remembered that she'd had the most horrendous crush on him. Looking back, she thought he might well have been her first love – even if he hadn't been aware of it.

Just then her meal arrived, and it looked and smelt amazing, diverting her attention away from Mack and onto her supper. She ate hungrily, polishing off the lot. When she eventually looked up from her plate, he'd joined his brother and the others.

As though sensing her interest, Mack turned his head towards her and their eyes met. Freya hastily looked away, embarrassed to be caught staring, but she soon risked another look (she couldn't help herself) and she almost yelped when she saw that he was heading directly for her. However, her consternation turned to relief and then to mortification when he walked past her table, and she realised he was actually going to the gents.

Feeling foolish, she finished her drink. She knew she should go home and go to bed. She had another long day ahead of her tomorrow, and she needed her rest.

Picking up her bag, she pushed her chair away from the table and was about to get to her feet, when she became aware of someone behind her. A sixth sense told her it was Mack.

Freya turned around.

Her eyes were at waist height and her gaze rose slowly, travelling up the breadth of his chest, lingering on the V created by the open neck of his shirt, before carrying on to his face. Her mortification knew no bounds as she realised that he was fully aware of her scrutiny.

'Hi,' Mack said. 'Leaving already?'

'I, er, yeah.'

'Can I buy you a drink, or do you have to be somewhere? My name's Mack, by the way.'

'Sorry, I have to go.' She lifted her jacket off the back of the chair.

'Pity.' He did look genuinely disappointed, but Freya wasn't fooled.

He'd been charming back then, too, full of boyish good looks and confidence. It seemed he still was. Maybe if he'd recognised her, she might have said yes. But there hadn't been a glimmer. He had no idea who she was, or that they used to go to the same school and lived in the same village. Had she changed so much, or hadn't she made enough of an impression back then for him to remember her? Anyway, why was she so bothered about Mack Burns when she hadn't seen him for fifteen years and hadn't thought about him for nearly as long? It wasn't as though she didn't have more important things to think about.

Feeling completely put out and too tired to make sense of her disjointed thoughts, Freya went home. She had always referred to her dad's house as home, even after she'd bought her first studio flat, the one where, if she stretched out her arms, she could have touched both sides of her kitchen at the same time.

But if that was the case, why did she feel like she didn't belong here, she wondered as she stepped into the tiny hallway. Abruptly, she felt a sudden yearning for London and the life she couldn't return to while her father needed her.

Chapter 5

Freya was stripping the sheets off her dad's bed the following morning when there was a rat-a-tat knock on the door. Curious, she went to answer it, and it took her a moment to realise that her visitor was Rhona from next door. Freya hadn't seen her for ages, not for a couple of years at least, but the woman hadn't changed a bit, despite being in her seventies now.

Rhona peered at her through a pair of round spectacles. 'Freya? Is that you?'

'How lovely to see you,' Freya replied. 'Won't you come in?'

'I've only popped by because I heard noises last night and saw the light on. I guessed it was you, but I thought I'd better chap on the door and check.' Her brows lowered. 'You can't be too careful these days.'

'No, of course you can't,' Freya agreed. 'Are you sure you won't come in? I was about to make a pot of tea.' She'd nipped out to the shop for milk and bread as soon as it had opened at seven o'clock, so she could have a cup of tea and a slice of toast for her breakfast.

'Go on, then, just a quick one,' Rhona said, and as she showed her in, Freya saw her eyes widen. 'You've been busy.'

Freya ignored the innuendo that her dad's house had needed a good clean. Filling the kettle, she said, 'Dad and

I owe you a huge thank you. Goodness knows how long he would have lain there if you hadn't heard him calling.' She switched the kettle on, then pulled out a chair. 'Please, sit down. Would you like a biscuit?' Freya had found an unopened packet in a cupboard.

'I'm watching my figure,' Rhona said, patting her plump tummy.

Freya, who wasn't, opened it and took two out, trying not to let her amusement show. Rhona had been 'watching her figure' ever since Freya could remember.

Rhona cocked her head to the side. 'How is he?'

'He's broken his hip, I'm afraid.'

'I thought as much. I could tell by the way he was lying. He didn't want me to phone for an ambulance, though, the silly auld eejit. But I did anyway.'

'And I'm very grateful.'

Rhona hadn't finished. 'I think he was hoping I'd be able to lift him!' She tutted and rolled her eyes. 'Will you thank him for the flowers? It was kind of him.'

'I will.'

'So, you're going to be here for a bit, then? Or will he be going to stay with you in London?'

'Milk?'

'Aye, just a wee drop.'

Freya poured the tea, then joined her dad's neighbour at the table. Rhona was looking at her expectantly and Freya realised she hadn't answered her question. 'I'll be staying here,' she replied.

Rhona raised her eyebrows and Freya simply knew that the news of her return to Skye, albeit on a temporary basis, would soon be all over the village.

'That's nice. I dare say he'll be glad of the company. He'll need it too, with a broken hip. How is he in himself?

I must admit, I've been a bit worried about him these past few months.'

'Oh? Why is that?' A slow dread crept into her bones.

Ever since she'd got here last night and saw how her father had let standards drop, Freya had worried that maybe he hadn't been coping. Were her fears about to be confirmed?

'He's not been himself,' Rhona said, 'but I can't put my finger on it.'

'Do you think he's ill?' Freya blurted.

Rhona thought for a moment. 'It's probably just old age. It comes to us all eventually. Look at me: I've got arthritis, high blood pressure, a cataract in one eye and my bowels haven't been right for years.'

Freya winced. She honestly didn't need to know that. 'I suppose you're right,' she said, thinking that if there was something wrong, the hospital would surely have picked it up, considering the number of times Dad's blood pressure, pulse and temperature had been checked this past week. But on the other hand, seventy-four wasn't *old* old.

Guilt pricked at her as she thought of the physical distance between them – nearly seven hundred miles and at least a twelve-hour drive. She should have made more of an effort to visit him, especially since he'd sold his boat six years ago. Retirement didn't seem to have agreed with him.

But she'd been so busy. She still was. Lecturing at the art college might mean long holidays, but she invariably spent those in her studio. It had taken hard work and determination to make a name for herself, and she rarely seemed to have any spare time.

Realising she was making excuses, Freya sipped her tea in silence.

Rhona said, 'Let me know when he's home and I'll pop round. Oh, and if my cat bothers you, shoo him away. Anyone would think I don't feed him.' She got awkwardly to her feet. 'Tell your dad I was asking after him.'

'I will,' Freya promised. 'He's being sent back to Broadford today, so I'll visit him later.'

As she showed Rhona out, Freya's thoughts turned to the jobs she needed to do, and her heart sank, as she realised she'd have to return to London shortly to fetch more clothes, because it looked like she was going to be here for a while.

—

Mack was pooped. Three trips a day throughout the summer months were enough for anyone, and he was looking forward to an afternoon off. Sea Serpent Boat Tours might be his business, but he was conscious of the need for downtime, both for his crew and himself, so he rostered time off for all of them. His crew took a full day once a fortnight. Mack allowed himself an afternoon, and even then, he often spent the time doing admin.

Although he was aware he needed to make enough money in the lucrative summer months to get him through the winter when decent days on the loch were fewer and there weren't as many tourists on the island, he wasn't intending to work this afternoon. He was going to go for a hike. The mountain behind his house was calling to him and, as much as he loved being on his boat, he was desperate to feel grass under his feet and to smell the heather.

After issuing instructions and reminders (which were met with shakes of the head, because his crew knew what they were doing), Mack took off just before the next trip went out.

Resisting the urge to go to the lock-up and do some paperwork, he jumped into his car and drove the short distance home. Once there, he didn't linger. After putting on his hiking boots, he made himself a piece, stuffing the bread with cheese, ham and salad, and grabbed a packet of crisps and a chocolate bar, before filling a flask with instant coffee.

Checking that his rucksack had waterproofs, a torch and a thermal blanket (in case of emergency), he popped in his picnic, then slung the bag over his shoulders and set off.

Located no more than ten paces from his back door was a path that would take him to the top of the mountain.

The first part of his hike was through woodland, a mixture of pine and deciduous trees, and the air was full of birdsong. But it was swiftly left behind as the gradient grew steeper and trees gave way to low scrub, then finally heather and tussocky grass, with the odd clump of stubborn gorse.

As he climbed higher, the view opened up, and he paused for a moment, squinting and shading his eyes with his hand as he tried, without success, to make out the *Sea Serpent* on the glittering water. Coorie Castle was clearly visible, though, and his gaze was drawn to the magnificent old building.

Perched on a hill above the loch, the castle rose out of the rock to tower over the landscape, although from here it looked like one of the doll's houses that Tara made. Its stonework was white and shone in the afternoon light; its many windows glinted and glittered, and he could just make out a flag flying from the top of one of the turrets.

To the side of the castle lay the craft centre; it had once been the service buildings for the castle, built many years after the monument itself. They had fallen into disrepair until Mhairi Gray, the elderly lady who owned the estate, had converted them into studios and created a craft centre out of them.

The village was spread out below, following the contours of the loch, the buildings dotted along the main road, with some to either side. He could make out the kirk, with its pointed spire, and the post office-cum-shop. It was easy to spot the pub, and he could also see his mum's house and his brother's. It was as though his whole life was laid out before him, everything and everyone he loved visible from up here.

This was why he loved coming here so much, no matter the weather. It grounded him and made him more aware of his place in the world. And on a day like today, when the sun shone out of a cerulean sky, it was pure joy.

The warm breeze was scented with heather, meadow-sweet, and the coconut and vanilla perfume of the yellow gorse flowers. He breathed deeply, letting the fragrance wash over and through him, and stayed there a moment, filling his lungs with the sweet, clean air.

Resuming his hike, Mack allowed his thoughts to wander, and they settled on the woman he'd spoken to in the pub last night. There'd been something familiar about her and he hoped he hadn't hit on her before. Might she be a regular holidaymaker to the area?

Abruptly, it came to him, and the knowledge stopped him in his tracks: the woman had been none other than Freya Sinclair.

Freya hurried into Broadford Hospital on Saturday afternoon clutching a bag for life, and headed for the ward. Spying her father in the bed furthest from the door, she made a beeline for him, but her feet slowed when she grew close.

His eyes were closed, his cheeks sunken, and he suddenly looked older than when she'd last seen him.

She bit her lip in distress, and it took her a second to gather herself; the last thing her dad needed was to see her upset.

Placing the bag on the floor next to his bed, she decided to sit with him until he woke, and while she waited, she would try to make inroads into her to-do list. She'd already informed Sean Pickles that she wouldn't be around during the summer (not that the college expected her to be) but she wanted to keep him abreast of what was happening, in case she didn't make it back to London for the start of the new academic year in September. It was well over two months away, but since no one could tell her how long it would be before her dad would be back on his feet again, she had to make sure the vice chancellor was aware of the situation, in case a slightly longer absence was necessary. She sincerely hoped it wouldn't be...

There was also Jocasta Black's offer to consider, and the woman was going to need an answer soon, but with everything that had happened, Freya hadn't had a chance to think about it properly.

Her thumb hovered over Hadrian's name and she was about to message him, when she decided against it. She would speak to him later in the privacy of her dad's house. Instead, she booked a flight back to London for tomorrow.

She needed to sort out her flat and, more importantly, her studio. Plus, she needed more clothes, and as she couldn't afford to keep the hire car indefinitely, she would have to drive her little van back to Skye.

Freya wasn't looking forward to the journey one bit, but it had to be done.

Feeling eyes on her, she glanced up to see her dad looking at her, and she got to her feet and bent over the bed to give him a kiss. His skin was dry and smelt of antiseptic. 'You're awake. How was the journey?'

'Not too bad,' he replied, but he couldn't hide a grimace, and she knew the transfer had taken it out of him.

'I've got to pop back to London…' she began, before realising how ridiculous she sounded: one didn't just 'pop back' from Skye. 'I need to fetch more clothes and—'

'Stay there,' he interrupted.

Freya blinked. 'You don't mean that?'

'I do. I can manage on my own. You've seen me with the walker.'

She had, and it had been painful to watch. Gone was the strong, striding father she knew, and in his place was a hesitant, shuffling old man. However – and Freya took comfort from this – her dad was making good progress, and although he would need her help for a while, she was confident that he'd be walking well in a few weeks, even if he did have to use a stick outside the house. And if necessary, she'd arrange for a cleaner to come in a couple of times a week and for him to have his shopping delivered.

She worried whether he'd be able to drive again, but they'd cross that bridge when they came to it. She needed to get him home first, and for that to happen she had to bring his bed downstairs. Thank goodness the bathroom was on the ground floor. In fact, she'd tackle the bed situation this evening, in case he was discharged early next week. It was better to be prepared than to leave things until the last minute, she reasoned, knowing she would be away for at least two days.

'There's no need for you to come back,' he insisted. 'You've got your own life to lead.'

He'd been singing variations of the same song all week, to Freya's growing irritation. Anyone would think he didn't want her there.

'We've been over this, Dad. I'm staying for as long as you need me.'

'But that's what I'm trying to tell you,' he argued. 'I'll manage.'

'You won't.' She could be just as stubborn as him, and she was determined not to back down. She could never be so selfish as to leave him on his own when he needed her, no matter how much he protested that he didn't. And if something happened to him, she'd never forgive herself.

'I'm staying and that's final,' she insisted. 'So get used to the idea. Anyway, it won't be forever, will it? You'll soon be as right as rain.'

As Freya got to her feet and began to unpack the bag, she almost missed the flash of guilt and sadness on her dad's face.

Her heart went out to him; it was going to be hard for such an independent and self-sufficient man to accept that he needed a bit of help – even if it would only be for a short time – and she vowed to make the next few weeks as easy as possible.

Chapter 6

Mack couldn't resist telling his mum that Freya Sinclair was back in town, so he called in on his way home. Strictly speaking, it wasn't on the way home at all and he could have phoned her instead, but he secretly harboured the hope that he might bump into Freya. He wanted a proper look at her, now that he knew who she was. Boy, had she changed! He remembered a flame-haired, skinny girl with brown eyes that were too big for the pale, freckled face they stared out of. But the woman he'd seen last night had been gorgeous. She'd really grown into herself, and she had oozed confidence.

As he marched back down the mountain, his feet sure and steady on the narrow rocky trail, Mack realised he knew very little about her, other than that she lived in London and taught pottery in a college. And hadn't his mum mentioned something about her work being in a gallery? He hadn't paid much attention, assuming that was what craftspeople did – display their stuff in shops and such.

He found his mother in the garden, weeding. She had a floppy sun hat on her head and a pair of ankle-high wellies on her feet.

'Are you expecting a heatwave or snow?' he joked when he saw her.

'It's Skye,' she replied. 'Any weather is possible.'

'Och, that's true enough.' It was nice at the moment, the evening warm and pleasant. Insects darted among the flowers, and sparrows argued in the bushes. Next door's cat lay sprawled on the path, taking a keen interest in the weeding process and one eye on the birds.

'Guess who I bumped into in the pub last night?' Mack said.

His mum straightened up. 'Freya Sinclair?'

'How did you know?' Mack was put out that she'd stolen his thunder. She hadn't had an inkling that Vinnie's daughter was home when she'd told him about the old man's fall yesterday.

Jean raised her eyebrows as the sound of a crash was followed by a loud yelp. The noise came from two doors up – Vinnie's house.

'Rhona told me. She spoke to her this morning. Freya's going to be staying a wee while.'

'What on earth is she doing?' he asked, wincing as an expletive floated on the air.

'Moving furniture, by the sounds of it. Why don't you see if she needs a hand?'

Mack was more than happy to, and he was off like a shot and chapping on Vinnie's door before he knew it.

Freya took a step back in surprise when she realised who was knocking, and Mack put on his most charming smile.

'Hi, Freya.'

'I'm surprised you've remembered my name. You didn't last night.'

'I didn't recognise you,' he replied, undeterred by her scowl.

She scoffed. 'I haven't changed *that* much.'

'Actually, you have,' he pointed out. 'You've grown up.' Then he wished he hadn't mentioned it, when his gaze involuntarily flickered down her body. Even in jeans and a T-shirt, she looked amazing. Her abundant curves were in all the right places and her waist looked narrow enough to span with his hands.

Unfortunately, she caught him looking and glared at him. 'What do you want?' she demanded, her tone on the unfriendly side. 'I'm in the middle of something.'

'So I heard.'

'Excuse me?'

'I was in my mum's garden. You swear like a fishwife.'

He was amused to see the freckles across her cheeks turn a deep copper colour as she blushed furiously.

'You would swear too if you'd just dropped a bed on your foot,' she retorted.

'Should I ask—?'

'No, you should not.'

'Do you need a hand?'

'I can manage.'

'It didn't sound like it.'

'You shouldn't have been listening.'

'I couldn't help it. You were loud.'

She closed her eyes, took a breath, then opened them again. 'Please tell me no one else heard me swearing?'

He shrugged. 'Can't say for certain. My mum heard.'

'Oh sh— dear.'

Mack grinned. 'Do you want a hand or don't you?'

He felt her eyes linger on his chest and arms, sending a pleasant warmth through him. He was used to women eyeing him up and liking what they saw, but when Freya reached out and gave his left bicep a squeeze, he almost jerked away in surprise.

However, his hope that she might be flirting with him came crashing down when she said, 'You'll do. If you were weedy, I'd be better off shifting it myself. It's upstairs.' Turning on her heel, she stomped ahead of him, giving him a perfect view of her bahoochie – and what a wonderful bahoochie it was.

He watched it go up the stairs, then stop when it reached the top, as Freya squeezed herself between a bed frame and the banister.

Giving the old brass bed frame an experimental push, he announced, 'It's stuck.'

The withering look made him flinch. 'I know.'

'You'll need to turn it on its side.'

'That's what I was trying to do.'

He bent down to peer at the offending piece of furniture. 'It might be an idea to take the headboard off.'

She waved an adjustable spanner at him. 'Now why didn't I think of that?' she drawled.

'Would you like me to have a go?' Mack flexed his muscles.

'Nah, I brought you up here to watch,' she snapped back, but when he smirked and she realised how that sounded, she blushed again.

Mack resisted the impulse to duck when she raised the spanner, thinking she was going to brain him with it, but she merely handed it to him.

Unfortunately, from his position at the top of the stairs, he wasn't able to reach the grub screws that bolted the headboard in place. Which meant he had to try to heave the cumbersome frame back, and hope he wouldn't damage the wallpaper in the process. It was already dented and had a slight tear, but he was wary of making it worse.

'If I take the weight, can you shuffle it back?' he asked.

Freya nodded, brushing the hair off her face before planting her feet apart and grasping the end of the footboard.

With some delicate shifting to and fro, enough of a gap appeared for Mack to squeeze through, and then he was on the landing, pressed against Freya as she held the bed steady to prevent it from moving again.

When he positioned himself in front of her to relieve her of the weight of the damned thing, he felt the heat and softness of her chest against his arm, and it sent a bolt of desire through him.

Down, boy, he silently told his libido. Now wasn't the time to be having those kinds of thoughts.

Freya moved back, putting some distance between them, but the scent of her lingered in his nose and he breathed it in.

'Are you OK there?' she asked.

'Grand,' he replied, jerking his head to indicate that she should step away, and in a matter of minutes he had the pesky bed into a position where he could get at the grub screws to loosen them. As he applied the spanner, it was clear why she hadn't been able to undo them herself. The blasted things were welded on, and it took all his strength to shift them. He prided himself on not cursing, though, despite being tempted to utter an expletive or two that would rival Freya's.

'There,' he announced triumphantly, when he'd managed to separate the headboard from the rails and the base. 'Let's get this downstairs, then I'll take the footboard out. Where do you want it?'

'The sitting room, please.'

He carted it downstairs and saw that she'd already cleared a bed-sized space in the sitting room. A sofa and two armchairs had been pushed together, and he could see how cramped the room would be once the bed was set up.

'How's your dad?' he asked, propping the headboard against the free wall.

'Getting there.'

'When's he coming home?'

'Sometime next week, hopefully.'

'We've got time, then.'

She narrowed her eyes. 'Time for what?'

'To take one of the chairs upstairs. It'll give you more room. You won't be able to swing a cat in here once we've got the bed down.'

'Swinging cats is the least of my worries,' she muttered.

He didn't bother pursuing that conversation, even though he'd heard what she'd said. Having her dad in the hospital must be a concern, and he guessed she wouldn't find it easy when he came home. Vinnie could be an ornery so-and-so, despite having a heart of gold.

Mack remembered the reason the old chap had given for hanging up his fishing nets; he'd claimed that he'd had enough of early mornings and heaving seas, and that he was fed up with being cold and wet. But everyone knew he'd been struggling for a while. Operating a trawler, even a small one, was damned hard work, and the body took a battering.

Now that the bed was apart, it took minutes to bring the rest of it down and put it back together again, then Mack carried the hefty double mattress down single-handedly, refusing Freya's offer of help. He was showing off a bit, but he couldn't seem to stop trying to impress her, despite knowing how shallow he was being. However, he suspected it would take more than muscles to impress Freya Sinclair.

When the job was done, and not wishing to outstay his welcome, he said, 'I'll be off – unless you need me for anything else.'

He saw her puzzled glance at the three-piece suite, crammed together with barely an inch between them. 'I thought we were going to take a chair upstairs?' she said.

'We are, but I'm going to need another body to shift it.'

'What am I? Cream cheese?'

Mack let out a laugh. 'Definitely not, but you can't—'

'Don't you dare tell me I can't do something,' she broke in hotly.

Mack held up his hands and backed away. 'I wouldn't dream of it,' he protested. 'I just don't want you to throw your back out, that's all. That sofa is heavy.'

'I thought we were moving a chair?'

'We were, but I've been thinking that removing the sofa will give your dad more room to manoeuvre his walker.'

Freya produced the first smile he'd seen from her the whole time he'd been there. 'Try telling *him* he'll need a walker. He seems to think he'll manage just fine with a walking stick.'

'If you don't remove the sofa, that's exactly what he'll have to use,' Mack pointed out. 'Believe me, he'll need the walker.'

'An expert on broken hips, are you?'

'My gran broke hers.'

'Sorry, I didn't realise.'

'Why would you?'

'Dad keeps me abreast of most things.' She was on the defensive again.

'My gran lived in Lochalsh. She died a couple of years ago. Pneumonia.'

'I'm sorry,' Freya repeated.

'Yeah, so am I. She was a grand old lady.' He gave himself a mental shake. 'Right, about that sofa…?'

Freya raised her eyebrows. 'I'm game if you are?'

It was a challenge. Mack picked up the gauntlet. 'OK, then.'

He didn't add, although he wanted to, that she couldn't hold him responsible if the task proved impossible. Or if she hurt herself – though he would do his damnedest to make sure that didn't happen. The hardest part would be having to lift it over the banister at the top of the stairs, and he not only hoped that he'd be strong enough, but he was also concerned that there wouldn't be enough clearance. If that happened, he would suggest storing it at his house for the duration. Goodness knows he had the room. In fact…

'I've got an idea. Why don't we save ourselves the hassle and I'll take it to my place?'

She stared at him in surprise. 'Um…'

'I can put it on the back of my truck, and I've got somewhere you can store it.'

This was true, but part of the reason for making the offer was that it would guarantee he'd see her again. OK, it wasn't much of a plan, but it was all he had, considering she'd blown him off last night.

'If you're sure,' she replied doubtfully.

'Do you want to give the stairs a go first?'

Freya caught her bottom lip between her teeth. It was a sexy gesture, and his libido gave him a little nudge.

She studied the stairs, and he could see the calculations going on behind her eyes. 'Could we?'

'I still think we need another pair of hands. It's going to be a two-man job. And, no offence, but you're not a man.'

She arched a brow. 'How observant of you.'

His lips twitched; he wasn't used to this kind of reaction from a woman and he was enjoying it.

She sighed, suddenly deflating. 'I suppose you're right.'

'I'll see if I can get someone to help tomorrow. It'll have to be in the evening, though.' He'd ask Cal or Carter.

'I won't be here tomorrow; I'm flying to London.'

'Oh, right.' The disappointment he felt at her news surprised him.

'I'll be back on Monday, so would Tuesday be OK?' she added.

'I'm sure it will.' He smiled at her. 'If there's nothing more I can help you with this evening, do you fancy going to the pub for a drink?'

Her gaze roved around the sitting room. 'I've got loads to do.'

'When you get back from London, maybe?'

'Maybe... Thanks for your help.'

'It's nae bother.' He was about to suggest swapping phone numbers so he could tell her what time he'd call on Tuesday, when her mobile trilled loudly.

It was sitting on a lamp table behind him, and as she reached past him to pick it up, he saw the name on the screen: Hadrian.

'Hi,' she said into the phone, holding up a finger to let Mack know she wouldn't be long. 'Yeah, tomorrow, landing about three... Dinner? I don't know. I've...' A sigh. 'OK, but I'm leaving early in the morning... You know why... I can't, *OK?*' This last was said with a measure of exasperation, then her voice softened. 'Me, too.'

Mack decided he'd better take his leave, and he waved at her to get her attention.

She looked at him as though she'd forgotten he was there.

'Hang on, Hadrian,' she said, as Mack mouthed, 'See you Tuesday.'

She dropped her arm to her side, the phone pressed against her thigh. 'What time?'

'Sometime after seven. I'll see myself out.'

She lifted the phone to her ear once more, but before she spoke into it, she said, 'Thanks again for your help with the bed.'

He shrugged, saying, 'No problem,' and stepped into the porch.

As he left, he heard her say, 'No one, just one of my dad's neighbours,' and he felt a pang as he realised how little impression he'd made on her, compared to the big impression she'd made on him.

Chapter 7

Freya threw her keys onto the coffee table and collapsed into her armchair. Resting her head against the squishy cushion, she closed her eyes and breathed deeply, trying to centre herself after the journey back to London.

She found it difficult to believe that she'd only been away just over a week. It felt more like a month.

Opening her eyes again, she willed herself to her weary feet. There was so much to do, and she really should get going.

She was halfway through sorting what she wanted to take, when the intercom buzzed.

'Party time!' Harini, who lived in the apartment directly above Freya, breezed into the flat in a swirl of long dark hair, full skirt and flowery perfume.

'Now?' Freya asked, bemused.

'No, silly, Friday.'

'What's the occasion?'

'Our one-year anniversary.' Harini followed Freya into the bedroom.

Opening a drawer and taking out a pile of underwear, Freya said, 'I thought you and Coretta had been together longer than a year. Congrats, by the way.'

Harini laughed. 'No, it just feels like it sometimes – but don't tell her I said that.' Her gaze fell on the open suitcase.

'Of course!' She slapped a palm to her forehead. 'It's the summer holidays, isn't it? Are you going somewhere nice?'

'Yes and no.' Freya dumped the armful of underwear on the bed and began to sort through it. 'I'm sorry, but I'll have to miss your party. I'm going to Skye for a while.'

Harini gave her a cautious look. 'How long is a while, and why don't you sound happy about it?'

'It isn't a holiday, unfortunately. My dad's broken his hip, so he needs looking after.'

'Oh, no! I'm sorry. Is he OK?'

'He will be. He's in hospital at the moment, but I'm hoping they'll discharge him soon.'

'Is that why I haven't seen you around for a few days?'

Freya nodded. 'I've spent the past week there, and I'm driving back tomorrow. I only popped home to pack.'

'Would you like a hand?'

'That's so sweet of you, but I can manage.'

'How long do you think you'll be gone?'

'I'm praying it won't be more than a couple of months, but it depends how quickly he recovers.'

'If there's anything I can do…?' Harini said.

Freya stopped what she was doing and gave her a hug. 'I'm sorry to miss your party.'

'There'll be others. You know us – we don't need an excuse.'

As Freya showed her out, she made a mental note to send the pair some flowers. In fact, she'd order a bouquet now, before she forgot.

While she was choosing a suitable card to go with it, Freya realised that she and Hadrian had been dating for almost two years, but their one-year anniversary had come and gone without so much as a whimper. Maybe neither of them had noticed it because they didn't actually live together, she mused.

Pausing, a blouse in her hand, Freya pulled a face: the prospect of sharing a home with Hadrian failed to send her into paroxysms of joy. She liked her own company too much, needed her own space. And Hadrian was too fastidious for her liking, which was why he tended not to spend the night at hers, preferring his own penthouse in Dalston. She had to admit that his flat was very nice. Situated in a modern building, it was minimalist and stylish, but what she loved most was the light. Hadrian had turned his spare bedroom into a studio and had paid a fortune to have a hole punched in the roof and a skylight put in. It was a room she seldom entered, as he liked to keep his creative life separate from his private life – something Freya found difficult to understand.

Her creativity *was* her life, and vice versa, and she could no more compartmentalise it than she could split herself in half. And that was why Hadrian found her in her studio, when he called to pick her up to go to dinner a couple of hours later.

—

Despite his reputation, Mack was selective about who he slept with. He didn't hop into bed with every woman he asked out. There had to be some kind of connection, and this evening, he wasn't feeling it. The woman's name was Tori (short for Victoria?), and she was pretty, vivacious and a mature student – if twenty-nine could be called 'mature' – doing a degree in marine something-or-other.

Mack felt every one of his thirty-five years this evening, as demonstrated by the suspicion that he was getting too old for putting himself about like a twenty-year-old. It didn't help that he was stone-cold sober, whereas Tori was necking vodka back like it was going out of fashion.

She was getting steadily plastered and the more alcohol she consumed, the flirtier she became. Mack had nothing against a woman being flirty – heck, he usually encouraged it – but tonight, with the noise and busyness of a rammed Portree pub around him, all he wanted to do was go to bed. On his own.

It was only ten to ten, and the night was still young, but his heart wasn't in it.

'Where did you say you were staying?' he asked, raising his voice to be heard. She'd mentioned it already, but he'd forgotten. When she told him, he realised it was a five-minute walk away.

'Shall we go?' he suggested, hoping that once they were outside, she would be happy to call it a night.

'Let's have another first. Mine's a vodka.' She finished her drink and waggled the glass at him. 'And why aren't you drinking?' She pouted.

'I'm driving, remember?'

Leaning closer, her lips a hair's breadth from his ear, she said, 'Driving where?'

'To Duncoorie.'

She giggled. 'Are we going to your place?'

'Er, no.'

'Then you won't be driving,' she shot back. 'Go on, have a drink and don't be so uptight.'

'I've got an early start in the morning,' he replied, his thoughts going to Freya. She'd said the very same thing. Idly, he wondered what she was doing now, then wished he hadn't, because she was probably with the guy she'd spoken to on the phone.

Since he'd left her yesterday, she had crept into his mind on and off, and he couldn't think why. Was it because he hadn't seen her for so long that—

'Oi!' Tori nudged his arm. 'Drink,' she reminded him.

He got to his feet. 'Do you mind if I take you home now?'

Tori peered up at him blearily. 'Ooh, aren't you keen! Is that why you're not drinking, so you can keep going all night?'

Mack blanched. 'I won't be staying. Let me take you home,' he repeated.

'Why?' She was pouting again.

'To make sure you get to your accommodation safely.'

'My friends are over there.' She pointed to the other side of the crowded bar. 'So there's no point in you taking me back, if we're not going to...' She trailed off and made a face.

Good grief! He knew she was on holiday and wouldn't be expecting more than a fling, but he would never give a woman the sort of ultimatum Tori had given him. She was basically telling him to sleep with her or bugger off.

However, he felt guilty for abandoning her after he'd asked her out, even if her friends were nearby, so he tried again. 'Are you sure I can't drop you off on the way?'

'I'm sure.' She was no longer looking at him and when he followed her gaze, he saw a group of men – and one of them was staring in her direction.

'I hope you enjoy the rest of your holiday,' he said.

'I'll try my best,' was her reply.

Mack hadn't made it to the exit before she was in the thick of the group. Shrugging, he went home to his solitary but infinitely more preferable bed.

Freya disentangled herself from the 500-count Egyptian cotton sheets and slipped out of bed.

Hadrian turned onto his side and propped himself up on his elbow. He was watching her dispassionately as she reached for her clothes. She really didn't feel like trekking halfway across the city at eleven thirty at night, but it was better than getting up at six a.m., especially on a morning when she had a long drive ahead of her.

Fastening her bra, she wished she hadn't allowed Hadrian to persuade her to go back to his place, but his flat was the nearest to the restaurant he'd taken her to, so that was where she'd ended up.

'Will you be back next weekend?' he asked, and she let out an incredulous sigh.

'Don't be daft.'

His eyes narrowed. He wasn't used to being called daft. But honestly! It wasn't like she was popping to Oxford or Brighton. Skye was almost the full length of the country.

'When, then?' Hadrian demanded.

'I don't know. I've got to go,' she said. 'I've got a long drive.'

'Maybe I'll visit. Inspiration, and all that jazz.'

'Not to see *me*?' she snapped, more sharply than she'd intended.

He chuckled. 'Of course to see you. That goes without saying.'

No, it really doesn't, she thought. 'I'll ring you when I get there, to let you know I've arrived safely.'

Hadrian yawned and stretched, the sheet slipping lower, exposing his toned stomach. Freya looked away.

He said, 'Message me instead. I've got a meeting this afternoon.'

'Who with?'

'No one you'd know.' This was Hadrian-speak for: *you might know them, but I don't want to talk about it.*

She said, 'It won't be this afternoon. It's a twelve-hour drive, and that's without stops and if the traffic is good. It'll be the evening before I get there.'

'Message me anyway. I'm going out to dinner.'

That didn't surprise her. Hadrian never ate in. If it wasn't for his spangly coffee machine, she didn't think he'd know where his kitchen was.

'Surely you can take a quick phone call?'

'Best if I don't.' He yawned again, and she wasn't sure whether he was genuinely tired or just bored with the conversation.

Fully dressed now, she said, 'I'll be away, then.'

He sat up, laughing. 'You sound so Scottish.'

'That's because I am.'

'More than usual,' he clarified. 'You know I adore your accent. I adore *you*.'

'Do you?'

'Do you have to ask?'

Actually, she did. Never once had he told her that he loved her. It was always *you're gorgeous*, or *I adore you*. Then again, she'd never said those three little words to him, either. Wasn't being in love supposed to be an all-encompassing thing? If so, she felt very far from all-encompassed. She liked Hadrian a lot. They were good together and she had fun when she was with him, but she wasn't entirely certain that what she felt for him was love. And if she wasn't certain, then it probably wasn't, was it? It didn't bode well for their relationship that she would miss her pottery wheel more than she would miss him. If she had to make a decision about which one to take with her if she went to New York, it wouldn't be Hadrian.

Perhaps this enforced break would do them both good. Anyway, she realised that if she did accept Jocasta Black's offer and moved to the States, their relationship wouldn't survive.

The thought saddened her, but she wasn't heartbroken or even heartsore. And that spoke volumes.

Chapter 8

'Are you sure you don't mind giving me a hand?' Mack was standing in Cal's tiny hallway, waiting for him to slip his feet into a pair of trainers.

Tara, his fiancée, leant against the door frame, watching.

'Mate, I'll always be in your debt,' Cal said.

Tara piped up, 'Me, too.'

'It was nothing—' Mack began, but Tara put her arms around him.

'I could have drowned out there,' she reminded him, glancing at the loch through the window, its water glistening in the early evening sun. 'I almost did.'

'The coastguard would have rescued you,' Mack said.

'You don't know that. Anyway, you risked your own life to save me, and I can't thank you enough.'

'What about me?' Cal broke in. 'Don't I get a mention?'

Mack chuckled at their easy banter. Those two were made for each other, but it had taken Tara 'borrowing' Cal's little boat and getting caught in a storm for the pair of them to realise it. Cal had enlisted Mack's help, and Mack had taken the *Sea Serpent* out to find her. Thankfully, she'd been unharmed, and Cal had sung Mack's praises ever since.

Tara slipped an arm through his. 'Can I come with you?'

Mack was surprised she wanted to. 'It's not going to be much fun – we're shifting a sofa.'

'I don't care about the sofa. I want to meet Freya.'

'OK, but she mightn't appreciate a bunch of people descending on her.' For some reason he felt rather protective of her.

Tara laughed. 'I'm hardly a bunch. Should I bring a bottle of wine?'

'This isn't a social thing.'

'It might be a nice gesture,' she persisted.

'You just want to be nosey,' Cal said, ushering her out the door. Mack followed, jangling the keys to his truck.

'Friendly,' Tara corrected. She turned to Mack. 'Cal says she grew up here, but moved away and is now living in London.'

'That's right.' He hopped into the driver's seat. Cal hung back so Tara could sit in the middle, then he got in.

'What's she like?' she asked.

'Nice.'

She scoffed, 'Is that it – *nice*?'

Mack stared steadfastly ahead. He knew Tara's game. She was trying to set him up.

She cried, 'You like her, don't you?'

Cal said, 'If she's under thirty and pretty, he'll like her.'

Mack shot his friend a quick look. 'She's *over* thirty, actually.'

'How old?' Tara demanded.

'Thirty-three, thirty-four.'

'Not that much over.'

'Shut up and let me concentrate on the road.' The road was practically empty, and Mack was aware of the pair exchanging looks. 'She'll only be here for a few weeks,' he told them, not sure why he felt the need to explain.

'Just how you like your women,' Cal said. 'No risk they'll get serious.'

'I feel sorry for her, that's all. Her dad is in hospital and she's having to cope on her own.'

'But she's from around here, isn't she?' Tara pointed out. 'I mean, she'll know people – her old friends and such. How about Jinny?'

Mack considered the question. 'You forget how small Duncoorie is. It's not as though there would have been loads of kids around. A handful maybe.' An image of Alice sprang into his head, and he pushed it away. 'Anyway, Jinny is a bit older than Freya.'

His sister-in-law was the same age as Carter, and they'd been inseparable since school. In some ways, Mack envied his brother: Carter and Jinny were blissfully happy. On the other hand, being tied down wasn't Mack's bag. While Carter had been stuck at home changing nappies, Mack had been out having fun.

Mack eased the truck into a space behind a small red van that was parked outside Vinnie's cottage, and got out.

'We should have brought wine,' Tara hissed, as he knocked on the door.

'As I said, it's not a social— Hi, Freya.' His heart stuttered at the sight of her, and he smiled widely to cover his sudden confusion. 'Are you ready for us to move your sofa?' he asked. Then, seeing her gaze flit to Cal and Tara, he added, 'I've brought reinforcements. Actually, *Cal* will help; *Tara* will just get in the way. Oh, and she's nosey.'

'Oi.' Tara elbowed him in the ribs.

And to make sure Freya didn't get the wrong end of the stick, he added, 'Cal is a mate and Tara is his fiancée.'

'Right. Er, come in.' Freya appeared to be flustered at the sight of so many people on her step, and he didn't blame her.

Mack led the way, Cal behind him and Tara bringing up the rear. He noticed that Freya had made up the bed in the sitting room and had cleared away some of the ornaments.

'How's your dad?' he asked.

'The worst patient ever. I think the nurses will be glad to be rid of him, and he's only been in Broadford for three days.' Freya wrinkled her nose.

Mack had an urge to kiss it and he looked away, wondering what that was all about. Yes, she was attractive and, yes, he fancied her, but kissing noses? In fact, he could kiss—

'Mack? Mack!'

'Huh?' He came back to earth with a jolt at the sound of Cal's voice.

'I *said*, which end do you want to take?'

'I don't mind.'

'In that case, you can take the heavy end.' Cal chortled.

Mack had walked right into that, which meant Cal would lead the way while Mack took most of the weight. Oh well, he supposed it would give him the opportunity to show off his strength and muscles when he heaved the sofa up those stairs.

Unfortunately, that plan didn't work out as he'd hoped, because Tara took charge, saying to Freya, 'How about putting the kettle on and leaving the men to it? The kitchen is through here, is it?'

The last glimpse Mack had of Freya was her quizzical expression as she followed Tara out of the room.

He stared after her and Cal followed his gaze with a smirk., saying, 'That's the way of it, is it? I thought you just wanted to get into her knickers, but Tara was right – you *do* like her.'

Mack stuck his nose in the air. 'I don't know what you mean. I'm doing this for Vinnie.'

'Yeah, mate, you keep telling yourself that.' Cal gave him a knowing look, then turned his attention to the sofa. 'Grab that end and let's get started. You owe me a pint, by the way.'

'What happened to you being forever in my debt?'

'It went out of the window when I saw those damn stairs.'

Thinking about it, a pint would be a good idea and maybe they could ask Freya if she wanted to join them.

—

Freya felt rather railroaded as she headed into the kitchen to put the kettle on. She'd been hoping that Mack would turn up this evening as promised, and she knew he'd be bringing someone to help, but she hadn't expected *two* someones, or for the second one to be quite so bossy.

Tara pulled out a chair, sat down at the small table and said, 'I hope you don't mind me tagging along.'

'Not at all. Coffee or tea?' One of the many things Freya had brought with her from London was her espresso machine and a supply of pods.

'Coffee, please.'

There was an awkward silence after Tara had selected a pod, and Freya busied herself making the drinks.

'I knew I should have brought wine,' Tara muttered. 'It would have broken the ice.'

Abruptly, Freya wondered whether she was giving off unfriendly vibes, and she immediately felt contrite. 'So, you and Cal are engaged?' she began, hoping to make amends.

It was the right question, as Tara beamed. 'We are.' She raised her left hand and waggled her fingers. A blue stone in a white setting glittered back.

'Congratulations,' Freya said. 'When's the wedding?'

'We've not set a date yet, but we've got a venue. The ceremony will be in the church in the village, followed by a reception at Coorie Castle.'

Freya let out a low whistle, thinking that wouldn't be cheap.

Tara said, 'Cal is the castle's estate manager and we live in the grounds, so it's the logical place to hold it.'

'You're not from Duncoorie, are you?' Freya estimated that Tara was a couple of years younger than her, but even so, she would have remembered her.

'Glasgow originally, but I lived in Edinburgh for a few years.' She made a face, so Freya concluded that the experience hadn't been pleasant.

'How about you?' Tara asked.

'Duncoorie born and bred. I went to university in London when I was eighteen and ended up staying there.'

'It'll be a bit of a change being back on Skye?'

'You can say that again!' Freya's reply was heartfelt. 'Needs must, though; Dad won't be able to manage on his own for a while. Luckily, I don't have to rush back for work.' Freya felt Tara's gaze on her ringless left hand and answered the woman's unspoken question. 'Or for anything else. No husband, no kids – although I do have a boyfriend.'

'Mack will be disappointed.'

'He will?'

'Uh-huh.' Tara nodded. 'Mind you, he's got the morals of an alley cat, so even if you didn't have a significant other, it might be best if you told him you did.'

Freya joined her at the table. 'He's not married, I take it?'

'Good grief, no! He's not the tying-down kind. His heart is in the right place, though. Seriously, if you need a hand or you're in a bind, Mack's your guy.'

A thud from upstairs, accompanied by some choice swear words, made Freya flinch. 'So I gather. It's kind of him to help.'

'He *is* kind,' Tara said. 'I understand you're a teacher? Lovely coffee, by the way.' Her mug was half-empty.

'Thanks. I'm a lecturer in an art college.' To be precise, she was a professor, but she never used the title, as she didn't believe it suited her.

'What do you lecture in?'

'Ceramics. What about you, what do you do?'

'I make doll's houses.'

Freya's interest was piqued. 'I used to love my doll's house when I was a kid.' She wondered what had happened to it. 'Have you got any photos?'

'Loads! You're going to regret asking,' Tara said, taking a phone out of her hoodie pocket.

'They're gorgeous!' Freya exclaimed when she saw them. 'And unusual, too.'

'I do commissions of people's actual houses, or whatever building they want,' Tara explained. 'If you're going to be around for a while, you might want to pay the craft centre a visit. You could have a look at my houses in the flesh, and the centre has an ace gift shop.'

'Craft centre?'

'At the castle.'

Oh, yes. Now Freya came to think of it, she recalled her dad mentioning that Coorie Castle had a craft centre, but that had been a few years ago and she'd totally forgotten about it.

Tara asked, 'Do you make pots and stuff yourself? Or do you concentrate on teaching?'

Tactfully done, Freya mused; some people might have said, 'Or do you "only" teach,' as though teaching was easy. Freya was beginning to warm to the woman.

'Both,' she told her.

'It's rewarding, isn't it? I don't teach as such, but I occasionally run a workshop.'

'That's teaching,' Freya replied firmly, and saw Tara glow with pleasure.

'I never thought of it like that,' the woman said.

'What other crafts are there?'

'We've got a glass-blower, a man who makes stained glass, a jeweller, a watercolour artist, a quilter, and loads more. Oh, and a *potter*.'

Freya was curious to see the craft centre – the pottery studio in particular – and a wave of longing for her own studio swept over her. She'd been trying to avoid thinking about how she was going to cope without the feel of clay in her hands for the rest of the summer, because it was too upsetting. And being back in London on Sunday, packing for Skye, had brought it home to her.

She'd spent the interminable journey telling herself that she'd be too busy to throw pots or make ceramic sculptures anyway, but she hadn't been able to escape the ridiculous sense of loss she felt. And it *was* ridiculous, because she'd only be gone for a short while – she'd be back in London before she knew it.

Her thoughts were interrupted by Mack and Cal.

'All done,' Mack said. 'It was a right bawbag to shift, but it's up there now.'

'Thank you. I really appreciate your help.' She gave Mack a wry smile. 'You were right – I don't think we'd have managed it on our own.'

Cal said, 'Tara, take note: you *can* admit to being wrong now and again.'

Tara got to her feet and walked over to her fiancé. 'I'll be happy to – *when* it happens.' She stretched to give him a quick kiss, then turned to Freya. 'Thanks for the coffee.'

Freya replied, 'Thanks for the company.' She'd enjoyed chatting with her and was sorry to see her go.

She followed them into the hall to show them out, and Mack hesitated by the door. 'We're off to the pub for a quick pint,' he said. 'Care to join us?'

Freya hesitated.

Tara gave her puppy-dog eyes. 'Please come! I guarantee these two will start talking about tides or football, or something equally riveting. I need saving from them.'

'You need *saving*?' Cal chuckled.

'I do! I really do.' Tara nodded. 'You don't know what these two are like when they get together, Freya.'

Freya smiled regretfully. 'Maybe another time? I've had a hectic few days and I'm bushed.'

'I'll hold you to that,' Tara said as Freya showed them out.

After they'd left, she made a mental note to buy the men a bottle of whisky each, and maybe some wine for Tara, because she'd made her feel so welcome.

Her spirits lifted for the first time since she'd heard of her dad's fall. Hopefully, being back in Duncoorie wouldn't be as bad as she feared.

Chapter 9

Mack's mind wasn't on the job, so it was lucky he knew his spiel off by heart. He'd taken out so many whale and dolphin watching trips that he could do it with his eyes closed.

OK, that wasn't *strictly* true. He could talk the talk without too much conscious thought, but he still needed to keep his wits about him, because a sea loch was a fickle mistress. At the northern end, an island at the mouth of the loch gave the landward side protection from the sea, but the tides could be dangerous, and submerged rocks were a hazard.

While keeping his attention on the water, the wind and the boat's location, Mack was able to deliver his well-rehearsed info over the loudspeaker system, telling his passengers about the Atlantic grey seals that were hauled out on the rocks. But a far too generous portion of his mind was on Freya.

There was something about her that intrigued him, although he couldn't put his finger on it.

In the pub last night, Cal, blast him, had taken every opportunity to wind him up, though why Cal was under the impression that Mack thought Freya was different to any other woman he'd set his sights on, Mack didn't know. As far as he was concerned, he'd not done or said anything to give his mate that impression, aside from offering to help shift a bed and a sofa. And that was only because his mother would have given him hell if he hadn't.

But somehow, Freya was preying on his mind. He couldn't seem to get her out of his head and he was baffled by that. He kept returning to the feeling that there was something about her...

Annoyed with himself, his gaze strayed to two women sitting near the cabin. They were giggling and looking his way. Mack smiled automatically as he continued describing the feeding habits of the seals, and received smiles from them in return. However, he had a golden rule of never mixing business with pleasure, so no matter how tempted he might be, he didn't hit on his paying customers. If he happened to bump into them in the pub later, that was a different matter. Not that he was boozing this evening, though. Contrary to popular belief (i.e. *Cal's*), Mack didn't spend all his free time in Skye's various drinking establishments, picking up women.

If he wasn't too tired, he might do a bit of work on his house when he got home. He'd bought it a few years ago, and it had cost him every penny he had and then some. And he'd been doing it up ever since.

As was so typical of many of the older dwellings in this part of Scotland, his house had been single-storey originally, but he'd put in a staircase, and was now in the process of converting the attic into a master bedroom with an en suite, and a study. There was another bedroom downstairs, which he currently slept in, and a family bathroom, so he was in no rush to finish the attic because he wanted to take his time and make sure it was done properly.

He was doing all the work himself, apart from the electrics and the plumbing, and there were only so many hours in the day during the summer months. Running three boat trips, seven days a week (weather permitting) meant he didn't have a lot of free time. Winter was the season to do the renovations; it was also the season to work on the boat, such as servicing the engine, clearing the hull of algae and making any necessary repairs.

Och, who was he kidding! He wouldn't be getting his toolbox out this evening. He didn't want to be indoors hammering and sawing, when he could spend the evening on his lawn, with a cold beer in his hand and listening to music.

—

'They're not all for me,' Freya explained, as the cashier gave her a sideways look when she put three bottles of Scotland's finest malt on the conveyor belt. One of them was, though, and she was planning on having a wee dram with her dad to celebrate him coming home at the end of the week, as the doctor seemed pleased with his progress and the wound was healing well.

Freya was looking forward to getting him home and having some semblance of normality. Normality for *him*, that is; nothing about being in Duncoorie was normal for *her*.

She'd soon settle into a routine, she told herself, aware that these past two weeks couldn't possibly be indicative of the next few. And although she was anticipating things being hard for a while, they should get easier the more mobile and independent her dad became. However, she'd already made a promise to herself that she wouldn't leave Skye too soon. She'd have to be convinced of his ability to cope alone before she returned to London.

Dad was going to find it hard, her being here. He was too used to his own space, his own routines and his own way of doing things, and she feared they might get on each other's nerves fairly quickly. With that in mind, she vowed to try to stay out of his hair as much as possible. Him being downstairs and her being upstairs should help, in the beginning at least, until he demanded to sleep in his own bedroom – which he would want to do sooner rather than later, she guessed.

Freya could continue to work, after a fashion. Obviously, she wouldn't be able to throw any pots or do anything with clay, but she'd be able to design new pieces. In fact, taking a step away from the studio might be good for her. She couldn't remember when she'd last had time to devote purely to designing, to think of nothing except colour and form. Skye was the perfect place to do that. The island had been such a massive influence on her early work, and it would be good to reconnect with it. She could view this enforced, extended visit as a chance to escape from city life, and think of it as a holiday and the opportunity to spend time with her lovely dad.

With the shopping now packed and paid for, Freya drove the thirty-minute journey from the supermarket in Portree back to Duncoorie. She was soon filling the cupboards, freezer and fridge with all kinds of goodies, some of which she knew her dad would turn his nose up at. Avocados were one, and chia seeds were another. But she'd made sure to include his favourites, and she smiled as she placed the bottle of whisky on the sideboard.

On second thoughts—

Freya took it back to the kitchen, not wanting it to be too easy to reach. The last thing she needed was for her dad to overindulge and have another fall.

Feeling like the whisky police, she put the bottle on top of a cupboard, then picked up the other two. Now was as good a time as any to deliver them, and she'd take a look at the craft centre while she was at it. She hadn't been to Coorie Castle for years, although she used to love the woodland behind it and the loch.

The loch…

It was time she made her peace with it. Freya hadn't been near it since she and her dad had scattered her mother's ashes, but if she was to be here for several more weeks, maybe she should. Living in London meant that she hadn't had to confront her grief often and when it did threaten to rise up, she dammed it behind a wall of busyness and activity. Usually, she would retreat to her studio, but sometimes she would throw herself into her college work, or she would visit a museum or see a play – anything to stop her thinking about her mother.

But whenever she visited Duncoorie, she was unable to escape her thoughts, her memories, her sadness. And not once in all those years had she felt any inclination to go down to the loch.

She set off, heading for the track leading from the village to the castle, following the shoreline, and she paused as the loch came into view. It was a glorious day, warm and peaceful. The sea was calm, the waves lapping gently against the rocks, and Freya sat for a moment, letting the stillness of the afternoon flow over her.

She abruptly realised how much she'd missed the glitter of the sun on the water, the birdsong in the trees, and the tang of salt and seaweed. She breathed deeply, drawing the air down into her lungs, and held it, letting it out slowly, closing her eyes.

Expecting grief to rise up and overwhelm her, she was surprised to find that it didn't, and her tension slowly drained away.

After a while she got to her feet and resumed her walk, her eyes scanning the ever-changing loch and the mountains on the opposite shore. All this and more had inspired her creativity when she'd first begun making ceramics, and the further she ventured from the house, the more she felt as though she was being transported back in time to when she was seventeen and preparing a portfolio to take with her to her interview at the very college where she now lectured.

Smiling ruefully, she recalled how keen she'd been to get away, how eager she'd been to experience the world and how desperate to make her mum proud. She still was. If only her mother could see her now… Never in a thousand years had Freya dreamt that she'd be lecturing in a renowned art college and have an offer to become the course director in another, while also having made a name for herself in the world of ceramics.

The path veered away from the loch and as she strolled to the end of it, she could see the castle's turrets poking up above the trees, and very soon the whole thing came into view.

She'd forgotten how magnificent it was. Despite having sites such as Buckingham Palace and the Tower of London practically on her doorstep, Coorie Castle exuded a wildness which was lacking in the historical buildings of England's capital.

Seeing this Scottish castle, she could easily imagine how it must have looked when it was built in the thirteenth century, its purpose to put the fear of God into the English invaders. She almost expected to see men with swords guarding the entrance and archers positioned at the top of the towers.

The place had changed since she'd been here last, and she wondered whether Mhairi Gray still owned it. She couldn't recall her dad saying anything about the castle changing hands, but the woman must be in her eighties, so she probably didn't.

Whoever owned it now had done a considerable amount of work. There was a paved area in front of what she remembered being disused outbuildings, and in the corner where the two wings of those buildings met was a cafe called Coorie and Cuppa, and Freya smiled at the old Scots word coorie, which meant 'cosy'. She also saw signs directing visitors to a maze, a duck pond, a children's play area and a woodland walk.

A quick scan of the studios told her that there were a variety of crafts on the site, from blown glass to silver jewellery, as well as the gift shop that Tara had mentioned.

One end of the long building, the one nearest, housed the largest of the workshops, and she wandered inside to see a glass-blower hard at work. It was hot in there, with several furnaces going, and she wondered how he stuck it. Today wasn't even particularly warm, yet the heat was stifling, even with a good few metres and a counter between her and the fires.

There was a printed sign explaining what the various furnaces were for, which she examined with interest, chuckling to herself when she read that one of them – used for reheating the glass to soften it so it could be worked further or kept hot enough to avoid it cracking – was called a 'glory hole'.

She watched for a while, fascinated as the man rolled a long pole with a blob of orange-white molten material on the end, the glass gradually changing shape, lengthening and widening as he worked it.

Eventually, her attention was drawn to the far end of the room where there was another glass workshop, and when she moved closer, she saw that the area was dedicated to stained glass. There wasn't quite as much drama here, so she contented herself with studying the many completed or semi-completed pieces that were dotted around the space.

Stained glass was something she would like to have a go at, and maybe she would when she found the time. Glass-blowing... not so much. The intense heat and the danger of burning herself put her off. She classed it in the same ballpark as blacksmithing – another craft she was too wary to try.

Freya emerged from the glass studios and went in search of the pottery, her heart lifting when she saw the array of ceramics displayed in the window. Pushing the door open, she went inside and was immediately transported. This was where she belonged, and her spirits soared.

The potter was hard at work, a bowl taking shape under his fingers while she watched, transfixed. No matter how many thousands of times she had seen this done, and had done it herself, it still felt like magic. She assumed every craftsperson felt the same when they transformed a blank page, a lump of wood or a piece of uninspiring metal into something different, new and beautiful. This was why she did what she did.

After watching him for a moment, her gaze roamed around the workshop, noting the barrel-shaped kiln. A pair of protective mitts lay on a nearby shelf, along with a pair of safety glasses, cones and items of kiln furniture. The studio's set-up was much like her own. There was a sink, an area for wedging the clay and hand-building, the wheel itself for throwing, and a glazing station.

There were bags to keep the clay moist, tools for throwing, decorating and trimming, a set of scales, pots of brushes, wareboards, bats for throwing, bowls, sponges, bottles of glazes, slips, and stains. Drying rails held greenware that had yet to be fired, and on other shelves bisqueware sat ready to be glazed. Several aprons hung on hooks near the door, and everything was neat and nicely arranged.

Freya's attention returned to the potter as, satisfied with his creation, he took a wire cutter and sliced through the base of the bowl, separating it from the circular wooden bat that sat on the wheel.

Only then did he look up from his work. 'Hi.'

'Hello. You've got a nice set-up.'

He smiled. 'Are you a potter?'

'I am.'

Getting to his feet, he picked up the bat with the freshly thrown bowl, and carried it to the drying rack. 'I'm Rob. I'd shake your hand, but...' He held up his clay-covered hands.

'Freya. Have you been here long?'

'About four years. I used to be a copper and pottery was my hobby, but now I do it full time. You?'

'I teach and I also potter.'

'Are you local? You sound Scottish.'

'I grew up on Skye, but I live and work in London now.'

'Back for a visit?' He was cleaning the wheel as he spoke, washing it thoroughly. 'Duncoorie is a braw place to escape the rat race for a while. I'm from Newcastle originally.'

'I thought I heard a Geordie accent.'

'We came here for a holiday once and fell in love with the place. Me and the missus decided to move to Skye when I left the police force. We live in Portree now. Duncoorie is too quiet for her. Not enough shops.'

Freya said, 'The craft centre seems busy.'

'It is, thank God. I sell through the gift shop, so the more visitors, the better.'

'I'll have a look at that later.'

'You should. There are some lovely things, real quality workmanship.'

'Like yours,' she said truthfully.

'Thanks, that's kind of you to say so.'

'I'll leave you to it. Nice meeting you,' she said.

'You, too. Maybe you could stop by again before you leave?'

'I definitely will. I'm going to be here for a couple of months.'

'Ah, that's the upside of teaching – the school holidays. But don't let my daughter-in-law hear me say that. She claims they're not long enough! She teaches primary kids. I wouldn't have the patience. What about you?'

'Higher education.'

'University?'

'Uh-huh.' She nodded.

'What subject?'

'Ceramics.'

'When you said you teach, I thought you meant in general, not that you teach *pottery*. Got any tips?'

'I doubt you need any.' She smiled. 'You clearly know what you're doing.'

'Well, don't forget to pop in again,' he said as she turned to leave. 'It'll be nice to talk shop with a fellow potter. My wife's eyes glaze over when I start talking about slips and stains.'

After promising him she would, Freya left to explore the other studios, but before she'd taken more than a step or two, she heard her name being called and glanced around to find Cal walking towards her.

'Have you come for a look around?' he asked.

'Actually, I've come to give you this.' She pulled one of the bottles of whisky from her bag and held it out.

He took it, turning it over in his hands. 'What's this for?'

'For helping move that sofa. I've got one for Mack, too.' She removed the other bottle and offered it to him. 'Would you mind passing it on, along with my thanks?'

He made no move to take it from her. 'You can give it to him yourself. I'm on my way to see him right now, so how about you come with me?'

Freya was taken aback. 'No, it's OK, you can give it to him.'

'I'm sure he'd prefer if you did. Come on, it's not far.'

He wasn't taking no for an answer, was he? And Freya had to admit that she wasn't averse to seeing Mack again. The attraction she felt for the man was undoubtedly an echo from her teenage years, but as she didn't intend to act on it, what was the harm? Anyway, Cal was right: it probably was more polite to thank Mack in person.

Cal strode towards a narrow lane leading past the castle, and she hurried to catch up.

The lane led directly down to the loch, and she fell into step with him. She soon heard the lap of waves against rocks, as a small crescent-shaped beach appeared in front of them. A wooden jetty jutted into the water and a boat lay above the high tide mark.

There was a building directly in front of her, which used to be an old boathouse, but now looked lived in and cared for.

'Oh, how lovely!' she exclaimed, when Cal told her that it had recently been transformed into self-catering accommodation.

'And this is my house.' He pointed to a whitewashed cottage with a wonderful deck facing the water. 'Although, technically, it belongs to Mhairi.'

'Does she still own the place?' Freya was incredulous.

'She does, and she continues to be very active in the running of the estate.'

As they neared the Range Rover parked outside the cottage, it beeped into life and Freya got in the passenger seat.

'Where does Mack live?' she asked.

'He's got a house not far from Muirporth Quay. That's where he moors his boat.'

Freya knew the quay well. Her dad used to moor his trawler there.

Cal was saying, 'He runs a whale- and dolphin-watching business – although I'm hoping he'll agree to the proposition I have for him. It's why I want to see him today. He should be returning from the last afternoon excursion about now.'

'You should have said! I don't want to intrude on a business meeting.'

Cal chuckled. 'You've been in the Big Smoke too long. It's hardly a meeting – a quick chat, that's all. It'll take five minutes.'

The informality of the island appeared to be another thing she'd forgotten, having become so used to the considerably more formal way of life of the college, where emails, conference calls and shared documents were the order of the day, and diaries were synced every other second.

Freya lapsed into silence for the rest of the drive, the journey bringing back so many memories. Her dad used to be a fisherman, landing prawns, crab and lobster for local pubs and restaurants, and he used to come home smelling of sea spray and fish, his face weather-beaten, his hands calloused. To tiny-Freya he'd seemed like a giant, invincible and never-changing. However, adult-Freya recalled the worry on her mother's face if he had been out on the loch when the weather turned.

When she'd been about ten or eleven, he used to take her out with him now and again, but although she'd enjoyed being with him and she'd been fascinated by the creatures he brought up from the deep, she'd hated the thought of the poor things being eaten. Which was daft, considering she used to happily eat chicken nuggets and ham sandwiches. She still liked chicken and ham, but her palate was rather more sophisticated these days, and nuggets definitely weren't on the menu.

Muirporth Quay hadn't changed much, Freya saw, when Cal turned off the coast road. The boats moored up alongside it looked roughly the same; the buildings were as she remembered them, just different signage, that was all.

As the car came to a halt, she noticed a sign saying *Sea Serpent Boat Tours*, and then she spotted the man who operated them, as her gaze was drawn to a vessel where loads of activity was taking place.

She drew in a sharp breath.

Mack was shirtless, wearing just shorts and a pair of calf-length rubber boots. With his hair tied back and his muscles gleaming with water or sweat – Freya didn't mind which – he looked hot.

When Cal guided her across the quay and she drew closer and could see him better, Mack's physique appeared even more impressive. He had a six-pack, for God's sake!

Freya hoped she wasn't drooling, and she hastily averted her eyes in case he saw the spark of desire she suspected might be lurking in them. She was aware of his curious gaze resting on her as he greeted Cal.

'We don't see you up this way very often,' Mack said to him. 'Do you have another damsel who needs rescuing?'

'No, but you'd be the first man I'd call, if I did,' Cal replied, then turned to Freya.

She took the hint and reached into her bag, withdrawing the bottle of whisky. 'This is for you, to say thanks for your help with the bed and the sofa.'

Mack's initial surprise was swiftly followed by a delighted smile. 'You shouldn't have.'

'I got one, as well,' Cal told him. 'She was at the castle, delivering it, and I suggested she took a drive out here with me, as I was coming to see you anyway.'

The surprise was back. 'You were?'

'I've got a proposition for you,' Cal said.

Freya, concerned that it might be a private conversation, said, 'Shall I wait in the car?'

Cal shook his head. 'No need. Stay here and enjoy the view.'

Heat immediately sprang into her face. Oh, hell! Cal must have noticed her reaction to the semi-clothed Mack, but there was no need for him to embarrass her like that.

Then she realised that Cal hadn't been referring to Mack at all, as he said, 'There's an osprey,' and pointed at the water.

Mack turned to look. 'Aye, there's a pair of them. I haven't been able to spot a nest, but they're doing a lot of fishing, so I think they've got chicks.'

'Which brings me to why I'm here,' Cal said. 'Mhairi and I have been chatting, and she wants to offer a bespoke *Colours of Skye* tour.'

'A what now?' Mack frowned.

'A tour of the loch and its natural wonders.' Cal spoke to Freya as he explained, 'I don't know if you're aware, but the castle runs short breaks, where people can try out several different crafts over the course of their stay. It's proving to be quite popular, and as an added perk,' he turned back to Mack, 'we were thinking we could offer boat trips around the loch, could serve as inspiration to the guests.'

Mack appeared to be confused. 'Why couldn't they just come on a normal excursion? Why would they need a special one?'

'Because your trips concentrate on spotting seals, dolphins and whales. The *Colours of Skye* trips would look for those things as well, but it wouldn't be the sole emphasis,' Cal replied. 'Our guests will be encouraged to look at the shape and colour of things like seaweed.' He laughed. 'I realise seaweed isn't sexy, but—'

'I know exactly what you mean,' Freya broke in. 'Creativity isn't just about the bigger things like the sky, the mountains, the deer. It's also about the little things, such as the colours of a mussel shell or the strata in a rock formation.' She stopped abruptly, excitement coursing through her. 'Can somebody let me know when the first trip is running, because I want to be on it.'

Mack was studying her. 'You *do*?'

'Definitely.'

He scratched his beard, and Freya watched his fingers comb through the golden hairs, resisting an insane urge to stroke it. The worrying thing wasn't *that* thought, but the one which followed quickly on its heels, one where she didn't want to stop at stroking his beard – she would want to stroke the rest of him. *All* of him.

Bloody hell! This was so unlike her. It must be due to stress. These past two weeks had been difficult, and the next few weren't promising to be much better, and everyone knew that stress had peculiar ways of manifesting itself.

Freya hastily reminded herself that she was in a relationship, and she vowed to phone Hadrian later. It would be good to ground herself in her normal life, because being on Skye was starting to become somewhat surreal.

'What are your initial thoughts?' Cal asked.

Mack scratched his chin again. 'I'm not sure.'

'Will you at least think about it?'

'I will, aye, but I'm pretty busy with my regular tours just now.'

'How about trying one, and see how you get on?'

Mack sniggered. 'You're the one who is trying – my patience, that is. Get away with you, and let me finish cleaning my boat.'

'I think you'll find that the lads have done it already,' Cal pointed out, jerking his head towards a couple of men nearby. 'This is just a suggestion, but you could put on an additional trip once or twice a week.'

'I work enough hours already! Are you trying to kill me, man?'

'Do you trust your crew?'

'Implicitly.' Mack's reply was immediate and emphatic.

'Couldn't they take out the boat for one of the trips? Then you could run the *Colours of Skye* one without doing any more hours yourself. There'll still be time for—'

Mack interrupted, 'Haud yer wheesht a minute and let a man think.' His eyes narrowed, and he called the two men over. 'What do you say to earning a bit extra?'

The men exchanged glances. 'Doing what?'

'Taking the boat back out.'

'This evening?' one of them asked.

'Now.'

'Why?'

'Because Cal here has got an idea in his head and he's pestering me about it.'

A shrug from the shorter of the two. 'Aye, it's nae bother.'

Cal's expression was one of confusion. 'But how can you run a trip if there's no one on it?'

'There *will* be someone on it,' Mack said.

'I can't go; I've got to get back.' Cal was shaking his head as he backed away.

But when Mack's striking blue eyes turned in her direction, Freya knew who he'd lined up to go on this excursion – *her*.

Chapter 10

Mack strode towards the lock-up, cursing himself. He didn't need any more work in the summer months, so why was he going back out on the loch when he should be going home and relaxing with that beer he'd promised himself? He was getting hungry, too.

'Excuse me? Excuse me!'

The sound of footsteps accompanied the voice, and he glanced over his shoulder to see Freya hurrying after him.

'I don't think this is such a good idea,' she said.

Neither did Mack, and his response was gruffer than it should have been. 'You were all for it a minute ago.'

'I was. I mean, I still am, but I'm not dressed for it.'

Mack stopped and turned to face her, trying to keep his gaze neutral as he scanned her from head to foot. Damn, but she looked good in those jeans. 'You're dressed fine.'

'I've only got trainers on.'

He wished that was true. A naked Freya Sinclair would be a sight to behold.

Och no, he shouldn't have thought of her naked, because now his libido had woken up and given him a prod.

'Trainers are OK,' he replied, his voice coming out somewhat strangled. Dear Lord, if this was what thinking of her naked did to him, God help him if he actually did see her without clothes on. He suspected he might spontaneously combust.

Thank God she couldn't read his mind, because she'd either think he was some kind of lech, or a teenage boy who hadn't kissed a girl yet. Neither image was one he wanted to convey, and he hoped his expression wasn't betraying his thoughts.

'But you've got rubber boots on,' she pointed out.

'I've just been hosing the boat down.'

'Ah, yes, OK.'

Acutely conscious that his chest was bare and that she was staring at it, Mack was about to resume his march to the lock-up, only for her to say, 'Shall we arrange it for another time?'

Hell, no! 'We may as well do this now. Cal will want a decision from me soon.'

Without looking, she called to Cal over her shoulder, 'You can wait a couple of days, can't you, Cal? *Cal?*'

She turned around and her huffed-out sigh told him she'd finally noticed that Cal had left. Something Mack was already aware of.

'He's gone,' she said incredulously. 'You're going to have to give me a lift home.'

Oh, was he now? He didn't think so. 'No can do. Not yet.'

'When?'

'After I've taken you out in the boat.'

'What if I refuse to go?'

'Then you wait on the quay until I come back.'

'You'd go out anyway?'

'I would and I will. It'll give me a chance to think about what these creative types might want to see, if some of the largest creatures on the planet aren't enough for them.'

'It's not so much about the wildlife. It's more about the—'

'Seaweed,' Mack finished for her.

Freya's expression was defiant. 'Have you looked at seaweed? I mean, *really* looked?'

'I've been up to my backside in the stuff,' he said. 'And it's all over the place, so… aye, I've seen seaweed.'

'Seeing isn't the same as looking,' she retorted.

'I thought you taught ceramics, not semantics,' he shot back.

'I do,' she replied slowly. 'Which is partly why I know the difference between the two. You see, I've been heavily influenced by Skye. I still am, to an extent. But…' She smiled, and it lit up her face. 'I think I need a refresher course.'

Mack considered her response, then said, 'So a boat trip right now *is* a good idea, then?'

'I suppose. I wish I'd brought my camera, though. My phone doesn't take good enough shots.'

'You can borrow mine.'

'Oh. Thanks.' She didn't sound particularly enthusiastic or grateful.

Mack smiled to himself, guessing she might be assuming it would be a cheapie supermarket special. Was she in for a surprise!

After a quick glance at the boat to make sure his crew was on board and preparing to cast off again, he turned to the lock-up's door and yanked it open. As he stepped inside, he realised Freya was right behind him. Stopping, he turned around to tell her to go wait by the boat, and Freya walked straight into him.

Her arms came up reflexively and her palms landed on his chest.

Mack sucked in a sharp breath at the electrifying feel of her hands on his bare skin. Her touch jolted through him, sending sparks travelling along his nerves to centre in his stomach.

Her face flushed pink and she hurriedly stepped back. 'Um, sorry. I didn't expect you to stop suddenly.'

'I didn't expect you to follow me inside.' Covering his confusion with banter, he quipped, 'But you're more than welcome to watch me change into some dry shorts.'

The pink deepened to scarlet. She looked incredibly sweet when she blushed, and he wondered whether her kiss would be equally sweet. He also wondered whether he would ever get to find out.

Freya was backing away, her expression one of profound embarrassment. 'Sorry,' she repeated. 'I'll, um, wait by the boat, shall I?'

Mack realised he was being a bit of a dick. Softening his voice, he said, 'I'll only be a minute. You'll enjoy the trip. I promise.'

He didn't blame her for looking sceptical after his less-than-stellar performance during the past few minutes.

Quickly changing into dry clothes, he grabbed his camera. He used it mainly to take marketing shots for his website, and he often took it out on the boat. The Nikon hadn't been cheap, but he'd spent an absolute fortune on a telescopic lens, because he'd discovered that trying to photograph a black blob of a dolphin with a normal lens was nigh on impossible.

It seemed it was going to come in handy again, and he was curious to see what kind of things would get Freya's creative juices flowing. Hell, he was curious about her, full stop.

When he got to the boat, Freya was chatting with Angus and appeared to have recovered from her embarrassment.

'I brought you this,' Mack said. 'It can get chilly on the water.' 'This' was the fleece he rarely wore but kept in the lock-up, just in case. He hoped it was clean.

'Thanks,' she said, slipping it over her head and pulling it on.

He passed her the Nikon. 'Will this do?'

She took it from him and studied it. 'Mine's a Nikon, too. The exact same one.' She looked through the viewfinder, then down at the LCD screen.

So much for his theory that she'd be impressed by his camera.

'They take some decent shots, don't they?' she said.

'Aye. Let's get you on board.' Mack jumped onto the boat first and offered her his hand, which she took after the briefest of hesitations. Once she was safely on the boat, he nodded to Angus. Mack trusted his first mate to know what he was doing, and he wanted to concentrate on Freya's creative process and what she wanted or expected to get out of this trip.

But what Mack really wanted was to get to know her better.

Much better.

—

Wild and windswept, her hair a tangled mess from the stiff breeze scudding across the open water, and with her face glowing from that same breeze and the evening sun on her skin, Freya felt more alive than she'd done in ages.

She zoomed in on the almost-black colour of the still water on the leeward side of a rock, the rock itself glistening with a thousand droplets. Then her eye was caught by the iridescent shells of the mussels, shimmering pale blue to the deepest navy, pearlescent in the early evening sun, and she leant over the side of the boat to get the best angle, her finger clicking the shutter time and time again.

Mack pointed out a piece of driftwood, mostly submerged, with barnacles clinging to it and strands of seaweed so fine and green they could be a mermaid's hair. Tiny fish darted around it.

Surrounded by the sights she'd forgotten, Freya took photo after photo: redshanks wading at the loch's edge, so called because of their distinctive red legs; a little egret on the wing, its snowy-white plumage gleaming and its bright yellow feet making it look like it was wearing a pair of little rubber boots; the streaks of cirrus cloud high in the pale blue sky above, reminding her of horses' tails in the wind. She must have taken a thousand photos and her brain was buzzing with ideas. The only sour grape in her overflowing fruit bowl of excitement was the knowledge that she wouldn't see them come to life until she returned to London.

Throughout the trip, Mack had been a quiet, unobtrusive presence by her side, only speaking occasionally to the guy at the helm to tell him where to go, and now and again asking her a question.

'Do you think it was worthwhile?' he asked her, when the boat was chugging back towards the quay.

'Definitely. I've got so many ideas!'

'Is this for your teaching?'

'No, it's for me. Although, I don't know when I'll have time to make any new pieces if I take the job I've been offered in New York.'

'New York, eh?' Mack's eyebrows raised. 'Doing what?'

'Working for the Black and White Art Academy. Their ceramics course director is retiring shortly, and basically, I've been headhunted.'

'It sounds impressive.'

'I'm still pinching myself. It's one of the leading art academies in the US and a dream job.'

There was a pause, then he asked, 'So you'll be moving to the States?'

'I hope so. They've only just made an offer and I've not seen anything in writing yet. And I have my dad to consider.' How often could she feasibly fly over to Scotland to see him? Maybe he'd like to visit her, and they could take it in turns.

'When will they let him out?'

Freya laughed. 'It sounds like he's in prison, doesn't it? And I'm sure he thinks of it that way; he's not the easiest of patients. I'm hoping they'll discharge him in a day or so.'

'Give him my best. He used to let me help on his trawler sometimes. Paid me peanuts, of course, but he taught me how to handle a boat.'

'I didn't know that.'

'You'd left for uni. Can I drop in on him when he's home?'

Freya beamed. 'I'm sure he'd love to see you.' She ignored the voice in her head telling her that she would like to see Mack just as much as her dad would.

She must phone Hadrian, she reminded herself.

Mack said, 'I'll drop you at home, then send you the photos.'

'I can't wait to see them.' She'd brought her watercolours and sketch pad with her from London, and she was itching to start designing.

How could she have allowed herself to forget how wild and beautiful her homeland was?

'Thanks for insisting on taking me out in your boat,' she said as they drove away from the quay a short time later. 'Are you going to take Cal up on his offer?'

'Maybe. I haven't decided yet. It seems like a lot of bother.'

'My experience hasn't convinced you?'

He gave her a sideways glance and shrugged, as he pulled out onto the road.

Oh well, it was his business, his decision. Nothing to do with her.

'Have dinner with me?' His suggestion startled her, and she didn't know what to say.

On the one hand, she was hungry, but she knew that as soon as she stepped through the front door, she would get out her sketch pad, and food would be the last thing on her mind. On the other hand, she needed to eat, and she knew she'd regret it later if she didn't.

However, considering how attracted she felt, having dinner with Mack was dangerous, and she suspected that food would still be the last thing on her mind.

'I'd better not,' she said.

'OK.'

To her irritation, he didn't seem bothered in the slightest. And it was his lack of concern that made her change her mind.

'On second thoughts, I don't feel like cooking, so it might be a good idea.'

'Up to you.'

'I will, then. Thank you.'

Having anticipated going home to shower, change and sort out her hair, Freya let out a yelp as Mack executed an eye-wateringly fast U-turn and headed back the way they'd come.

'Where are we going?' she demanded. 'The village is that way.' She jerked a thumb over her right shoulder.

'I know. We're going to mine.'

'What? *Why?*'

'Because that's where dinner is.'

'I didn't agree to have dinner with you in *your house*,' she spluttered.

'What's wrong with my house?'

'What's right with it?' It struck her that she was in a stranger's car, being taken to his place, and no one knew where she was.

Mack sighed. 'What has Cal told you? Whatever it is, he's lying.'

Freya bit her lip. 'He hasn't said anything.'

'My place might be a work in progress, but it's perfectly liveable. And while I'm making dinner, you can download the photos.'

Freya's panic subsided into mild concern. 'This is a working dinner, then?'

'Kind of. It'll save me doing it later.'

'Promise to take me home afterwards?'

Another sideways look. 'I was hoping you'd spend the night.'

'*What?!*' Her shriek was loud enough and shrill enough to shatter glass.

Mack slapped the steering wheel with his palm and guffawed. 'Got you going,' he crowed. 'Of course I'll take you home.'

Freya glowered. She didn't find his joke funny in the slightest. 'What if I want to go home right now?'

'Then I'll take you home *right now*. Just make up your mind, because I'm hungry.' Pulling into the side of the road, he twisted in his seat to look at her.

'What are you planning on cooking?' she asked.

'Thai prawn curry with rice.'

Freya's mouth dropped open. She hadn't been expecting that. A rib-eye steak or a pork chop maybe, with chips. Peas, if she was lucky. Thai prawn curry sounded delicious, and she was quite hungry, so... 'OK.'

'OK, what?'

'Please.' Cripes, it was like being a kid again and having her parents drilling manners into her. He needn't be so snotty, though.

'I mean, which do you want to do – go home now, or come to mine for food?'

Ah, right. 'Yours.' And with a wry smile at her silliness, she added, 'Please.'

She and Mack were clearly not on the same wavelength. They had nothing in common, not even a sense of humour, which was fortunate, considering how attractive she found him. For a brief fling, he would be ideal – good-looking, considerate, sexy as hell – but not for anything more serious.

However, as she wasn't in the market for either, it was irrelevant.

Reminding herself she had a boyfriend who was far more in tune with her than Mack could ever be, Freya resolved to enjoy the meal, then put him firmly out of her mind.

Chapter 11

A few seconds later, Mack pulled up alongside a house set on a hillside with views over the loch. It was a lovely spot, but Mack's nearest neighbour probably wasn't within screaming distance, and a frisson of unease shivered through her as Freya realised just how alone she would be with this man.

Oh, for goodness' sake, she told herself. She'd known Mack since they were kids. OK, she mightn't have known him well, in that they'd never hung out together, but they'd gone to the same primary and secondary schools. Anyway, his mum lived two doors up from her dad. Mack was hardly a stranger or a serial killer. She'd been living in the city too long, seeing danger around every corner.

'Didn't you used to live near the post office?' she asked.

'That was years ago. Mum sold the house when I moved out. Said it was too big for her, now she's on her own. Carter was already married by then.' He showed her into a little porch, and she looked around curiously.

'Bathroom's through that door there.' He pointed to a door directly in front, with a set of stairs next to it.

To her right, through an open door, she could see a bedroom, and to her left was a sitting room. When she followed him into it, she saw there was a kitchen beyond, with a boot room-cum-utility room leading off it. The house was modern and light, with white walls, yet had a cosy feel. She'd been expecting something rougher, more in keeping with his job maybe, and she chastised herself for being so judgemental.

'Make yourself at home,' he told her, unlacing his work boots. She noticed he was wearing odd socks, and the sight was strangely endearing.

Slinging her bag onto the sofa, Freya removed the fleece she was still wearing and folded it carefully. 'Would you like me to launder it?'

'Was it dirty?' He looked worried.

'No, but I've been wearing it, so…' She suddenly felt its lack. Despite not being cold, she'd found it comforting. When he'd first given it to her, she'd felt self-conscious wearing something of his, and she hadn't been able to prevent herself from sniffing it. It had smelt of him. Now the fabric only smelt of the outdoors, with a vague hint of the Paco Rabanne perfume she favoured.

'Och, it'll be fine,' he said.

She placed it on the arm of the sofa and wondered what to do with herself.

Mack didn't have any such worries. 'Let me log on to the computer and you can have a play with the photos while I fetch the prawns.'

'Excuse me?' Weren't they in the kitchen, ready and waiting? *Please don't tell me he has to go out and buy some*, she thought. *Or worse, catch them!*

'Tavish will have dropped them off for me on his way home.'

'I don't understand.'

'He leaves them in the byre – the old cowshed out the back. This used to be a farmhouse long ago, you see. Anyway, I've got a fridge out there, just for the purpose.'

'Ah, I see.'

'The food will be ready in half an hour, if that's all right?'

'Brilliant. I'm hungry.'

'Aye, I thought you might be. So am I.'

While he set up the computer, she scanned the room: wooden floors, log burner, battered leather sofas, artwork on the walls. One of the pieces caught her eye. It was a stunning picture of a loch, with a small beach and mountains behind. Made mostly of sea glass, there were also some shells, small pebbles and driftwood, and it was gorgeous.

'There you go,' Mack said, and gestured for her to take his seat at the computer.

He left her to it, and she was soon engrossed in the task of sifting through the photos she'd taken earlier. Gradually, though, an enticing aroma began to distract her, until eventually it made her tummy rumble and her mouth water. If the smell was any indication, this meal promised to be delicious.

Mack popped his head around the sitting-room door. 'Five minutes?'

'Perfect, I'm almost finished. Can I help with anything?'

'It's all under control, but thank you anyway.'

'No, thank *you*. It smells divine.'

'Wait until you taste it first, before passing judgement.'

'I'm sure it'll be delicious,' she insisted, following him into the kitchen where a table only big enough for two had been laid.

'Sit down,' Mack said, flicking a tea towel onto his shoulder as he took the lid off a wide pan and stirred the aromatic golden contents.

Freya's tummy gurgled loudly, and she winced. Thankfully, Mack didn't appear to notice. He was busy dishing up the food into bowls: rice first, topped by the curry, and finished with a scattering of something green (parsley?) and a flatbread on the side.

'Here you go.' He placed the bowl in front of her.

Freya stared at it greedily. 'I'm so looking forward to this.'

'Me, too.' He sat down opposite and picked up a fork. 'Get stuck in.'

Freya didn't need telling twice. She dived into her meal, almost inhaling it as it was so good.

'Do you do much cooking?' Mack asked, after the first few mouthfuls had been hungrily devoured.

'When I remember. I have an awful habit of forgetting to buy groceries, or if I do buy them, I forget to cook them. I usually eat on campus when I'm at work. At home, I either grab whatever's still in date or order in, unless…' She ground to a halt.

'Unless, what?'

'Unless I'm seeing Hadrian, and then we usually eat out.'

'Hadrian…?'

'He's my boyfriend.'

Mack's expression didn't change, but she sensed he was disappointed.

He broke off a piece of flatbread and dipped it in the sauce.

'Been together long?' he asked, before popping it in his mouth.

She must have imagined his disappointment, because now he just looked mildly interested.

'A couple of years.'

'I expect you're missing him.'

Not as much as I should, she thought. 'A bit, but I only saw him on Sunday, so I've not had much time to pine. Sometimes we don't see each other for days.'

'You don't live together?' He looked surprised.

'My flat is on the ground floor, with a studio attached. His is a penthouse, with no room for a kiln.'

'You have your own kiln?' More surprise.

'I do. It's essential – renting space in a kiln would be impractical.'

'Isn't there one in the college you could use?'

'There are several, but they're for the students, as are the drying rooms. But even if I could use them, I wouldn't. I need my own studio, my own kiln and my own space.'

'I see.'

Freya could tell that he didn't, so she explained. 'I wouldn't want to risk anything getting damaged, or fired at the wrong temperature, or… Any number of things can, and do, go wrong when making pottery, and I want to try to minimise the risk, so having my own studio is essential. My kiln has got a 500-litre capacity and weighs half a tonne. It also needs good ventilation, so a penthouse is definitely not the place for it. Besides, Hadrian doesn't like that my ceramics end up all over my apartment. He's more of an acrylics man. Pottery is too messy for him and takes up too much space.'

'I see. Would you like a glass of pop? Coke, or dandelion and burdock?'

Freya laughed. 'Do they still make that?'

'Aye, and cherryade.'

'Oh, God, *cherryade*.' She groaned. 'I used to *love* that stuff.' And suddenly the conversation turned away from her London life, and the vagaries of her and Hadrian's living arrangements, to the remembered tastes of childhood.

'Old Mrs Ferkin at the corner shop used to make her own tablet,' Freya said, after the meal was finished and Mack was cleaning it away.

She'd offered to help, but he'd turned her down with an, 'Och, it'll only take but a minute.'

'Do you remember?' she asked.

Mack grinned. 'It was the best. I can almost taste it. Mmm, sweet, buttery, caramelly...'

'Is caramelly even a word?' Freya laughed. 'Gosh, I could eat a piece of it now.'

'I've got a Wagon Wheel you can have.'

'Dandelion and burdock pop, and Wagon Wheels? What are you – ten?'

'Hey, don't knock it till you try it.'

'Go on, then,' she said, and he refilled her empty glass with more of the bubbly pop and took a Wagon Wheel out of the fridge.

'I like them cold,' he said. 'Anything chocolatey has to be cold.'

'Uh-uh.' She shook her head. 'Room temperature, you heathen.'

'Chilled, Sassenach.'

'I'm no Sassenach, as well you know!' she objected with a laugh. 'Have you been watching reruns of *Outlander* by any chance?'

'Never seen it.'

'You don't know what you're missing. Sam Heughan is to die for.'

'I've heard of him. Doesn't he make the Sassenach Whisky?' Mack said. 'But in case you haven't noticed, I'm not into men, so I don't think I'm missing much.'

Oh, God – *that was it!* Mack Burns had a touch of Jamie Fraser about him, the longish blond hair and beard notwithstanding. An image of the *Outlander* actor flashed into Freya's mind, with one of Mack and his delectable chest following hot on its heels. There wasn't a lot to choose between them...

Abruptly, she got to her feet. 'It's time I made a move.'

'Got what you need?' He jerked his chin towards the sitting room.

'Yes, thanks. Thank you for taking me out in the boat and for the loan of your camera.'

'You're welcome.' He grabbed his work boots and stuffed his feet inside.

'And thanks for dinner,' she added.

'Aye, well, we both had to eat.'

God, he even spoke like Sam Heughan. How come she hadn't noticed it before? And those eyes: bluer than the waters of the loch on a summer's day, they were even more arresting than the actor's.

'Come on,' he said. 'Let's get you home.' And she realised she'd been wool-gathering.

Neither of them said another word until Mack pulled up outside her dad's house.

'Thank you,' she said again, cringing at how formal she sounded.

'You're welcome.'

She noticed that he waited until she was safely inside before he drove off, and she was touched by his chivalry. Not that she was in any danger in this quiet village backstreet.

It was as she ran a bath and poured in the bubbles she'd bought earlier did she understand that, actually, she *was* in danger. But it wasn't a stranger she needed to fear. It wasn't even Mack Burns. It was *herself*.

Freya, wearing pyjamas and a fluffy dressing gown, looked at the clock on the mantlepiece and wondered whether now was a good time to phone Hadrian. It was only ten fifteen, so he was sure to be up. Hadrian was a night owl, rarely going to bed before midnight – unless it was to make love – whereas Freya was usually ready to crash out well before then.

Might he be out, though? There was a strong probability that he would be – and if so, would he want to talk?

Oh, sod it. She'd take her chances, and if he was too busy, then at least she'd tried and he couldn't accuse her of not caring.

Curling up on the sofa, she tucked the dressing gown around her feet and picked up her mobile. But before she rang Hadrian's number, she saw she'd had a missed call from her dad.

Hoping nothing was wrong, she debated whether to call or message him, not wanting a ringing phone to disturb the other patients on the ward. And if he'd only wanted a chat, he might actually be asleep by now, so the message won.

> Sorry I missed you. Call me now if you want? Or I'll phone you in the morning xxx

Her phone rang almost instantly, making her jump. 'Hi, Dad, is everything OK?'

'Can't sleep.'

'Oh, dear. Why's that?'

'Dunno.'

'You sound down.'

'Just fed up, that's all. I want to go home.'

'It won't be long now. Didn't you tell me that the doctor thinks you're doing well?'

Her dad grunted, which she took as an affirmative.

She said, 'I did a big shop this afternoon after I saw you. Got some of your favourites, and a bottle of malt. I also got a bottle each for Mack and Cal.'

'Who?'

'Mack. You know, Jean's son. Remember me telling you that he'd helped me move your bed downstairs? And they shifted the sofa into your room to give you more space in the sitting room.'

'You didn't tell me any such thing.'

'I did. I told you this afternoon.' She shook her head, exasperated. 'You weren't listening, were you?'

'No, sorry.'

She'd noticed that he had a habit of doing that lately. Trying to engage his interest, she said, 'You'll never guess what I've been doing this evening! I went out on a boat.'

'Whatever for?'

She heard him stifle a yawn.

'It's a long story. I'll tell you about it tomorrow. Can I bring you anything?'

'My navy jacket and those cord trousers I like to wear, the ones from Marks and Spencer. And a shirt.'

'You're convinced they're going to send you home soon?'

'They said so, didn't they!' he snapped.

Freya took a calming breath. She knew he didn't mean to be sharp with her. 'You're tired, Dad. I'll let you go to sleep.'

'I told you – *I can't.*'

'Could you ask the nurse for something?'

'Bugger, I need to pee now.' He sounded so cross that Freya had to suppress a laugh. Oh, dear, he wasn't an easy patient, was he? Never mind, they'd muddle through, and she was sure he'd feel better once he was home.

He hung up, and Freya's thumb hovered over Hadrian's number.

Making up her mind, she pressed it.

'Freya!' Hadrian shouted, and she moved the phone away from her ear. It sounded like he was in a nightclub or a bar. She could hear loud music and even louder voices.

'Where are you?' she asked.

'Hang on, I can't hear you.' A couple of seconds later the noise level dropped considerably and Hadrian said, 'That's better, I can hear you now.'

'Where are you?' she repeated.

'The Bustle Club.'

She'd never heard of it. 'Who with?'

'Just some people. You don't know them.'

Try me, she wanted to say, but then she realised she wasn't particularly interested.

'You got to Skye safely, I take it,' he said.

'I messaged you, like you asked.'

'Did you? I didn't see it. I miss you.'

It didn't seem like it. 'I've only been gone three days.'

'Is that all? It feels longer.'

Freya was flattered, until he added, 'It's probably because I've been so busy. You wouldn't believe what happened yesterday.'

He then embarked on a long story involving a fellow artist, which Freya stopped listening to after the first minute.

When Hadrian finally drew breath long enough for her to get a word in edgeways, Freya took the opportunity to say, 'My father will be coming home soon, thanks for asking.'

'Are you annoyed with me, babe?'

Was she? Hmm, yes, she was. If the shoe had been on the other foot, the first thing she would have done would have been to ask about his ill parent. The second would have been to ask about *him*.

Hadrian had done neither. He really could be a self-centred sod sometimes.

Weariness swept through her. She was too tired for this. She wanted to go to bed and sleep for a week.

She had no idea what he had been saying when she interrupted him. 'Sorry, I'm going to have to hang up. I'm asleep on my feet. I've had a frantic couple of days.'

'Why? What on earth have you been doing up there? Too much sightseeing?'

Freya snapped. 'I don't need to see the sights. I used to live here, remember? For your information, I've been sorting my dad's house out ready for when he comes home from hospital. It's not been easy.' She was close to tears.

Maybe Hadrian heard her distress, because he said, 'I'm sure it hasn't. Sorry, babe, that was insensitive of me. Ignore my weird sense of humour.'

Right now, she wanted to ignore *him*. 'I'm tired, Hadrian. I'll speak to you tomorrow.'

'Don't be like that. I didn't mean it. Talk to me for a minute. Has it been really hard?'

'Yes.' She sulked for a moment, then relented. 'There was one nice thing, though. I went out on a boat today. I kind of got railroaded into it, but the fresh air and change of scenery did me good. I was a guinea pig for a new venture.' She proceeded to tell him all about it, ending with, 'It really fired up my imagination. The colours here are out of this world. I'd forgotten how stunning they are: the many different blues and greys of the water, the—'

There was a muffled rustling sound on the other end of the phone, and it dawned on her that he wasn't listening. He was doing what he often did when he was on a call – he was speaking to someone else while holding his phone against his chest.

Freya fumed in silence for a second or two, until he came back on the line. 'Sorry, babe, I lost you for a minute. What were you saying about photos?'

'It doesn't matter, I'll tell you another time,' she said, knowing full well that she probably wouldn't.

'OK. Night, babe. Miss you.'

She wasn't sure she believed he did. Or was she just being crabby because she was away from home, worried about her dad and bone-tired? That must be it, she decided after she ended the call.

Dropping the phone on the sofa, she rested her head against the cushion, uttered a deep sigh and closed her eyes, feeling rather sorry for herself.

Suddenly, Freya sat up.

There was a noise at the front door. Not a knock, but a kind of thud, as though someone had bumped against it. Might it be Rhona's cat, asking to come in?

Not liking the idea of the animal being outside all night, especially on the street, she heaved herself off the sofa and went to take a look. The road her dad's house was on wasn't busy by any stretch of the imagination, but all it took was one car.

Opening the door, she whispered, 'Puss, puss...' But it wasn't a cat that was on her step.

It was a bottle of cherryade pop and some chunks of tablet, wrapped in cellophane and tied with a length of tartan ribbon.

Chapter 12

'You know she's famous, right?'

Mack narrowed his eyes and stared at Jinny. He'd dropped into the castle to see Cal, but Jinny had spotted his truck before he'd got out of the cab and had beckoned him over. He was early, having run some errands that hadn't taken as long as he'd thought, so he had a bit of time to spare before Cal expected him.

Having lured him into the cafe with the promise of coffee and cake, his sister-in-law was now in the middle of quizzing him about what he thought of Freya.

He'd just finished telling her that Freya had taken loads of photos when she was on the boat yesterday, and that not only did she teach, but she also had her own studio complete with a half-tonne kiln, when Jinny dropped this particular bombshell on him.

'What do you mean, *famous*?' he asked.

'As in well-known, renowned, her ceramics in demand – that kind of famous. Hang on.' She played with her phone for a moment, then turned it around so he could see the screen. 'That's her website.'

He took it from her and examined it. 'Flipping hell, is that price in *pounds*?'

'It is.'

'I'll be jiggered. I'd never pay that for a vase. It's a weird shape for a start.'

Jinny rolled her eyes. 'Heathen!'

It was the second time he'd been called that in less than twenty-four hours.

'Why are you looking so glum?' she asked.

'I don't look glum,' he protested. 'This is my normal expression.'

'Aye, right-o. Is it because she's got a boyfriend? If so, Tara got the impression it wasn't serious.'

'Why's that?' he asked, knowing he'd regret asking, but curiosity getting the better of him.

'Apparently, she's not too bothered about rushing back to London, so it *can't* be serious, can it?'

'That might be the case, but she's not staying on Skye. As soon as Vinnie's better, she's away. She's been offered a job in New York.'

'She's moving to *New York*?'

He shrugged. 'Or back to London. She's not decided yet.'

'You sure talked a lot on the way home.' Jinny waggled her eyebrows.

'We were on the loch for a wee while,' he hedged.

'From what I heard, the pair of you didn't actually speak much when you were on the boat, but you were sniffing around her like a stag after a hind.'

'You paint a lovely picture. Who did you hear that from? Was it Angus?' Mack would have his guts for garters.

'Never you mind.'

'It was either him or Graham.'

'Does it matter?'

'I don't want my crew yammering about my private life.'

'I thought you were doing Cal a favour? I didn't realise taking Freya Sinclair out on your boat was *private*.'

'I was, and it wasn't.'

'So you can't have a go at Angus or Graham for saying anything, can you? Besides, I thought you would have been proud to be likened to a stag.' She placed her hands on her head, fingers spread wide, and wiggled them. 'What would you be, a fourteen-pointer? A sixteen?'

'Since when do you know so much about red deer antlers?'

'I know lots of things. Did you know that the stags with sixteen or more points on their antlers are called monarchs?'

'I did, actually. Can we talk about something else?'

'We certainly can. Why don't we talk about how you managed to find the time to have an in-depth convo with Freya?'

Mack groaned. Carter always said that Jinny could be like a dog with a bone, so he decided to come clean, and it wasn't as though he had anything to hide.

'She had some Thai curry at mine afterwards,' he admitted.

Jinny's eyebrows shot up so fast that Mack was surprised they didn't escape Earth's gravity.

He said, 'I cooked while she sorted out the photos. It saved me a job.'

His sister-in-law's smile was knowing. 'Is that how you're going to play this?'

'I'm not playing anything.'

Abruptly, she sobered, her gaze fixed on his face. 'No, I don't believe you are. It's about time you found someone special, Mack.'

'I don't need anyone special. I wish everyone would stop trying to marry me off! I'm fine as I am.' It came out as a growl.

Jinny opened her mouth to say something, but closed it again, which was just as well, because he was done with the conversation.

Getting to his feet, he said in a softer voice, 'I'd better go find Cal – he's expecting me and I'm late, thanks to you. We must do this again sometime. I enjoyed our little chat.'

'Liar.'

She was laughing at him, and he couldn't help but laugh back. Jinny might be as irritating as hell, but he thought the world of his sister-in-law.

When he entered the castle, Mack asked the woman on the reception desk where he could find Cal, and she informed him that he was with Mhairi in the parlour, and that Mack was to go on through.

Mack had a soft spot for Mhairi and a great deal of respect for her. She still took an active role in the running of the castle, despite her advanced years, and her business acumen was second to none. She was as sharp as a tack, yet she was also warm and generous. He intended to tell Cal that he was turning down the offer and although he knew Mhairi wouldn't hold it against him, he couldn't help feeling he was letting her down.

'Mackenzie, my dear!' Mhairi cried as soon as she saw him step into her parlour.

This was the hub of the castle, where Mhairi conducted her business, made decisions and held meetings. There were old paintings on the walls, a marble mantlepiece and antique furniture, including the desk she used, which was probably worth a fair bit.

She wasn't sitting at it now, but was perched on one of the two chintzy sofas, her back ramrod straight, her legs neatly crossed at the ankle. She held out both hands, and

Mack walked across the room. Taking them in his, he bent to kiss her cheek.

It was like an audience with a senior member of the royal family, without the bowing.

'Tea?' she asked, letting go of his hands and reaching for the teapot sitting on a low table between her and Cal.

Mack gave Cal a nod of acknowledgement, then said, 'No thanks, I'm not stopping. I've just come to tell Cal—'

'Nonsense! There's always time for a cup of tea.'

Mack glanced at Cal, who raised his eyebrows and shrugged, and Mack knew when he was outgunned so he took a seat, saying, 'That would be grand.'

He watched her pour the tea into a delicate china cup, which sat on an equally delicate saucer. When she handed it to him, he took it from her with a rattle. Worried he might spill his drink, he balanced the saucer on his knee.

Mhairi began, 'Cal tells me you've taken your first client out on the *Colours of Skye* tour.'

Mack gritted his teeth and shot Cal a venomous look, sensing he was being set up. 'Not exactly. I had a trial run.'

'How did it go?'

'All right, I suppose. The lady seemed to get something out of it.'

'Would you say it was a success?'

'Difficult to tell, what with it being only the one person and only the first trip.'

'In that case, you must organise another. I've been canvassing opinions among my guests and they think it's a good idea.'

Wait till he got Cal on his own…

He said, 'Mhairi, I'm not sure this will work. My boat takes fifty-three and it runs at between 90 and 95 per cent full capacity at this time of year. For me to put on an additional excursion, what with the fuel, the additional staff costs, the—'

Interrupting him, Mhairi said, 'I've worked out some figures, and of course I wouldn't expect you to do this for nothing. You have to make a profit. Cal?' She inclined her head, and Cal placed a sheet of paper on the table.

Mack looked at it, swiftly working out the figures in his head. They added up. 'Your guests would pay this?'

Mhairi smiled. 'They would. I don't think you appreciate quite how exclusive our clientele is.'

'Why wouldn't they just book on a normal trip?'

'As I said, they enjoy exclusivity.'

Mack shook his head, bewildered. He was aware that staying at the castle wasn't cheap, and that it catered to what his mum referred to as 'the more discerning guest' and what he silently called 'those with more money than sense', but for them to pay four times what he normally charged for a whale-watching trip was beyond his ken.

'I'll consider it,' he said, cautiously.

Mhairi inclined her head again. 'That's all I ask.'

Assuming he was dismissed, Mack carefully placed his untouched tea on the table and made to stand.

'There is something else,' she said. 'I wonder if you could arrange for Ms Sinclair to pop in and see me? I want to chat to her about her experience yesterday and ask her whether any improvements can be made from the client's point of view.'

Mack was taken aback. 'Can't Cal do it? I hardly know the woman.'

'You probably know her better than Cal, considering you spent some time in her company yesterday. Anyway, I expect you to be there as well. You will be, won't you? Please indulge an old lady and say you'll come.'

Mhairi might look like a pussycat, but she was a leopard underneath the sweet, gentle exterior. And that leopard had sharp claws; once she got them into a person, she didn't let go easily.

'I've got a lot on,' Mack hedged. 'Work... and stuff.'

'Tosh! You don't work in the evenings. We'll have dinner. Seven p.m. sharp.'

'Tonight?'

'Is that a problem?'

'It's a bit short notice.'

'For whom?'

'For me, for one.'

'Had you anything planned?'

'No, but Freya might.'

'There's only one way to find out. Ask her.'

Mack knew when he was beaten. He had come here to tell Cal that he wasn't interested in operating the castle's bespoke tours, and he was leaving having been strong-armed into it by a little old lady half his size. Not only that, but he'd also agreed to have dinner at the castle this evening with a woman who he feared he liked more than was good for him.

Freya wasn't in. The disappointment Mack felt was balanced by an equal measure of relief. Deciding it was best not to delve too deeply into the reasons behind either emotion, he turned away from her door to get back in his truck.

He'd send Cal a message telling him that dinner was a non-starter for this evening and let *him* pass on the news to Mhairi.

Hesitating, his fingers curled around the truck's door handle, Mack gazed at Freya's step and wondered what she'd thought of his little gift last night. He had no idea what daft impulse had made him pop into the shop after he'd dropped her off. He should have gone straight home but…

'Have you lost something?' Freya's voice made him jump, and he glanced around.

She was nowhere in sight.

'Up here,' she called, and he looked up to see her leaning out of the sash window, peering down at him.

'Hi,' he mumbled, at sixes and sevens.

'I was in the bath,' she said.

Mack swallowed. Nope, he wasn't going to go there.

'I had to dash upstairs to put some clothes on before I answered the door.'

Dear God…

She continued, 'I thought you were from social services. They're coming today to assess the house.'

'Sorry to disappoint you,' he said, craning his neck.

'Wait there, I'm coming down.' Her head disappeared, and the window slammed shut.

A couple of seconds later, the front door opened and she was standing before him in a pair of cut-off jeans and a vest top. Her hair was tied back, copper tendrils escaping to frame her face, and her cheeks were pink and her feet bare.

Mack fought the urge to take her in his arms and kiss her senseless.

Och, he was the one who was senseless, having these ridiculous thoughts. Freya was not casual-fling material, a tourist who would be here today and gone tomorrow. And neither was she a local — not that he'd risk having a relationship with anyone who lived nearby, because he wouldn't want to give them the impression he wanted a steady girlfriend.

Freya was somewhere in between. Unclassified. Out of bounds for both reasons. She might be gone sooner or later, but she'd be here for long enough to derail his orderly existence. Plus, he had a suspicion that if he let her, she might come to mean more to him than any woman ever had.

Then there was the irrefutable fact that she had a boyfriend, and he wasn't in the habit of poaching on anyone else's patch.

Her expression unreadable, Freya said, 'Thanks for the pop and the tablet.'

'I was in the shop for some bits and bobs, saw it and thought of you.'

'That's kind of you.'

'It was nothing.' He shuffled self-consciously from foot to foot, hoping what he was about to say next wouldn't come out wrong or be taken the wrong way. 'I've just come from the castle. Mhairi wants you to have dinner with her this evening. She wants to pick your brains about yesterday's trip.'

'Dinner at the castle? As Mhairi Gray's guest?'

'Aye, that's the gist of it.'

'I've always wanted to see inside.'

'Now's your chance.'

'Can you tell her, yes, please, and thank you? Or should I phone the castle to confirm?'

'No need. I'll let Cal know.'

'Maybe you should pass on my mobile number, in case there's an issue?'

She gave him her number, and he called her back on it to ensure he'd typed it in correctly. Or that's what he told himself. It had nothing to do with her now having *his* number. Though why she'd need it, he hadn't figured out.

'See you tonight,' he said, opening the truck's door.

'Will you be there?'

'Aye. It concerns me too. Apparently, I'll be running these trips, whether I want to or no. A word of warning – what Mhairi wants, Mhairi gets. Be on your guard, that's all I'm saying.' And with that, he hopped into the truck.

Let her make of that what she will. At least she couldn't say she hadn't been warned.

—

Freya closed the front door and leant against it. Dinner at the castle, eh? She was rather surprised to be asked, and even more surprised that it was Mack who had done the asking. Wait till she told her dad – he'd be well impressed.

She wasn't sure Hadrian would be, though; a castle in the wilds of Scotland wasn't his kind of thing. She would tell him anyway, and she'd be sure to make a point that it was work-related, in case he still thought she was up here enjoying herself.

Another knock on the door startled her.

'Come in,' she said when the ladies from the local authority identified themselves, and the next twenty minutes consisted of them taking notes and advising her what they could and couldn't do to help her dad.

They recommended that a stairlift be put in, along with a shower stall, or one of those baths that you get into while the water fills it; they also advised about installing handrails by the front and back doors, and suggested replacing the sagging armchairs with ones which had firmer seats at the very least (they did mention one of those electric chairs that raised or lowered at the touch of a button). Then they departed, leaving Freya with her thoughts whirling and a to-do list longer than her arm.

Was there really any need to have a new bath or a shower put in? And a stairlift?

Her dad would undoubtedly have difficulty walking for a while, but he'd soon be able to get up and down the stairs and in and out of his own bath, so was all this strictly necessary?

Anyway, knowing the speed at which local authorities moved, he'd have been back on his feet for months by the time anyone came to measure up. Plus, he would probably be discharged tomorrow, so all these adaptations would be installed far too late to be of any use to him. And would he want any of them anyway?

One of those electric riser chairs might be a good idea, though, and while she was eating a hastily prepared lunch, Freya looked online to see what was available and how quickly she could get hold of one.

Not quickly enough, it seemed. None of the websites she visited had anything available immediately. The shortest lead time was three weeks, the longest twelve. Her dad needed it now, if it was to be of any use to him.

Trawling an online auction site gave her more joy, although she didn't particularly want to bid on one then have to wait until she knew whether she'd won the item.

Shelving that for a moment, she went on to see what else might help him during the first few weeks at home, and before she knew it, she had purchased a bath seat that swivelled, a raised loo seat, a couple of handrails (and a special curved one for the stairs), and several other bits and pieces which she thought may come in handy.

No doubt her dad would shout at her when he saw them, but he'd soon get over it when he realised that they were there to make his life easier. And with next-day delivery, everything should arrive tomorrow. Now all she had to do was visit him to tell him her news.

'I couldn't get you a chair, though,' Freya said, after telling him about the recommendations that social services had made.

Her dad's expression hardly changed; he was trying not to let his displeasure show but she could see the irritation in his eyes.

'Why did you buy all that? It's a waste of money. They told me I can't have a bath for six weeks. I have to have a strip wash.'

Freya made a mental note to order him a plastic chair, so he could sit on it in the bathroom to have a wash.

'I told you I'll be fine,' he added, grumpily.

'If it helps you, it's worth it.' Freya chuckled, adding, 'It could be worse, Dad – I could have arranged for you to have a stairlift installed.'

'Don't you bloody well dare!'

'Don't worry, I didn't. Although the two women who did the assessment seemed quite insistent.'

'I don't need a bloody stairlift. Or a raised toilet seat.'

'Tough. You're having one. It's being delivered tomorrow. Which reminds me, do you think they'll discharge you tomorrow?'

'I expect so. They'll want the bed. What did those women say? The ones from the council? Did they mention me?'

'Of course they did! You're the reason for the assessment. Dad, are you OK?'

'Do I look it? I've been stuck in here for days on end.'

'I hope you aren't giving those poor nurses a hard time.' Freya tried to keep the admonishment light because she knew how frustrated he felt at being in hospital, but he needn't be quite so curmudgeonly.

Her dad looked away and refused to meet her eye, and she guessed he knew he was being unreasonable. It wasn't anyone's fault that he was in hospital, and everyone was trying their best.

Now that she'd got the practical side of things out of the way, it was time to share her other news. 'I've been invited to the castle to have dinner with Mhairi Gray tonight,' she announced, and was gratified to see him perk up as she explained why.

'You can't stop working, can you?' he said, patting her arm then giving it a squeeze.

'Gotta keep my hand in,' she joked. 'This isn't anything to do with work, though, but I'm not turning down the chance of a meal at Coorie Castle!'

She'd read on the castle's website that only the castle's guests ate there. You couldn't just book lunch or dinner – you had to be a resident – which made the invitation even more appealing, considering she wouldn't get to sample the food any other way.

'You must tell me all about it,' her dad said.

'I will,' she promised.

Freya intended to make the most of the experience, because once her dad was home from hospital, she knew that all she would be doing for the next few weeks was caring for him and making sure nothing impeded his recovery.

Chapter 13

It's lucky I thought to pack something smart, Freya mused as she took the one and only dress she'd brought with her from London off the hanger. It was plain blue linen with buttons down the front, and she had a feeling she might have bought it because it reminded her of a denim shirt. The cut and style were classic, so she hoped it would do. It would have to, because she didn't have anything else.

She'd tamed her hair into a sleek bun, rather than the hastily gathered-up mess she usually had on the top of her head, and she'd even applied some make-up to her eyes and lips. She never bothered with foundation because it would have to be thicker than the bark on an old oak tree to successfully cover her freckles. A squirt of perfume, and she was ready.

It was a shame she'd spoil the effect by rocking up in her little van, but the vehicle was practical for transporting her ceramics, and practicality trumped appearance.

Grabbing her leather biker-style jacket, she headed out the door, anticipation making her quite giddy. It wasn't the poshness of the venue making her feel this way (she wasn't into that kind of thing); it was the thought of centuries of history within those thick walls: paintings, tapestries, antique furniture, sculptures and – of course – ceramics. Freya was salivating over the prospect of seeing all the treasures the castle undoubtedly held, as much as at the thought of the food she was about to eat. If the sample menu on the castle's website was any indication, she was in for a culinary treat.

To be honest, she was a bit apprehensive about meeting Mhairi Gray. The woman had been a well-known, although somewhat elusive, figure in Duncoorie when Freya was growing up. And although Freya had played in the woodland and had explored the loch's shoreline near the village, she'd rarely ventured into the castle's grounds.

Mhairi Gray hadn't encouraged visitors, but from what Freya's dad had told her over the years, the rumour was that Mhairi had run out of money, so had been forced to make the castle earn its keep. How true the rumour was, Freya had no idea, and neither did she particularly care. She was simply grateful for the opportunity to see inside the place.

This evening, the castle's car park was considerably less full than yesterday afternoon, which wasn't surprising, since the craft centre was now closed. The cars which were there were parked in a separate area, with a sign that said: *Residents' Parking Only. Please inform reception of your vehicle's registration number when booking in.*

After taking a quick look at some of the vehicles, Freya drove her van into one of the many vacant bays in the main parking area, feeling self-conscious. She didn't belong in a place like this, and she revised her initial feeling that Hadrian wouldn't like it here – this would be right up his alley. Not the craft-centre bit, obviously, but the castle itself.

As she got out of the van and glanced around, she thought it strange that an artist such as Hadrian wouldn't want to mooch around somewhere like the craft centre. But it wasn't his kind of thing at all. The only mooching he did (if she could use a word like that when referring to her boyfriend) was around upmarket, expensive and hip London galleries.

Hadrian liked to be seen in places like that; it was where he was happiest. Freya wasn't keen on them at all. Her happy place was her studio, when she was up to her elbows in clay. She did enjoy seeing her work displayed, though, but wasn't keen on the attention she received, whereas Hadrian revelled in it. The attention he got for *his* work, obviously, not hers.

Oh dear, was she doing him a disservice? If people could listen in on her thoughts, they'd be perfectly within their rights to assume she didn't like him much, when in fact she liked him fine.

Freya had been about to step through the castle's grand entrance, when she froze.

Liked him *fine*? That was hardly the basis for a romantic relationship, liking someone *fine*.

The realisation gave her a shock, but now wasn't the time to think about the epiphany she'd just had. She'd mull it over later. But it seemed she had a decision to make, especially since she was almost certain she was going to take Jocasta Black up on her offer.

Putting Hadrian to the back of her mind, Freya entered the castle and was immediately transported back in time.

The hall was wide, its walls covered by wood-panelling partly hidden by portraits of stern-looking people, a coat of arms and a couple of large tapestries depicting hunting scenes. The floor was tiled with marble, a crystal chandelier glittered overhead, and a sweeping staircase lay directly ahead of her.

Freya twirled slowly on the spot, taking in as many details as she could, filing them away for future reference.

The castle wasn't all Bonnie Prince Charlie, though. There were nods to the present day in the form of a reception desk with a computer. The guy who was sitting behind it smiled at her, and she approached hesitantly, feeling rather out of her depth.

'Hi, I'm supposed to be having dinner with Miss Gray?' She hated that she made it sound like a question, but she wasn't entirely convinced that it wasn't a mistake, or that Mack had got it wrong and she was actually meeting with Cal, and dinner wasn't involved at all.

'Freya Sinclair?' he asked.

She nodded.

'Come this way. She's expecting you.'

Freya's eyes were out on stalks as she followed the guy through a series of interconnected rooms, and when he finally halted outside a door and gently tapped on it, she was thoroughly lost. Without waiting for a reply, he turned the handle and held the door open for her. But just then, Freya became aware of footsteps behind and when she looked around, expecting to see a member of staff, she was surprised when she saw it was Mack.

Oh, my, he looked gorgeous! Open-necked white shirt, with the sleeves rolled up exposing his forearms, faded blue jeans (but not the scruffy kind) and tied-back hair...

Freya found herself staring, and she swallowed and looked away. Seeing him had given her a jolt of the nicest kind. The sort of jolt that made her heart go tippety-tap and her breath catch in her throat. The sort of jolt that sent her ovaries into overdrive.

Bloody hell! What was wrong with her? She really must control her reaction to him. It was getting out of hand.

An imperious voice jerked her out of her fugue. 'Are you coming in, or do you intend to eat out there?'

Mack arched his brow and said, 'I think we're being summoned. After you.' He gestured for her to go first and she wished he wasn't being a gentleman.

Lifting her chin, Freya walked into the room and her gaze was immediately captured by a tall, white-haired woman with high cheekbones and piercing blue eyes, who said, 'Hello, dear, I'm Mhairi Gray. It's nice to see you. You too, Mackenzie.' She held out a slender hand.

Freya shook it. 'Thank you for inviting me. You have a lovely home.'

'It is rather grand, isn't it. You know Cal, don't you?'

'I do. Hello, again.'

Cal gave her a wave then turned his eyes on Mack. 'You scrub up OK, Mack. One of these days we'll see you in a suit.'

Mack scoffed. 'I highly doubt it.'

'What about a kilt?' Mhairi asked. 'You like getting your legs out.' She gave them a pointed look, adding, 'It's nice to see you fully clothed for a change.' She turned to Freya and continued, 'I don't object to seeing Mack's legs, but he does tend to flaunt them.'

Freya barked out a laugh which she hastily turned into a cough.

He glowered. 'I do not. I like shorts, that's all.'

Mhairi stared at him over the rim of her silver-framed spectacles. 'Let's enjoy our meal, then we'll talk business. Take your seats, please.'

Mack pulled out a chair for Freya and she sat down, admiring the crisp white tablecloth, the silver cutlery and the lead crystal glasses, none of which would be out of place in any of the top London hotels. This was seriously posh, and she felt rather awkward.

After the first course had been served and Freya had taken a sip of the miniscule portion of pea and mint soup, Mhairi said, 'Freya, my dear, I believe you father has recently had a fall. How is he? On the mend, I hope?'

Freya placed her soup spoon neatly on the edge of her plate before answering. 'He's fractured his hip, but I'm hoping he'll be discharged tomorrow.'

'I expect he's looking forward to coming home. Please give him my regards. It's not going to be easy for him for a while, but I'm sure he'll recover swiftly with you to look after him. If there's anything I can do to help, please don't hesitate.'

'That's very kind of you. I'm fine at the moment. Mack and Cal have been a great help.'

'Ah yes, moving furniture.' Mhairi pressed her lips together. 'As one gets older, falling does become a worry. But then, lots of things become worries, and what one could cope with easily when younger becomes more difficult as one ages.'

Cal shot his employer a concerned look. 'Is everything all right?'

'Of course. You've nothing to worry about; I'm as fit as a fiddle. However, I am realistic.'

'You would tell me if something was wrong, wouldn't you?' Cal persisted.

Freya realised that he genuinely cared for the old lady and that their relationship went deeper than employer and employee, and it warmed her heart.

Mhairi waved a dismissive hand in the air. 'You know I would. Now, can we move on from the dreary subject of old age? I want to ask Freya about her wonderful pots.

I understand you're becoming quite famous in ceramic circles?'

Freya's cheeks grew warm. 'I'm doing OK.'

'She's being modest,' Mhairi said to the others. 'Maybe we could ask Freya whether she would like to run a workshop here – as a one-off, of course. Rob isn't keen, so I'm sure he wouldn't mind.' She turned her bright gaze on Freya. 'I realise you have commitments elsewhere, but if time allows maybe you would consider it? Or perhaps a talk? Hmm, that might be an option.'

Freya had been starting to relax, despite the formality and the castle's rather intimidating owner. Mhairi was a gracious and genteel host, if somewhat regal, with old-world manners. Cal appeared totally at home in her company, although Freya sensed that Mack was a fish equally as out of water as she. It kind of bonded them together in some small way, as they kept meeting each other's gaze, usually with a smile and occasionally with a hint of mild panic when faced with so many choices of cutlery.

But now Freya was tense once more. So much for not discussing business until after the meal! They hadn't finished the first course yet and the old lady was already bargaining harder than a dodgy market trader.

'Um, I'll have to see how it goes with Dad,' Freya hedged. 'I'm not going to be able to leave him alone for long at first.'

'Understood...' Mhairi said, and Freya thought that was the end of it, until she added, 'But when you are able, we'll discuss it, yes?'

Like a rabbit caught in headlights, Freya froze, not wanting to discuss it at all, and she wondered how she could politely turn the woman down. It seemed rather rude to refuse, when she was enjoying a meal at her table.

A tap on her ankle from Mack's foot made her realise that Mhairi was staring at her expectantly, waiting for an answer.

'Er, yes, of course. We'll chat again when he's better.'

Another tap, this time slightly harder, and she glared at Mack, who was grinning at her.

'Liar,' he mouthed, and she scowled at him.

The rest of the meal went considerably smoother – for Freya at least. For Mack, not so much.

After Mhairi had expertly and knowledgeably quizzed Freya on what she had been looking for when she was out on the loch, what had caught her eye and what she thought the hotel guests would gain from the experience, the old lady turned her gimlet gaze on Mack.

It was Freya's turn to grin as he shifted uncomfortably at Mhairi's ability to counter all his arguments for not trying at least one official *Colours of Skye* excursion.

'What have you got to lose?' Mhairi asked.

Mack pulled a face and Freya pressed her lips together to hold in a giggle. Poor Mack, she felt rather sorry for him – he clearly didn't stand a hope in hell when it came to the owner of Coorie Castle. Freya definitely wouldn't like to get on the wrong side of her.

'That's settled,' Mhairi announced with a satisfied smile, delicately dabbing her lips with a linen napkin. 'Coffee?'

'Lovely,' Freya said, placing her own napkin next to her plate. The food had been wonderful and she was so full that she could barely move.

After the coffee and some exquisite handmade chocolates to go with it, she was seriously concerned that she would fall asleep at the table. It had been another busy day (recently, every day was hectic) and she was ready for bed, even though it was still light outside and it wouldn't be dark for another hour. Having lived down south for so many years, she wasn't used to the days being quite so long. But she didn't want to appear rude by leaving yet, with the meal not long finished, so she decided to take her cue from Mack.

However, it was Mhairi who made the first move. 'I think it's time I retired to bed. I find I don't have the stamina I once did. These days I tire more easily.' She made to rise and Cal leapt out of his seat to pull out her chair.

'Thank you, Cal. Give Tara my love. It's a pity she wasn't able to join us for dinner this evening. Another time, perhaps? And you must come again, Freya, my dear. It was a pleasure to meet you.'

Mack got to his feet and Freya followed suit. She said, 'It was a pleasure to meet you too, and thank you so much for inviting me. The meal was divine.'

'Not up to London standards, I suspect.'

'It most definitely was,' Freya assured her. Mhairi was being modest. 'I can't think of a time when I've had better,' she added.

'You're so kind. Why don't you and Mack get off? I'd like a quick word with Cal.'

Freya bade them both good night and accompanied Mack out of the castle.

Despite her tiredness and full tummy, she was reluctant to leave and she turned around to gaze at the old building.

'It's gorgeous, isn't it?' she said. 'But maybe gorgeous is the wrong word. Magnificent is better. To think it's been standing for the best part of eight hundred years.'

'Aye, and it'll probably stand here for another eight hundred.'

'I hope so. There's something quite humbling about so much history. I'd forgotten that.'

Mack chuckled. 'Isn't there the same amount of history in London? I was under the impression there was rather more of it.'

Freya wrinkled her nose. 'You know what I mean.'

He nodded slowly. 'I do. It's the raw power of a place like this. It can get lost in a place like London, I think.'

'Have you been there?'

'I have, but I wasn't keen.'

'It can be a bit of a culture shock,' Freya acknowledged, even for her, who had loved the city from the very first time she'd visited it. She still did. It was so alive, so vibrant. And the culture was to die for.

Still, now that she was back on Skye, she really should make the time to reconnect with nature; it would do wonders for her work, and since the boat trip, she'd been buzzing with ideas.

Her thoughts went to her studio and the items that were still waiting to be fired. It wouldn't hurt for them to dry for a few more weeks, but it pained her to think that she wouldn't be there for a while. She was itching to get back to it.

'I really did get a lot out of the boat trip,' she said softly. 'I think other people will, too.'

'I'm not sure *I* will,' Mack grumbled, but she could tell it was half-hearted.

'Go on, you'll love it,' she teased. 'And think of the extra money.'

'It's not all about money,' he countered. 'Do you make your pots purely for the money?'

'Absolutely not! I do it because I love ceramics.' Pots indeed! She made much more than pots.

He said, 'That's my point exactly, but it helps that I earn a living from doing what I love.'

His gaze met hers and they grinned at each other, Freya feeling a warm glow that he 'got' her. It *wasn't* about the money (although it helped) and neither was it about the recognition. It was about the act of making something unique and beautiful out of a lump of clay.

She imagined that for Mack, it was being out on the water, at one with the wind and the tides, on a fickle sea under an ever-changing sky. She could appreciate the rawness of it, the beauty and the majesty.

'Would you like to go for a walk?' he suggested. 'It's a glorious evening for it.'

It was. The sky was silvered where the sun's light had dimmed, darkening imperceptibly to steel, then indigo. There was already a smattering of stars to the east and more would appear as the remaining light faded. The breeze was light, although it would pick up away from the shelter of the castle.

She asked, 'Where did you have in mind? It'll be dark soon.'

'There's a duck pond. We could stroll around that.'

Freya blinked. She'd been half-expecting him to suggest going down to the loch. 'They'll be asleep,' she pointed out.

'Who will?'

'The ducks.'

'We can tiptoe.' His expression was serious.

Freya giggled. 'You're being silly. I thought the whole point of walking around a duck pond was to see the ducks.'

'I don't mind not seeing them, if you don't.'

'How about we take a stroll down to the loch instead?'

'I assumed you'd had enough of the loch yesterday.'

'Actually, I didn't realise how much I've missed all this. I'm going to miss it even more when I leave.'

This surprised her. In all the years she'd lived in London she hadn't felt homesick once. What she'd felt was heartbroken and incredibly sad. She'd missed her mother more than words could say, and she missed her dad too. But she hadn't missed *Skye*.

'You won't be leaving for some time, though, will you?' he asked, as they made their way down the lane.

'No,' she replied slowly.

They arrived at the sliver of beach, and she breathed in sharply at the sight of the inky water and the dark mountains on the opposite shore. With the sun having set behind them, they looked forbidding and mysterious. She'd forgotten what a magical place this was.

Crouching, she dug her fingers into the coarse sand, letting the grains trickle through her fingers.

'Don't worry, the time will fly by,' he said, and she realised he'd taken her silence for dismay that she wasn't returning to London sooner.

'It's not that,' she said. 'I just wish I could do some work while I'm here. I'm lost without my pottery. I did consider packing a few bits of equipment when I was in London, but I decided against it. Although hand building can be done with a few simple tools, it can be messy and I don't think my dad would appreciate me taking over his kitchen. There's also the problem of storing the clay while I work on it, plus I'd need somewhere to dry it.' Freya wrinkled her nose. She was missing her studio badly. She couldn't imagine how she was going to cope without it for the next few weeks.

'You could use my place, if you like,' he said.

'*Your* house?'

'The byre. I keep a few bits and pieces in it, but there's room to spare.'

'You're very kind, but I couldn't impose.' Her refusal was automatic.

'Don't be daft. You won't be imposing. You can come and go as you please, as long as you don't steal the fish out of the fridge.' His eyes twinkled, teasing her.

'No, honestly, I couldn't.'

'You *could*,' he insisted. 'You need a space to work and I've got one. What's the problem?'

'I don't have any tools with me and neither do I have any clay.'

Mack chuckled. 'That's what the internet is for. Surely you can buy what you need online?'

'I suppose I could.' It's what she normally did.

She thought about his offer, and the more she considered it, the more attractive it became. Making her mind up, she said, 'Thank you, I will, and I promise I won't steal your fish. You must let me give you something for your trouble, though.'

Freya wasn't prepared for the flash of irritation in Mack's eyes, nor for the firm set of his lips before he replied, 'I don't want payment. That's not why I offered.'

Realising she'd insulted him, she hastened to say, 'I know you don't, but—'

'No buts. This is what we do around here; we help each other. Or have you forgotten?'

She had, but she didn't want to admit it. The city was so different to Duncoorie and although she had friends there and knew at least two of her neighbours, she wouldn't expect such generosity from someone she hardly knew.

'Thank you,' she said simply.

'The byre isn't locked; just come and go as you please.'

'It won't be for a couple of weeks.'

'No matter.' Mack turned his face to the sky.

The breeze had freshened, and broken cloud scudded overhead. Freya shivered. The days might be warm, but the evenings could turn chilly.

Mack noticed the small movement. 'Home time, I think. I've an early start. Mind you, all my starts are early when the forecast is good.'

'So have I. I'm hoping Dad will be discharged tomorrow.'

'If you need anything, just ask. You've got my number.'

'I will,' she promised as they turned to walk back to the castle and their respective vehicles. 'Good night, Mack. I've enjoyed myself this evening.'

'Aye, Mhairi lays a good table.'

That wasn't quite what Freya had meant, but she decided it was best to go with his interpretation, because what she'd *actually* meant was that she'd enjoyed seeing him again, had enjoyed their walk and had enjoyed his company. So it was probably a good thing he'd misunderstood her.

Freya glared at the message from Hadrian, wishing she hadn't sent him photos of her boat trip or mentioned having dinner at Coorie Castle. It consisted of one word – *sightseeing* – followed by a laughing-face emoji.

She replied. *Work, actually*.

> Out on a boat? Work?

> Inspiration.

> Dinner at a castle? Surely not work.

> Feedback

> Was the food good?

> Yes. Yummy.

It's a bit old-fashioned, though was his reply and Freya imagined Hadrian scrolling through the castle's website with a sneer on his sculpted lips. He didn't do old-fashioned.

> Does it smell of mothballs?

Freya rolled her eyes. *Do you even know what mothballs smell like?*

Another laughing-face emoji.

> Thought not.

Do you? he asked.
No. She smiled to herself. *Envious?*

> Of you having dinner in an old pile like that? Not really.

> Did you go somewhere nicer this evening?

> I ordered in.

Bet my dinner was nicer than yours. Was there a poking-out tongue emoji, she wondered.

> Got more sightseeing planned?

Freya pursed her lips, annoyed that Hadrian was persisting with the idiotic insistence that she was there on a jaunt. She knew he was trying to cheer her up, but honestly! A bit of sympathy and understanding wouldn't go amiss.

With a *Good night*, she closed all the apps down and tossed her phone on the bed, then as she cleansed her face and changed into her PJs, she resolved to tell him they were over. She should do it soon, she decided, and although she continued to be reluctant to end it over the phone, she couldn't make the long journey to London and back, so the only option was to call him. Not now, though. She'd had a long day and was tired, and she'd only just had a conversation with him.

She would do it tomorrow.

Decision made, Freya felt rather despondent. Hadrian had been part of her life for the past two years, so she supposed it was only natural to feel glum.

However, it wasn't Hadrian who invaded her thoughts as she drifted off to sleep – it was Mack.

Chapter 14

Freya scurried around the house one more time, making sure everything was perfect – or as perfect as she could make it, considering she'd had to improvise a fair bit. No doubt her dad wouldn't be pleased with the way she'd organised his sitting room, but beggars couldn't be choosers and she'd done her best with what she had available.

Earlier this morning, Rhona had knocked on her door to tell her that she'd seen a card in the window of the post office with a riser chair for sale, along with a commode, so Freya had hurried to the main street to see for herself. She'd bought the chair (not the commode, though) and having wrestled it into the van with some considerable cursing, mostly under her breath, it now sat next to her dad's bed, angled towards the TV.

It meant that the room was more crowded than she would like, but there was little she could do about that, unless…

Freya shook her head. She'd imposed enough on Mack already – she couldn't ask him to help her move one of the armchairs into her dad's bedroom. Anyway, it wouldn't be long before it would have to be moved back down again. From what she'd read online, Dad should be able to manage the stairs by himself in a few weeks, if not before.

Crossly, she recalled the visit from the two ladies from social services and their recommendation that she had a stairlift installed.

Honestly! Where did they find these people? Dad didn't need one and he certainly didn't want one, although she had every intention of persuading him that a rail going up the stairs would be a good idea. After all, he wasn't getting any younger. Future-proofing, it was called; however, she suspected there would be a limit to how much future-proofing her dad would allow.

She wished she'd been able to put the handrails up before he came home, because she had a feeling he'd object to those too, so that was an argument waiting to happen. It would have to happen on another day, though, because right now she was too concerned about her dad getting home safely.

With worry a low-grade whine at the back of her mind, Freya drove to the hospital. After finding a parking spot, she dashed inside and was relieved to see her father fully dressed and sitting in the chair next to his bed, waiting for her, his bag at his side.

'Have you got everything?' she asked, giving him a kiss.

He nodded.

'I'll just check.' She opened the bedside cabinet. It was empty.

'Stop fussing,' he grumbled. 'Can we go?'

A nurse appeared. 'All set, Vinnie?'

'Yes. Please, can I just go?'

She laughed. 'He reminds me of my wee dog when I take him to see the vet. He can't wait to leave and pulls on the lead like billy-o until we're outside.'

Vinnie gave her a baleful stare.

'I know, I know,' the nurse said. 'You want to go. Let me call a porter.'

'I don't need a porter.'

The nurse said firmly, 'Yes, you do. He can wheel you out while your daughter brings the car round.'

'It makes sense, Dad,' Freya argued.

He sighed, then nodded.

She followed the nurse into the corridor. 'Is there anything in particular I should make sure he does, or doesn't, do? The internet has given me a wealth of info on broken hips, but…'

'There's a fact sheet in his bag, along with his tablets, and he's got his first outpatient appointment with the physio booked.' The nurse hesitated, then said, 'He's had a major operation and the road to recovery will be long, especially with—'

'Nurse? *Nurse!* We need a bedpan over here!' a woman yelled, and the nurse glanced down the corridor. 'It's urgent! Hurry.'

'I'm being summoned. Have a safe journey.' And with that, she was gone, leaving Freya wondering what she'd been about to say.

Assuming it couldn't have been important, she returned to the ward to wait for the porter. In no time at all her dad would be home, and Freya could get on with the job of nursing him back to health.

'Dad, go sit down, I don't need any help.' Freya was preparing lunch. It was only soup and a crusty roll, but her father appeared to think she needed supervising. 'It's minestrone,' she said. 'Your favourite.'

'I like Heinz. That doesn't look like Heinz.' He shuffled closer to the stove and peered suspiciously at the pan.

'I made it myself,' she told him.

'Is that what you were doing? I wondered what the noise was.'

'I was chopping vegetables.' She dipped a clean spoon into the soup. 'Here, have a taste. It's rather yummy.'

Vinnie sipped at it cautiously. 'It isn't Heinz,' he repeated, and her heart sank.

'Shall I nip out and get you a tin?' If it made him happy, she'd fetch him one from the corner shop. She'd eat a bowl of the home-made one herself, and freeze the rest so it wouldn't go to waste.

'You've made this now.'

'It's no bother. If you don't like it, I can—'

'I didn't say I didn't like it. All I said was that it's not Heinz.'

He hadn't had to say it; the implication had been enough.

'Where's your walker?' she asked, realising he didn't have it with him.

'I don't need it.'

'You *do*,' she insisted. 'You can't rush these things, Dad. It'll take time to get back on your feet.'

'I'm on my feet now,' he pointed out. He was, but precariously. He was holding on to the worktop for dear life.

'I'll get it,' Freya said, and went into the sitting room. When she returned to the kitchen, she found him by the little table, trying to pull out a chair.

'Let me.'

'I can do it!' he shot back crossly.

Freya planted the walker in front of him and reined in a sigh. Getting cross back at him wasn't going to help matters, but he'd only been home an hour and he was already trying her patience. She needed to do some plain speaking.

'Dad, the way you're carrying on, you're going to have another fall and then where will you be? Back in hospital, that's where.'

Slowly and carefully, Vinnie lowered himself into the chair, using the table for support. His face was drawn, his skin grey. He needed food, then he needed to rest. After that, she'd make sure he did his exercises, and if she had time she'd try to find a drill in the shed. Those handrails weren't going to put themselves up and she was worried about him coping in the bathroom. The raised toilet seat should help, but she'd feel happier if he had something to hold on to instead of the wash-hand basin.

She noticed her dad patting his shirt pocket. 'If you're looking for your glasses, you left them in the sitting room,' she told him.

'I know. I'm after my tablets.' He produced a blister pack with a flourish. 'Got them.'

'Shall I pour you a glass of water?'

'Aye, that would be grand.'

'You should have said you needed to take your painkillers. I would have fetched some for you.' She felt awful, thinking he'd struggled out to the kitchen to get a drink. She should have anticipated that and made sure he had a jug within easy reach of his chair.

She said, 'Why don't you go back to the sitting room? You'll be more comfortable there, and if your hip hurts too much, you can have your soup later.'

Freya had broken her arm when she was a child, and she hadn't forgotten the unbearable ache and how sick it had made her feel.

'I'll have it now,' he said.

'It's no bother, Dad, I can—'

'They're not painkillers. They're my cholesterol tablets.'

'Ah, I see.' The vice chancellor was on medication for high cholesterol, and he was also on tablets for his blood pressure. She wasn't surprised that Sean Pickles's blood pressure was raised, since he had a stressful job – or so he kept telling her.

Reassured that her father wasn't in pain, and that the cholesterol tablets were nothing to be concerned about, Freya turned her attention to the soup once more. 'Would you like butter with your roll?' she asked, then had second thoughts. 'Are you allowed butter if you've got high cholesterol?' Sean was always telling her how he adored cheese but wasn't allowed to eat it.

'I've not got high cholesterol. My cholesterol is fine.'

'But you just said—'

'That's what the tablets are for, so I can eat like a normal human being and not like a rabbit. Aye, I want butter.'

That told me, she thought, taking the butter dish out of the fridge and putting it on the table a tad more forcibly than she'd intended.

'Watch you don't break it,' Vinnie grumbled.

Giving the soup a final taste, Freya deemed it ready, so she ladled a generous portion into two bowls and took her seat at the table.

They ate in silence, Freya ignoring the tremor in her father's hand as he lifted the spoon to his mouth. The daft old sod was trying to do too much, too soon. Stubborn, that's what he was, and proud. He'd never admit that the journey from Broadford this morning had taken it out of him.

Freya reconsidered her plan to put up the handrails today. Having a rest was more important for her father right now, and he didn't need to be disturbed by drilling. He'd probably refuse to have a nap if she suggested it, so she'd have to use cunning if she wanted to get him to rest.

'What do you usually do in the afternoon, Dad?'

'Not much. Watch a bit of TV, potter in the garden if it's fine, read the paper if it's not. I fetch one every morning, along with any bits I might need. It gets me out of the house.'

'Would you like me to fetch you a paper after lunch?'

He huffed. 'They don't have many in. They'll all be sold by now.'

'We could watch a film?'

Her dad huffed again. 'I don't like the modern stuff.'

'I'll find an old one,' she assured him, hoping there'd be something on. 'Or we could watch a documentary?'

'I wouldn't mind listening to *The Archers*.'

'OK, we'll do that, then.'

'I don't need babysitting,' he stated, using the last of his roll to wipe his bowl clean. For someone who'd complained that the soup wasn't Heinz, he'd managed to polish off the lot. He added, 'Haven't you got anything to be getting on with?'

Freya hesitated. She did, although she wanted to keep an eye on him. At the same time, she knew she wouldn't be able to concentrate if he had *The Archers* on full blast. She could work in the kitchen, she supposed, then she'd be on hand if he needed anything. But to be honest, she wasn't in the right frame of mind for designing, although hopefully things would settle down in a day or two, when her dad became more used to having her around.

He pushed his bowl away. 'Thanks, lassie, it was tasty.'

'Glad you enjoyed it. Go through to the sitting room and I'll bring you a cup of tea and a biscuit.'

'What kind of biscuit?' His tone was suspicious.

'I bought one of those tins with an assortment, so you can take your pick.'

'I don't like my tea too strong,' he reminded her, getting to his feet with considerable difficulty.

Freya wanted to help, but knew he had to do it on his own. It was hard, though, and she was forced to look away until he was upright and holding on to the walker.

With a heavy heart, she watched him shuffle out of the room. How had he got to look so old? She knew it was because of his hip, and only temporary, but it was a distressing glimpse into the future. One day he would be old for real, and the thought made her feel incredibly sad.

Freya glanced up from her drawing pad as the sound of laughter filtered into the kitchen from the sitting room. A visit from Rhona was just what her dad had needed to cheer him up. His neighbour had been chatting with him for nearly an hour, filling him in on the goings-on in the village, while Freya had made herself scarce after supplying the initial cups of tea and plate of biscuits.

Rhona was a better tonic for Dad than an hour's nap, although Freya suspected the fatigue would catch up with him soon. Never mind, he could have a snooze in the chair before tea, then after they'd eaten, they could settle down to watch some TV before bed, though she assumed it would be an early night for both of them.

'More tea, anyone?' she asked, popping her head around the door.

Rhona heaved herself to her feet, the sagging armchair briefly holding her captive. 'Not for me, hen, I'd best be away. I only popped in to see how your dad was and to thank him for the flowers, and he's kept me gabbing.'

'I'll see you out,' Freya said, as the elderly woman headed for the small hallway.

'I'll pop in again, Vinnie,' Rhona promised.

'See that you do,' Vinnie called. 'And thank you, lassie, I don't know what would have become of me if you hadn't heard me caterwauling.'

At the door, Rhona paused. 'He's looking better than the last time I saw him, and he'll look better again with you to take care of him. He's been letting himself go a bit, has Vinnie. I said the same to Jean the other day.' She clutched Freya's arm. 'You be sure to take good care of your dad – he's the only one you've got.'

'I will,' Freya replied.

After Rhona had left, guilt nibbled at her. She really should have visited him more often. But she'd always found it so difficult being back on Skye, and especially being in this house. It echoed with memories of her mother and she'd found it easier to stay away. Her poor father had borne the brunt of her selfishness.

Ironically, now that she'd been forced to spend more time here than she'd done since her mother's funeral, the pain was lessening. The ache in her heart would always be there, but it no longer tore at her with sharp claws whenever she caught sight of the dresser that her mother had loved so much, or the rose bush she'd planted in the garden, or the teapot she'd bought in the church jumble sale and had treasured because it was rumoured to have come from the castle. Or the hundreds of other things that brought memories of her mother welling to the surface.

Freya peeped into the sitting room, closing the door softly when she saw that her dad's eyes were closed. A little sleep would do him the world of good.

Returning to the kitchen table, and her pad and paints, Freya resumed her seat. However, she didn't pick up the brush she'd been using. Instead, she stared into space, thinking of all those times when she could have visited him but had been too busy. It wasn't a lie – she *had* been busy. Life had been hectic and would be even more hectic if she moved to the States, but he wasn't getting any younger, as his fall had brought sharply home to her.

Never had Freya felt so torn. She knew what her dad would say – he'd tell her to go, to follow her dreams, because if she didn't, she'd always regret it.

A thought occurred to her. A direct flight from New York to Edinburgh took about seven hours and from there she could either get an island hopper flight, or rent a car to get to Skye. That wasn't long, considering the distance. Twelve hours door-to-door? Maybe less.

The more Freya thought about it, the more doable visiting Dad from New York became. She'd have to make sure she made the effort and didn't slip back into her old ways of letting life get the better of her, but she'd have to do the same if she stayed in London because she was determined to keep a closer eye on him.

Feeling somewhat nearer to making a decision, Freya returned to her task with renewed enthusiasm. Despite the upheaval of the day, she'd had a productive hour or so, as the germ of a whole new range had begun to take root. When the materials she'd ordered arrived, she would definitely take Mack up on his kind offer of using his byre.

–

'He's home, then,' Jean announced, as Mack walked into his mum's kitchen.

'Who is?'

'Vinnie.'

'Oh, good. How is he?'

'Rhona says he's looking a bit frail, but that's only to be expected, considering what he's been through.'

'How's Freya?'

His mum sent him a sharp look. 'All right, I think.'

'Should I call in and see if he needs anything?'

'You could. I expect he'll appreciate that. We can both go, if you like. I made a sponge cake earlier – I could take him a couple of slices.'

'Good idea.'

'What's Freya like now? I haven't set eyes on her since she was a girl. From what I can recall, she was a bonnie little thing: red hair and freckles.'

Yeah, she still is bonnie, he thought. Very bonnie. He said, 'She's nice.'

'Just nice? I heard you took her out on the boat *and* made her tea after. And how was dinner at the castle?'

Mack realised that he hadn't spoken to his mother for several days, but it came as no surprise to discover she already knew what he'd been up to. 'Don't read too much into it. Mhairi was behind both the boat trip and dinner.'

'At the castle, aye, but I don't think she twisted your arm about tea at your place.'

'I felt sorry for her, what with her dad being in hospital.'

'Did you now? Make yourself useful and lay the table.'

Mack grinned. His mum said the same thing to him every time, as though he'd forget that laying the table was his job.

'It's about time you found a decent woman and settled down,' she said.

'What's for tea?'

His mother huffed. 'Did you hear what I said?'

'I heard. I'm ignoring you.'

Jean opened the oven and peered inside as a cloud of steam billowed out.

'Mum, I asked you, what are we having for tea?'

'I heard. I'm ignoring you.' She threw his words back at him with an arch of her eyebrows.

Mack tutted. 'The difference is, *I'll* know in a couple of minutes what we're having.'

'Then you don't need me to tell you,' she shot back.

Damn, his mother could be trying at times. Mack relented. 'Yes, I like Freya; no, I didn't have to cook her tea; no, it wasn't because I felt sorry for her. But…' He met his mother's eye. 'She's not for me. For one thing, she's got a boyfriend, and for another, she's been offered a job in America. And for a third, I'm not the settling-down type. I like my own company too much.'

'Ah, now, that's because you haven't spent time in the *right* company.'

'I'm spending time with you, aren't I?'

She flapped a tea towel at him. 'Don't be cheeky.'

'I wasn't,' he protested, watching her take a baking tray containing two pieces of golden battered fish out of the oven. 'Ooh, a fish supper. Nice.' His mouth watered. 'What I meant was, I haven't found anyone to compare to my mum.'

The look she sent him was pure disgust. 'The wee tourist lassies might fall for that tripe, but I don't. Butter some bread.'

'Yes, Mum.'

'And mind your manners.'

'Yes, Mum.'

Another glare.

Mack blew her a kiss, and she rolled her eyes.

If he was hoping that would be the end of it, he was mistaken. Throughout the meal, she quizzed him – thankfully not all about Freya.

When they'd finally finished eating and the remains of their meal had been cleared away, Mack was relieved. 'Come on, let's go satisfy your curiosity,' he said, and his mother's eyes lit up.

Freya seemed pleased to see them, if somewhat surprised. 'Haven't you got anything more exciting to do on a Friday evening?' she asked Mack, after inviting them in.

Jean said, 'He's away to the pub later. I'll sit with your dad if you want to go along.'

Freya looked taken aback, but before she could say anything, Vinnie called from the sitting room, 'I don't need a bloody babysitter.'

Silently, Freya pursed her lips with a slight shake of her head, and Mack wondered whether the old gent had been giving her a hard time. She looked tired, and he guessed that today hadn't been easy for either of them, even though she was no doubt relieved to have her dad home.

Jean sailed up to his chair. 'Look at you, you daft sod. Fancy breaking your hip.'

'Yeah, fancy,' Vinnie growled.

'I've brought cake, so be nice,' she warned.

'Och, now you're talking.' Vinnie smiled stiffly at her. 'Put the kettle on, Freya.'

Mack asked, 'Need a hand?' as he followed her into the kitchen.

'What I need is a drill. You don't happen to have one, do you?'

'I do. What do you want to drill?'

'Handrails.'

'I'll put them up for you in the morning.'

'I can put them up myself. I just need a drill, that's all.'

'I never said you couldn't, but I'm very particular who I lend my tools to.' He wasn't, but he wanted to help and guessed this might be the only way she'd let him. He was coming to realise that Freya Sinclair was stubborn, proud and independent, just like her dad.

'I won't break it,' she protested. 'I know how to use a drill.'

'Nevertheless…'

'Fine.' She sighed. 'If you insist on putting them up, you can. I'm not going to argue.'

'I'll take one of the armchairs upstairs at the same time,' he offered. 'It's a bit crowded in there.'

'It's a bit crowded in *here*,' he thought he heard her mutter.

'Pardon?' he said.

'Nothing. Thank you, that would be helpful.'

He smiled. 'Haven't we been here before?'

'I suppose we have.'

'No whisky this time, please.'

'Don't you like whisky?' Her eyes widened, as though it was unheard of for a Scot not to like whisky.

'Of course I do. But a simple "thank you" is enough. If you keep buying folk bottles of the good stuff every time they lend a hand, the corner shop will run out.'

He wasn't offering to help because he wanted payment. He was doing it because that was the neighbourly thing to do.

Mack ignored the naggy voice in his head taunting him that the *real* reason was because it would give him an excuse to see her again.

Chapter 15

With her dad settled in his chair, Freya laced up her Doc Martens, grabbed her phone and some money, and dashed out the door.

If she was honest, she was glad to be away from him for a few minutes. This morning had been quite fraught; actually, the fraughtness (if that was a word) had begun last night, after Mack and Jean had left. Dad had wanted to watch TV, which was fine by Freya, but as she'd had little interest in the programme, she'd spent an hour or so on her phone, answering emails, checking her website and social media, and catching up on a couple of blogs she followed.

She'd had earbuds in so as not to disturb him, but her dad had objected nevertheless. He seemed to resent her not watching TV with him, but when she'd put her phone to one side, he'd accused her of sulking. Freya had most definitely *not* been sulking, but his constant picking at her had resulted in her feeling quite petulant by the end of the evening.

As she scurried along the road, heading for the shop and a newspaper purchase, she recalled how crabby he'd been last night as he was getting ready for bed. She'd seen that he was struggling and she'd tried to help, but it had only made him crabbier. And this morning hadn't been any better.

Reminding herself that he must be finding it difficult, she vowed (yet again) not to take it personally. He was used to his own space, and had his own routine and his own way of doing things. She might be his daughter and he might love her unconditionally, but she was getting on his nerves.

'Stop fashing me,' he'd said, more than once since he'd come out of hospital, and she had a feeling he'd be saying it a few more times before she returned to London.

Although she didn't want to fuss, it was hard not to, especially since she had to constantly remind him to use his walker.

'Just until you're more confident on your feet,' she'd told him this morning, after discovering him heading towards the bathroom by way of holding on to the wall. The glare he'd given her could have felled a sheep at fifty paces.

'Aw, hen, how's your dad?' Mrs Davy in the shop asked when Freya approached the counter to pay for the newspaper.

'Getting there slowly, thanks for asking,' Freya replied.

'I meant to tell you the other day, when you popped in, that you've turned into a bonnie lass. I bet Vinnie's glad to have you home.'

Freya wasn't entirely sure that was the case. Resentful was probably a more apt description. Telling herself that her dad's mood would improve as he became more mobile, she paid for the newspaper, assured Mrs Davy that she'd let her dad know she was asking after him, and hurried home.

To her surprise, she discovered Mack's truck parked behind her van, and when she went into the house, she heard laughter coming from the bathroom.

'I had to use a boathook to nab it, with Angus holding on to my legs to stop me toppling in,' Mack was saying. 'I wouldn't have minded, but it was only a cheap one. She could have picked up another easy enough, without me having to risk a soaking.'

'What are you talking about?' Freya asked, taking in the scene at a glance. Her dad was perched on the toilet seat (thankfully with his trousers on) and Mack was holding a handrail against the wall with one hand and had a pencil in the other.

'A daft woman and her daft hat,' Mack said. 'We'd barely cast off and it blew off her head into the loch. She demanded I went in after it. You can imagine what I said – under my breath, of course.'

'Stick to fish, lad,' Vinnie said. 'They don't answer back. I could never be bothered with people. Too contrary.'

Mack chuckled. 'I should have known she'd be trouble when she told me she expected to see orcas or she wanted her money back. Did she think I kept a tame one in my pocket?'

'Some people just aren't right in the head,' Vinnie tutted.

'Tell me about it,' was Mack's heartfelt reply.

Pleased to see her father in better spirits, Freya took his newspaper into the sitting room and stopped dead.

One of the armchairs was missing.

Retracing her steps, she said to Mack, 'Have you taken a chair upstairs already?'

'I have. It only took but a minute.'

'Thank you.' Blimey, he didn't hang about; then she realised that he probably had to get to work. 'What time does your first trip go out?'

Mack tilted his arm to see the dial on the diver's watch he wore. 'About now.'

'Shouldn't you be on it?'

'You heard what Mhairi said: they can manage without me. I'm beginning to feel redundant.'

Vinnie said, 'Join the club, lad.'

Mack screwed a bit into the drill and tightened it. 'You miss it, don't you.' It wasn't a question.

'Wouldn't you?'

'Aye, I would. I'm surprised you don't have a wee skiff, to keep your hand in.'

'It's not the same.'

'No, I suppose it isn't, although you could always fish for your supper. Cal, the daft wee bugger, catches them and throws them back, then goes and buys fish from the supermarket.'

'I could eat a nice bit of fish for my dinner,' Vinnie said.

Freya said, 'There's some smoked basa in the freezer. We can have it with quinoa and salad, but I'll have to take it out now if it's to defrost in time for tea.'

'*Quinoa?* What the hell is that?' her dad demanded.

'It's a bit like couscous.'

'Couscous?' He shuddered. 'I'd prefer chips.'

'You can have chips if you want.'

'And I don't want salad. I want peas. And I don't want it for tea, either. I want it at dinner time.'

'Mmm… battered cod, chips and mushy peas,' Mack said. 'I could go for that myself.'

The two men exchanged glances, then stared at her hopefully.

Freya took the hint. She stared back with narrowed eyes, her focus on Mack. 'I thought you said you didn't want payment?'

'I don't. I can buy my own fish and chips.'

'But you want *me* to go and get them.'

'I'll fetch them myself as soon as I've finished this. I was merely wondering whether you'd like to join us.'

Freya threw up her hands; she knew when she was beaten, and she was clearly outnumbered. 'I'll go.'

'It's not open yet,' Mack said.

Freya was confused. 'It opened at seven, didn't it?'

Her dad piped up, 'Not the supermarket, hen, the chippy. We don't want *you* cooking it, we want proper fish and chips from the chip shop.'

'Thanks a bunch,' she spluttered.

'Och, you know what I mean. I don't care how good a cook you are, you can't beat a proper fish supper.'

Freya had to admit that her dad was right, and the appeal of the frozen basa dimmed significantly. A fish supper it was, then. She rarely ate fish and chips from a chip shop, and on the odd occasion when she did, Hadrian always turned his nose up. Food eaten out of paper wasn't to his liking, and he'd never been able to get his head around the way she referred to the meal as a *fish supper*, even if it was eaten at lunch time.

'It'll give me time to finish up here,' Mack was saying. 'I'll put this handrail up, then if you could show me where you want the others—?'

Vinnie said, 'It's nonsense, if you ask me. I don't need bloody handrails.'

Mack chuckled. 'Give it a couple of weeks, yeah? If you find you're not using them, I'll take the bloody things down.'

'And leave me with holes in the wall?'

'I can fill in the holes.'

'I'll fill you in, you cheeky wee bugger.' But her dad was smiling as he said it.

Freya thought it was actually a good job that Mack was putting them up, because if *she* had installed them, her father would have been far less amenable and might have refused point-blank to have them.

Driven out of the bathroom by the high-pitched screeching of the drill, Freya retreated upstairs to check on her father's bedroom, and smiled when she saw that Mack had taken the trouble to place the armchair at an angle to the sofa, so it didn't look like it had been dumped there. It was almost like her own private sitting room, she thought, deciding it would be an ideal place to retreat to when she and her dad needed a bit of space from one another, which she feared might happen a lot.

It was weird, but ever since her dad's fall, Freya'd had the feeling he didn't want her here and was doing his best to get rid of her. She appreciated that it might be embarrassing to have his daughter look after him, but if *she* didn't do it, there wasn't anyone else. He'd just have to suck it up.

'Where do you want the next one?' Mack called, and Freya trotted downstairs to show him.

While he was putting that up, she'd clean—

She halted. The bathroom was clean and tidy. Bless him, Mack had cleaned up after himself, and his kindness touched her. He didn't have to do that, but he had, and it was incredibly sweet of him.

Trying not to hover, she waited for him to finish, and when he began to pack away his tools, she said, 'Cod and chips, and a pot of mushy peas?'

'Have you got brown sauce?' he asked. 'You can't have mushy peas without brown sauce.'

Freya took a look in the cupboard where her dad kept his jars and condiments, and found a bottle that was half-full.

'We have,' she said. 'Could you put some plates in the oven to warm, while I pop to the chippy?'

Heading out for the second time today, Freya felt grateful to Mack – his presence had lifted her dad's spirits. Hers, too. She no longer felt as glum as she had earlier this morning, and although she guessed it was only a temporary reprieve, she'd take what she could get.

Her mouth watering, she ordered three fish suppers, and as she waited for them to be wrapped, she spied a large bottle of dandelion and burdock pop in the fridge, so she grabbed it. With a piece of creamy, buttery tablet for afters, this lunch was turning out to be quite a feast.

When she got back, she found the plates in the oven and the table laid, with a bottle of vinegar and the salt cellar placed in the middle. Her dad sat in one of the chairs, a blister pack of tablets in his hand.

Freya wasn't sure how many he took a day, but it seemed a lot.

Oh, well, the GP must know what they're doing, she thought, and if taking this many cholesterol tablets meant that her dad could enjoy his fish and chips, she was all for it.

'I haven't seen you in the byre yet,' Mack said, as they tucked into their food.

Vinnie glanced up from his plate. 'The byre?'

'I've offered Freya the use of it while she's in Duncoorie,' Mack explained. 'For her to make her pots in.'

Vinnie asked, 'What pots?' He turned to Freya. 'Why are you making pots?'

A finger of fear trailed down her spine. 'That's what I do, Dad. I'm a potter.'

'I know *that*,' he snapped, 'but why are you making pots in Mack's cowshed?'

Oh, that's what he meant! For one awful second, she'd thought he was having trouble with his memory and the spectre of dementia had raised its head.

She said, 'I'm not. Not yet, anyway. But when you're more mobile, I'm going to do a bit of hand building.'

'Why?'

'Because I don't have a wheel. I didn't bring it with me.'

Irritably, Vinnie shook his head. 'You won't be here long enough to make anything.'

'I'll be here for a couple of months, Dad,' she reminded him yet again. 'Maybe longer. We'll have to see how it goes.'

'I can manage fine on my own.'

'Not with a broken hip, you can't,' she argued. Were they destined to have this same argument every day until she left? She bloody hoped not, because she was tired of it already. 'Anyone would think you didn't want me here,' she muttered.

Vinnie put his fork down. 'I don't. You've got your own life to lead. There's no need for you to be stuck here with me.'

'I don't look at it as being *stuck* here. I look at it as helping my dad because he needs it.'

'I don't.'

'Will you stop it! I'm staying and that's final. It's the summer holidays so I don't have to be in college until

September, so please don't worry that I'm having to take time off work. And being here has given me some real inspiration, so you're actually doing me a favour.'

His glare was, unsurprisingly, disbelieving, but everything she'd said was true. Technically.

'What about that boyfriend of yours – Hadrian? What does he say about you being so far away?'

'He understands,' she replied. Even as she said it, she didn't believe it, but she wasn't going to tell her father that she and Hadrian were over in front of Mack. Anyway, she owed it to Hadrian to tell him first, before she told her dad, who would probably be pleased, because he didn't seem keen on him, despite never having met him.

Maybe that was the reason? Freya always visited her dad alone, because Hadrian invariably had other plans whenever Freya mentioned going to Skye.

Vinnie grumbled, 'You should be there with him, not with me.'

Freya pressed her lips together and focused on her plate. *Goodness knows what Mack is making of this*, she thought, embarrassment heating her face.

Mack changed the subject. 'I'm taking my first *Colours of Skye* trip out the week after next,' he said, then went on to explain to her dad what that meant and what it entailed, giving Freya time to compose herself.

She didn't know whether that had been his intention, or whether he'd felt uncomfortable being on the outskirts of a family spat, but she was grateful to him, nevertheless.

'I thought it was next week?' she said.

'So did Mhairi, but I managed to push it back a week. She's persistent, I'll give her that.' Mack chuckled. 'I've never known anyone so determined to get her own way.'

Vinnie snorted. 'You have, you've met my daughter.'

'Dad!' Freya turned to Mack and mouthed, 'Sorry.'

Mack merely smiled and changed the subject again, but this time the topic wasn't such a welcome one.

'Have you made a decision about New York yet?' he asked, and Freya flinched.

Closing her eyes briefly, she drew in a slow breath, opening them to find both men staring at her.

Mack looked stricken, and she guessed he'd realised that she hadn't told her dad. She'd wanted to wait until he was stronger before she mentioned anything.

Confused, Vinnie said, 'New York?'

She decided it was best to tell him now, and she hoped he wouldn't be too upset at the thought of her living on the other side of the Atlantic.

Hesitantly she said, 'I've been offered a job as course director at the Black and White Art Academy in New York.'

'Is that a promotion?' His eyes were bright, and to her relief a smile lit up his face.

'It most definitely is! I'll be heading up their ceramics department, and when it comes to ceramics, the academy is one of the best.'

'Better than where you are now?'

She nodded. 'I haven't agreed to it yet and I haven't even seen a contract, so it's not definite, but I'm tempted.'

'And so you should be! Aw, hen, I'm so proud of you! And your mother would be too, if she were alive.' There were tears in his eyes, which made her own fill up.

'I'll still see you regularly, Dad. I've checked flights and—'

'Don't mind me, you have to do what's best for you and your career.' Vinnie beamed at Mack. 'Who'd have thought that my wee girl would be working for a New

York academy, eh? Didn't your mum always say that you can do whatever you set your mind to? *Of course* you have to go. I'm chuffed to bits, lassie, and I'm so proud of you.'

Freya hadn't been aware of how tense she was, until she heard her dad say he was proud of her, and having his approval meant everything.

It made saying yes to Jocasta Black that much easier.

New York, here I come!

Chapter 16

The clay was off-white and smooth to the touch as Freya removed it from the wet cloth she'd wrapped it in to keep it moist and pliable, after it had been delivered yesterday.

It was a warm afternoon and she was in her dad's garden, seated at the rickety outdoor table on which she'd placed a wooden board that she'd found in the small but incredibly full shed. It was held in place by a pair of rusty old clamps which she'd also found in there.

The familiar feel of the clay had an immediate soothing effect, and she couldn't wait to get started. But before she did, she went inside and popped her head around the sitting-room door to see whether her dad wanted anything.

Bless him, he was fast asleep, his head resting on the back of the riser chair, the TV on low.

Satisfied that she wouldn't be disturbed for a while, Freya turned her attention back to the clay. She loved every part of the process of making an inert grey lump come to life: from wedging the raw material, to taking the final product from the kiln and praying it hadn't cracked.

After breaking off a lump of the wet clay, she placed it on the digital scales, adding more to it until she arrived at a nice round number, then she moved the scales to the side, picked up the clay and slapped it down on the board several times.

Although this process was an essential start to any pottery session, as it knocked air bubbles out of the clay, it also served to get her in the zone, and it was an excellent stress reliever. There was nothing quite like repeatedly bashing a lump of clay onto a hard surface!

Satisfied that she'd given it enough of a pummelling, Freya patted it into a rough circle, then used a wire to slice the clay into horizontal sections, ending up with six flat patties. Working quickly because she didn't want the clay to dry out, she misted each patty with water, then donned a pair of thin disposable gloves and a respirator.

Carefully opening a packet of dark pink powder, she weighed out the amount she needed, then sprinkled it evenly over five of the patties, followed by another spray of water. As soon as she'd stacked the circles of powder-covered clay on top of one another, with the non-powdered one on the very top, she removed the respirator and took a gulp of air. Despite being outside, she hadn't wanted to take any risks. The powder (or mason stain, as it was called) was incredibly fine, and inhaling it could lead to all kinds of nastiness.

Keeping the disposable gloves on, Freya picked up the stack of clay patties and began squeezing them together, gradually mixing the stain and the clay together, occasionally giving it another squirt of water.

As so often happened when she was working (although how having this much fun could be called 'work' was something she often asked herself), she lost track of time, and it was only when she re-wrapped the now heather-coloured clay in a damp cloth, popped it inside a plastic bag and then into an airtight container to sit overnight, that she realised two hours had sped by.

She also became aware that she had an audience. Her dad was standing by the back door, watching her. He had a faraway look on his face, but quickly snapped into focus.

'Have I told you how proud I am of you?' he said, and Freya's heart melted.

'You have.' Her eyes filled with tears, and she left the box of clay where it was and walked towards him, her arms outstretched. He gathered her to him and she rested her head on his shoulder. 'I love you, Dad,' she whispered into his neck.

'And I love you, my gorgeous wee girl.'

Sniffling back tears, she said, 'I'm not so wee now.'

He rubbed a hand up and down her back. 'You'll always be wee to me, no matter how old you get. I wish your mum had lived long enough to see her little girl going off to America.'

'So do I.' She missed her mum dreadfully; she always would.

Vinnie cleared his throat, and his voice was hoarse when he asked, 'Have you thought any more about it?'

'I've thought of little else,' she admitted.

'When do they want an answer?'

'Soon.'

'When would they want you to start?'

'They've not given me a date, but the chap I'll be taking over from is retiring at the end of the year, so I expect I would start in January.'

He pulled back to look her in the face. 'What are you waiting for? And don't say you're waiting for me to get better to tell them yes, because if you are, I'll put you over my knee.'

'That won't do your hip any favours,' she joked.

'I'll do it anyway.'

Freya kissed him on the cheek, his whiskers bristly. 'I believe you.'

'Is Hadrian holding you back? Because if he is...'

'It's not Hadrian.'

'What is it, then?'

'It's me. What if I'm not good enough?'

'You *are* good enough.' He sounded positive.

'How can you be so sure?'

'Because I know you. When you set your mind to doing something, you do it. And you throw your heart and soul into it. Go tell them yes, Freya. Opportunities like this don't come often.'

Her dad was right: they didn't. What *was* she waiting for?

Freya said, 'Let me put this lot away and get cleaned up first, then I'll send them an email.'

'That's my girl! Now, what's for tea? I'm starving.'

'I can do us salmon and cucumber sandwiches, with some sea salt and cracked pepper crisps. How does that sound?'

'Super.'

She watched him slowly retreat into the depths of the kitchen, then she returned to the task of clearing up. She would take her equipment to Mack's place later – after dropping him a message first, of course, in case it wasn't convenient. He may have told her to pop in whenever she wanted, but she had no intention of taking the mickey.

She hoped he'd be OK with that, because although the weather had been kind to her this afternoon, this was Skye, where no two days – or even hours – were the same, and she wanted somewhere dry and safe to store her material.

When Mack's phone buzzed, he didn't expect it to be a message from Freya, wanting to know whether she could drop some stuff at the byre later. He pinged a thumbs-up emoji right back, then wished he'd taken the time to compose a proper response.

After rushing through the end-of-day chores and ensuring the boat was set up for tomorrow morning's excursion, he shot off home, intending to give the byre a swift tidy, but when he pulled up to the house and saw Freya's van outside, he realised she'd beaten him to it.

His heart leapt, and he blew out his cheeks in irritation. There was no need to be quite so happy to see her. It wasn't as though it was going to lead to anything. Even if there was a chance it might, he wouldn't want to take it – the risk was too great. He didn't intend to be hurt again by getting involved with a woman who wouldn't be around for long.

Ignoring the irony – that a woman who wouldn't be around for long was *exactly* the kind he usually focused on – Mack climbed out of the truck and headed for the byre.

He found Freya standing in the middle of the former cowshed with a large plastic tub in her arms.

'Hi,' he said.

She let out a yelp and nearly dropped the box she was holding. 'Don't creep up on people like that!'

'Sorry, I assumed you'd heard the truck.' It wasn't the quietest of vehicles, being over fifteen years old and with a blowy exhaust. He'd take a look at it as soon as the next storm hit, when the boat would be unable to go out.

She said, 'I was too busy wondering where to put this.' She jerked her chin at the tub.

'Tell me what you need.'

'A table or two, a stool, a shelf...'

'I'm sure I can manage that.' Mack strode over to his workbench and began putting away the tools sitting on top of it. He'd dumped them there because he couldn't be bothered to put them back where they belonged, which was supposed to be on the hooks attached to a board on the wall above.

Glancing at Freya, he caught her frowning. 'Will this not work?' he asked, tapping the bench.

'It will, but I don't want to put you out.'

'You aren't. I'm not in here much in the summer – too busy out on the boat.' He made a face, feeling guilty. 'I'm sorry if I landed you in it with your dad. I didn't realise you hadn't told him about New York. Let me...' He stepped forward to take the tub from her and set it down on the bench's rough scarred surface.

'It's OK. No harm done.' Her smile was genuine, so he guessed she wasn't saying it just so he wouldn't feel bad. 'He's thrilled to bits for me.'

Her teeth worried at her bottom lip and his gaze was drawn to her mouth. It was a very kissable mouth.

Dragging his eyes away, he placed a hand on the box. 'Is this it? Or do you have more?'

An apologetic expression stole across her face. 'I do have more. Quite a bit more.'

He got the feeling she wasn't comfortable with this arrangement and would prefer her own space – which he could understand, as she probably felt beholden to him.

'That's no problem. I'll give you a hand bringing it in,' he offered, and her expression cleared.

Expecting the back of her small van to be crammed with stuff, he was surprised to see it virtually empty. There were three more of the same kind of plastic tub she'd already brought in, plus a length of wood and a bag of clothes with what looked to be a respirator resting on the top.

'Is this all of it?' he asked.

'Is it too much?' She looked worried again. 'I can keep most of it in the van, if you prefer.'

'I was expecting much more than this. Where's your wheel?'

'I don't have one. I mean, I do, but not with me. I don't need a wheel for what I'll be doing.'

He must have looked as flummoxed as he felt, because she said, 'Didn't you ever make little pots out of clay when you were a kid? There's this spot at the other end of the village where the burn enters the loch, which has some clay deposits. When I was about eight or nine, me and my friend Alice used to make pots and let them dry in the sun.'

Mack flinched. He remembered Alice all too well. Alice, his first love; Alice, who had moved to Aberdeen when her father got a job there; Alice, who'd told him she was leaving and had gone without a backward glance, breaking his tender young heart in the process.

It had taken him a long time to get over her. A succession of girlfriends had helped, and he hadn't thought about her in ages, but hearing her name suddenly brought it all back. Especially since he had a feeling of déjà vu. Freya was another woman who wasn't going to be around for long…

Keeping his tone light, he said, 'I can't say I did, although I know where you mean. I preferred grubbing about at the water's edge, looking for wee beasties.'

'How about in school? Mrs Blake got everyone in the first year to make pots and stuff by hand.'

Mack's mind flashed back to the art room, and he chuckled. 'Now you come to mention it, I do recall making an odd-shaped bowl once. It could hardly be called a thing of beauty.' His eyes widened and he cursed silently. 'I'm not saying that your vases and such are ugly, or that they're weird shapes. They're… They're…'

'Weird shapes.' She giggled. 'That's OK, they're supposed to be.'

'They're actually quite beautiful,' he said.

She was laughing at him. 'You can't walk it back, so don't bother trying.'

'Ah, shite.' He was mortified.

'I'm teasing,' she said. 'Beauty is in the eye of the beholder, as they say, so I don't expect everyone to like my work.'

'But I do like it,' he protested, and when she arched an eyebrow, he insisted, 'I *do*.'

'OK, I believe you.'

'You do? Thank goodness for that!'

She threw her head back, exposing the creamy column of her slender neck, and laughed. 'No.'

'You're a hard, unforgiving woman. It was just a slip of the tongue,' he protested, thankful that she didn't seem upset. He hastily changed the subject. 'When are you likely to be leaving British shores for the Wild West?'

'Not until the end of the year. I emailed the academy earlier to ask her to forward me the contract. I'm sure it'll be a standard one, but I want to read it through and make sure there aren't any nasty surprises before I sign on the dotted line. I won't be handing in my notice to the college until September and, with a January start, they should have enough time to find my replacement.'

'I bet they'll be sorry to lose you,' he said gallantly.

'Even though I make ugly pots?'

'You're making fun of me.'

'Yup.'

'Meany.'

'If you can't take it, don't dish it.'

'You do want to use my byre, don't you?'

'You'd go back on your offer?'

'I might.'

She shook her head. 'I don't think you would. You're too nice to go back on your word.'

Nice? She thought he was *nice*? He'd prefer sexy or irresistible, charming, even. Nice was so bland.

Blowing out his cheeks, he reminded himself that she had a boyfriend. She hadn't been flirting, she was just being friendly. He, though, most definitely *had* been flirting. Which was something he'd have to get a grip on before she noticed. Either that, or make himself scarce whenever she was around – which may be a fair bit, he concluded as he watched her unpack the tools of her trade and arrange them on the workbench.

Oh, bugger, how could he have been such a bampot! But it was done now, and he couldn't revoke the offer. He would simply have to hold his growing attraction for her in check and remember that she'd be out of his byre and out of his life before the autumn weather put the brakes on his whale-watching business.

But whether she would be out of his mind was a different matter entirely.

Chapter 17

Freya couldn't believe that it was already a month since the phone call informing her that her dad had suffered a fall and been admitted to hospital. The time had flown. Admittedly, the first week had been a blur of hospital visits and hotel rooms, and the second hadn't been much better, what with her dash to London, the long drive back to Skye, and then getting her dad's house in a fit state for him to come home to.

And that was just the physical stuff. The emotional side of things had been equally difficult, especially since her father had been under the impression that he could manage fine on his own and that she was surplus to requirements.

But as she'd hoped, the pair of them had settled into a routine, and she put it down to her dad finally accepting that he wasn't able to do everything he used to without support, and that he wouldn't be able to for some time. The fall had knocked him for six, and the healing of the wound and the knitting of the bone were only part of it. He had a tremor in his left hand that she wasn't happy with, but he assured her it was a leftover from when he'd damaged his wrist a couple of years ago. She couldn't remember him telling her about it, despite him insisting that he had, and he claimed that using the walker had aggravated it, as he wasn't used to putting so much pressure on the joint.

As well as that, he still seemed rather unsteady on his feet, even with his walker, and not sleeping was also an issue for him; and for her too, because she was on constant alert in case he got up in the night – which he did at least once, and sometimes three times. It was exhausting for both of them.

He blamed it on a weak bladder and the joys of growing old, and challenged her to find anyone over the age of sixty who slept through the night. Needless to say, Freya wasn't going to accept the challenge. Instead, she filed it away in a box in her mind labelled: *I hope I don't get like that when I'm old*. She also added irritability and forgetfulness to it, because her dad seemed to have both of those qualities in abundance, and there was only so much that could be excused by his fall and the subsequent operation.

Despite it all, they were muddling along together, with Freya doing her best to make life as easy as possible for him, and escaping to Mack's place whenever she was able, although never for very long.

It was Mack who had invited her out this evening. It wasn't a date, obviously, but as friends. He had a pint in the village every Friday with his mates and had suggested she came along if she fancied a night out, so she hadn't visited her makeshift studio today, as she didn't like leaving her dad alone twice in one day, the only exception being her daily walk to the shop for his newspaper.

'Have you got everything you need, Dad?' she asked for the second time in as many minutes.

Vinnie tutted. 'You've just asked me that.'

'I know, but I'm making sure. Humour me, OK? I'll have my phone with me, so call if you want anything.'

'You've *always* got your phone with you,' he grumbled. 'All you youngsters do.'

Freya bit back a smile. She was hardly a youngster, but he was right, she did keep her phone close, and that was because she was still waiting for the contract to come through for the job in New York. She wasn't in any hurry, but it would be nice to run her eyes over it.

Vinnie aimed the remote control at the TV. 'Shouldn't you be off?'

'Mack is going to call for me. He's having tea with his mum.'

'He's a good lad, is Mack.' Her dad found the channel he wanted and settled back in his chair. 'You look nice.'

'Thanks.' She'd made an effort, happy to dress up for once. It seemed a long time since she'd worn anything other than jeans or dungarees, and trainers or her well-worn and much-loved Doc Martens. This evening she was wearing a skirt, her hair was down instead of scooped into a bun, and she was wearing more make-up than her customary swipe of mascara.

Freya was aware of the irony: when she was in London and going out to dinner a couple of times a week, attending exhibitions, meetings and galleries, or giving lectures, she'd resented having to 'dress up', wanting nothing more than to don a pair of paint-daubed dungarees and tie her hair up. Yet now she was grateful for a reason to wear a skirt. Go figure!

A knock on the door alerted her that Mack was outside, and she grabbed her phone and keys, stuffing them into the pocket of her denim jacket, then bent to give her father a kiss.

Vinnie waved her away. 'Be quiet when you come back. I'll be in bed.'

'I won't be late.'

'Enjoy yourself. I worry about you stuck here with me, day in, day out.'

'Stop that,' she replied. 'I'm not stuck, as you put it, I'm looking after you.'

'I don't need—'

'Looking after,' she chimed in. 'I know, you keep telling me.'

'Stay out as long as you want. I'll be fine.'

Of course he would. How much mischief could her dad get up to in his own sitting room on a Friday evening? He'd eaten a good tea, he was in his pyjamas, and there were drinks and snacks in the kitchen if he was peckish. So why was she fretting?

When she left the house, she found Mack leaning against her van, his arms folded, his legs crossed at the ankle. He was gazing at the sky.

The sight of him made her pause, and her breath caught, as it often did when she saw him. He was one good-looking guy, with his tanned skin, sun-bleached curly hair and eyes the colour of the sky he was staring at.

'Anything interesting up there?' she asked.

'Does that cloud look like a dog to you?'

Freya looked up. 'I can't see it.'

'There.' He unfurled himself and stood close to her, pointing. 'That's the head, there's the nose, and that bit is the eye.'

Mack was wearing aftershave. It was woody and citrussy, and smelt divine. Freya tried not to breathe.

'Och, it's gone,' he said. 'The clouds are moving fast.'

'Are we expecting rain?' She hadn't listened to the news or the subsequent weather forecast, as she'd been too busy getting ready.

'This is Skye, we're always expecting rain,' he joked. 'Maybe not tonight, though I won't swear to it.'

She fell into step beside him as they strolled down the road. 'Aren't you fisherman types supposed to be able to sense it? Dad always claimed he could tell when the weather was about to turn.'

'You realise he probably listened to the shipping forecast, right?'

Freya laughed. 'Now you come to mention it…' The shipping forecast had been an ever-present background hum in their house when she was growing up. That, and *The Archers*.

The pub was as busy as it had been the last time she'd been in, and the same group of people were sitting at the same table, but this time she was going to join them.

Cal was there with Tara, together with Jinny and Mack's brother, Carter. She also recognised Rob the potter, and the glass-blower. Angus and another guy, who was part of Mack's crew, were propping up the bar.

'Drink?' Mack asked. She opted for a glass of cider and, after he'd gone to the bar, she draped her jacket over the back of a chair and sat down, feeling self-conscious.

She needn't have worried, because she was immediately welcomed into the group, as both Tara and Jinny began speaking to her at the same time.

'How are you?' Tara asked, as Jinny said, 'I remember you from when we were kids. I was quite a bit older than you, though.' She laughed. 'I still am – unless I'm going backwards!'

Freya couldn't help but smile at the warm welcome. 'You married Carter, didn't you?' she said to Jinny.

'For my sins.' She glanced fondly at her husband. 'Don't tell him, but he's the best thing that ever happened to me, apart from the kids. We've got two.'

Tara added, 'Jinny manages the gift shop at the castle's craft centre. I'd better introduce you to everyone. This is Gillian, who runs the cafe; next to her is Fergus, who does glass-blowing, and Shane, who does stained glass. Then there's Giselle, who makes sea-glass pictures, and Isla, who is our needle felter; and Rob is our potter. Everyone, this is Freya Sinclair.'

A chorus of hellos greeted her, and she said hi back, then caught Rob's eye.

'Freya *Sinclair*?'

'Er, yes.'

'*The* Freya Sinclair? You *must* be. I can't imagine there are many Freya Sinclairs who are potters. You should have said!' He turned to the others. 'Freya Sinclair's work is really good. I mean *really good*!'

Embarrassed, Freya blushed. She had no idea what to say to that.

'I love your work,' he continued, and she blushed even more.

Jinny said, 'Tara told me about you, so I looked at your website – your pieces are gorgeous! A bit pricey, though.'

'Jinny!' Tara cried. 'That's so rude.'

Jinny grimaced. 'I didn't mean it to be. I'm simply stating a fact. Freya's stuff is way out of our league. Her prices are London gallery prices.'

Mortified, Freya said, 'Sorry.'

'Gosh, don't be! They're worth every penny. They're stunning and I can see where you get your inspiration from

– they're the epitome of Skye.' Jinny turned to Tara and winked. 'It says so on her website.' Then back to Freya. 'Have you visited the castle's gift shop?'

Tara rolled her eyes. 'Always the salesperson…'

'I haven't,' Freya admitted. 'I didn't get a chance.' She gave Cal a meaningful look. If he hadn't whisked her away to see Mack, she would have had a good nose around.

'You must! We've got such a lot of lovely stuff, and you could treat yourself to coffee and a cake while you're there.'

'I'll go tomorrow,' Freya promised. As long as her dad didn't need her for anything, a visit to the castle and its craft centre would do her good.

-

Mack strolled over to Graham, a couple of pints in his hands. 'For you,' he said, giving one to Graham and placing the other on the bar. 'Tell Angus this is for him.'

'Cheers, Skip.' Graham slurped it thirstily.

'Stop calling me Skip.'

'OK, Skip.'

'I thought your name was Mack,' a voice said, and Mack turned to see a pretty blonde woman standing behind him. It took him a moment to place her. Then he realised he'd dated her last summer, but couldn't for the life of him remember her name.

'Hi,' he said. 'Long time, no see. It *is* Mack, but this bozo thinks it's funny to call me Skip. What are you doing here?'

She gave him a puzzled look. 'I'm on holiday.'

Ah, a tourist. For a moment he'd thought she might have been from Portree. 'I know,' he said, thinking on his feet. 'But there are so many wonderful places in Scotland, I don't think I'd go to the same place twice.'

She looked hurt. 'We come here every year. I told you that. I said, *see you next year*. Remember?'

Oh heck... His eyes found Cal's, who was watching with interest from his seat at the table, and he sent him a pleading look.

Cal took the hint and sauntered over. 'Mack, mate, I need a word. In private.' He smiled at the woman. 'Sorry, it's a work thing.' He shoved Mack towards the gents and, once inside, said, 'You owe me.'

'Thanks. She's a tourist and I went out with her last year, but I didn't expect to see her again.' Mack stepped to the sink and washed his hands.

'It's not nice when the shoe is on the other foot, is it?' Cal said.

'Eh?'

'Freya. I reckon you've got it bad, mate.'

'What are you on about?' He shook off the excess water, then shoved his hands under the dryer.

'Freya – you've got it bad.'

'You're talking rubbish.'

'I've seen the way you look at her.' Cal made puppy-dog eyes at him.

Mack scowled. 'Do you know how gormless you look?'

'It's the way you look at Freya.'

Mack shook his head. 'You're wrong.' He stepped away from the dryer, wondering why the damned things never dried properly, and wiped his hands on the backside of his cut-offs instead.

'Am I? I reckon she's got under your skin.'

'No chance.'

'Have it your way, but I know I'm right.'

'You're not. Just because you're all starry-eyed and drooly, don't assume everyone else is.'

'Drooly?'

'Yeah, you drool over Tara.'

'I do not!'

Relieved that he'd managed to turn the conversation away from himself, Mack thumped Cal lightly on the back and slipped out the door.

The woman was thankfully nowhere in sight.

But as he made his way back to the table, he saw Freya laughing with Jinny and Tara, and he knew Cal was right: he *did* look at her like a love-struck puppy. The problem was that he felt a bit like one too.

He'd better watch his step – falling in love wasn't on his agenda, and especially not with *her*.

Mack and Freya had only just left the pub and hadn't gone more than ten steps, when the first fat raindrops hit. Ten steps more, and the heavens opened.

With a squeal, Freya grabbed his hand and began to run. Mack hesitated for a split second then allowed himself to be towed along as she made a dash for it. He didn't like to tell her that no matter how fast they ran, the soaking they were about to get was inevitable. But when she dived into the bus shelter, he was glad he hadn't said anything.

He was disappointed when she immediately let go of his hand, though. It had felt warm and soft, even if her grip had been firmer than a weightlifter on steroids. Resisting the impulse to reach for it again, he shoved his hands in his pockets.

Shaking the drops from her jacket, Freya said, 'I'm hoping this is only a passing shower, but I get the feeling it's in for the night.'

Mack did too. 'Shall we give it five and see whether it eases up?'

The rain was dropping vertically, tamping onto the ground in a steady downpour, and a small river had formed in the gutter.

'At least we're on our way home,' she said, then groaned. 'Oh no, you've got further to go than me. If it doesn't ease, you'll be drenched. I'd offer to drive you, but I've had too much to drink.'

'That's the whole point of walking,' he said. 'Don't worry, it won't be the first time I've had a soaking going home from the pub.'

'Shall I see if my dad's got a waterproof jacket you can borrow?'

'It's fine. I'm used to being wet, it's part of working on a boat.'

She said, 'Remind me to carry a brolly with me at all times. I'm not as keen on the wet as you seem to be.'

'Don't get me wrong, I don't like it, but I can ignore it.'

She laughed. It was throaty, what Angus would call a 'dirty' laugh, and his pulse leapt.

'Could you honestly ignore that?' She flung an arm up to the sky. If anything, the downpour was getting worse.

'Perhaps not,' he admitted, wondering when it was going to let up and hoping it wouldn't be too soon. He was enjoying her company and didn't want the evening to end. Enjoying it too much, perhaps.

'So,' he said brightly, scratching around for something to talk about. 'You're off to the craft centre tomorrow?'

She beamed. 'I am, and I'm really looking forward to it. Seeing other artists at work is always a treat, and I didn't manage to have a proper look around last time because Cal dragged me off to Muirporth Quay.'

'Am I to assume that your first port of call will be the pottery studio?'

'Not necessarily. It might be the cafe. Jinny made the mistake of mentioning cake.'

'They do good food,' he acknowledged. 'I've eaten there a few times myself.'

'Would you like to come with me?'

Mack cringed. 'I wasn't angling for an invitation.'

'I didn't think you were.'

She *didn't*? Now he felt even more of an eejit. 'I wish I could,' he said, 'but I'll be out on the boat.'

'Pity, I would have treated you to a slice of something yummy, since you won't allow me to pay you for using the byre. Maybe another time?'

'I'd like that.'

'I could probably stretch to something more substantial, like a slap-up dinner?'

He didn't want her thanks, and he certainly didn't want her to feel that she owed him anything, but he wasn't going to pass up the opportunity to go out to dinner with her. He had no intention of letting her pay, though, so that would be a discussion if, and when, the dinner actually took place.

'Would you consider going to the castle again?' he asked, an idea beginning to form.

'I would; the food was divine, but they don't accept outside bookings. You have to be a guest.'

'Mhairi makes an exception for locals. I'll ask her, shall I? I think she owes me one.'

'Oh, that's right! I forgot to ask. How was your first photography trip?'

'It was OK, actually. Only five people were on it, but Cal said that the feedback was positive, and there are more booked onto the next one. It makes a change from hoping and praying that a bottlenose will show its face.'

As he finished speaking, Freya hugged herself and shivered. It may be summer on Skye, but the rain was cold.

'Come on,' he said, 'let's make a move. You're getting chilled, and if we wait for the rain to ease, we could be here all night.'

The possibility of spending all night with her gave him goosebumps. *Stop it*, he growled silently. He really needed to sort himself out; lusting after her wasn't going to do either of them any good.

Freya was already wet, so they walked quickly rather than ran, and by the time they reached her door, her hair was dripping and rainwater was running down her face. He guessed he looked equally as bedraggled.

Freya fumbled a set of keys out of her pocket, openly shivering, and although he wanted to linger, she needed to go inside and dry off.

'Are you sure you don't want to borrow a coat?' she asked, her teeth chattering.

'I'm sure. Get yourself inside before you catch your death.'

'I hate the thought of you—'

'I can't get any wetter,' he pointed out.

'But if you catch a chill, I'll blame myself.'

Mack grinned and shook his head. 'Stop fussing.'

'You sound like my dad. He keeps telling me off for fussing.'

'Do you think he might have a point?'

Freya rolled her eyes and pushed the door open. 'Don't forget to ask about dinner at the castle.'

He assured her he wouldn't forget, then waited for her to go inside.

He was nearly at his own front door before he realised it was still raining.

Chapter 18

Thankfully, the rain cleared overnight and the following day dawned bright and sunny. As Freya walked along the path from the village to the castle, the air smelt of salt and wet grass. It was one of those days when it felt really good to be alive.

She didn't seem to have suffered any ill effects from the dousing she'd had yesterday, although it had taken her a while to warm up. While she'd dried off and changed into her pyjamas, she hadn't been able to stop thinking about poor Mack, who'd had a decent walk before he reached his own house. She hoped he was all right, and she'd been tempted to phone him to ask, but she wasn't sure whether it was appropriate. She was fairly sure he wouldn't have taken it the wrong way, but the problem was she was fairly sure she *meant* it the wrong way. Her enquiry wouldn't have just been be a polite one, from one friend to another; it would have been an excuse to speak to him again.

Lying in bed last night, trying her utmost to fall asleep, Freya couldn't help wondering why she'd suggested taking him out for a meal. On the surface it had been a reasonable thing to do, to thank him for allowing her to use his byre, but considering the attraction she felt for him and the way he was beginning to invade her thoughts when she least expected it, it wasn't wise. She should have just bought him another bottle of whisky, or three. Dinner at the castle, just the two of them, would be far too intimate.

And there the castle was, its turrets rising above the trees.

So eager was she to see the rest of the studios (and visit the pottery again) that she decided the cafe could wait. She would treat herself to a small slice of cake and a cappuccino afterwards, and she would even ask them if they could box up a slice to take home to her dad. Actually, come to think of it, she'd ask them to box up two slices: her dad could have one and Mack could have the other. She didn't plan on going to the byre today, but she'd go tomorrow and take him his slice of cake then.

Rob beamed when she entered the studio and hurried forward. 'Hello, again. Have you come to have a chat about running a workshop? Mhairi mentioned it when I saw her this morning.'

'Er, no. I'm not sure I'll have the time,' she said. 'Or how long I'll be in Duncoorie. You see, my father's broken his hip and he's going to need a fair bit of help for a while, but as soon as he's better, I'll be going back to London.'

'That's a shame. I would have loved to have seen you in action.'

Freya laughed. '*In action?* I'd hardly call throwing a pot an exciting spectator sport.'

'I've heard you are hand building because you don't have access to a wheel.'

'I am and it's great fun. I don't do it often enough. I do miss my wheel, though, but it won't be for long. I'll soon be back in my own studio – fingers crossed.'

'If you find you're getting withdrawal symptoms, you're welcome to use mine.'

It was very generous of him, but she wouldn't invade his space. She knew how precious she could be when it came to her own studio, and how she wasn't keen on anyone else touching her things. Despite the principles of ceramics being the same, each potter had a slightly different way of doing things and a slightly different set-up.

'Thank you, that's kind,' she said. 'Maybe I will.'

Rob shuffled his feet. 'Could I ask your advice?'

'Of course.' She looked at him expectantly.

'I struggle to get height on pieces, especially when it comes to vases. I get them to a certain height and the necks become twisted.'

'Do you mean when you do collaring?'

'Yes.'

'How wet are your hands?'

'I keep a sponge handy.'

'Good.' The teacher in Freya kicked into gear. 'Tell you what, why don't you show me and maybe I can see where you can make an adjustment or two.'

Rob was obviously an experienced potter, and it amazed her that no matter how long you'd been making ceramics, there was always something to be learnt. She was more than happy to share her knowledge, and in return if she could scrounge tips from others, she would.

He ushered her towards his throwing station and handed her an apron. Then he pinned a bat onto the wheel and set it spinning, and unwrapped a lump of clay and slammed it down.

Freya watched him throw a wide cylinder, studying the placement of his hands as he gathered the clay from the bottom, pulling it up with his palms.

'OK, I think I can see what's happening,' she said, as the structure began to topple. 'If you leave the pulls a bit thicker, you'll be able to stretch the clay without it collapsing. Don't allow it to become too thin, and keep the pulls gentle.'

'Like this?' The clay was transforming from a short cylinder into a much taller one before her very eyes.

'Exactly like that. Now, rotate your wrists, like this.' She held up her arms to demonstrate, moving her hands upwards and her palms inwards, and watched him do the same. 'That's right. Don't worry if you feel it start to wobble; the trick is to re-centre it as you lift it. See the bit that's bulging? Right there?'

'Here?'

'Yes, keep your eyes on it and with each rotation, push it in. You've got to keep pushing it in, so you don't let the wobble take hold, because that's when it'll collapse. Good, good… You've got it.'

When the clay was at a height of about half a metre, she said, 'Stop pulling. Now you can shape it. Don't use your fingers, use a stick – it'll ensure the neck remains open. I think you were trying to thin the collar too much before shaping it.'

'I was!' he cried, and she was delighted to see how pleased he was with the finished result.

After he'd removed the vase from the wheel and carried it very carefully to the drying rack, he stood back to admire it.

'You really should run a workshop here,' he told her.

'No, *you* should.'

'But I can't—'

'Yes, you can,' she interrupted. 'Start with a beginners' workshop and a simple thrown pot. Or how about hand building for kids? You'll be amazed how rewarding it is.'

'I'm not as skilled as you.'

'Not at collaring perhaps, but what about your glazing?' She pointed to an elegant bowl in the studio's window. 'That's exquisite.' Pride shone in his eyes as she added, 'We can all learn from each other. No one knows everything.'

'You really think I could run a workshop?'

'Absolutely!'

'Oh, wow. Maybe I will.'

Freya fished around in her bag and handed him a small embossed card. 'My email address is on the back. *When*,' she stressed the word, 'you run your first one, I'd like to see some photos, and I definitely want you to tell me how brilliantly it went.'

'Thank you so much. I will.'

'Good luck, though I'll probably see you around because I'll be in Duncoorie for a few more weeks yet.'

'If you're ever in the pub, I'll buy you a drink.'

Freya grinned. 'Don't think I won't hold you to that, because I will.'

Happy that she'd been able to help, she left Rob's studio, eager to see the rest of the craft centre.

The next studio made her smile, for in the window were the most glorious and exquisitely detailed doll's houses. This must be Tara's work, she surmised, and with a spring in her step, she went inside.

Tara glanced up, a professional smile on her face, but when she saw who it was, she did a double take and her eyes lit up.

'Freya! You came!' She leapt to her feet and hurried towards the counter, leaning across it to give her a hug. 'What do you think?'

'I think you're extremely talented,' Freya replied honestly.

'Not about my doll's houses, silly. I was talking about the craft centre as a whole.'

'I haven't looked round all of it yet,' she admitted. 'I've only been into the glass workshops and the pottery studio next door.'

Tara beamed. 'Why doesn't that surprise me?'

'I remember these old buildings being mostly derelict when I was a kid. It's lovely to see them restored and put to good use.'

'It certainly is,' Tara replied. 'The minute I saw this place, I knew I wanted to work here.'

'I don't blame you. I wouldn't mind working here, either.'

'It's a pity we can't persuade you to stick around.'

'I wish I could, but I can't,' she replied. 'As soon as Dad is back on his feet, I'll be off.'

'To New York?'

'Not straight away. I'm hoping to start my new job in January, but I haven't had a contract through yet and neither have I handed in my notice. There'll be an awful lot to sort out before I leave.'

In her quieter moments, Freya had run through in her mind what needed to be done. Handing in her notice would be easy; deciding what to do with her apartment was much trickier. Did she want to sell it, or did she want to rent it out? It would be nice to have a base in London, in case she decided to return one day; actually, there was no *in case*, because she had the feeling she wouldn't spend the rest of her life in the States. She would come back to Britain at some point, so the most sensible thing would be to rent out her property in London, so she didn't have to try to find somewhere to live when she did eventually return. Anyway, renting it out meant that she could come back any time she wanted with a minimum of fuss if, for whatever reason, living in America didn't work out.

Freya chatted to Tara for a few minutes more, then left to explore the rest of the centre.

The other studios were equally fascinating, and she spent some time in each before making her way to the gift shop and Jinny.

Jinny was delighted to see her. 'What can I tempt you with?'

Freya's gaze darted greedily around the shop, briefly alighting on something that caught her eye, before swiftly moving on. By the time she'd finished her initial scan, there were at least a dozen things she would have loved to buy. In fact, she was so spoilt for choice that she was having trouble deciding on any one thing. Or any *two* things, for that matter.

Then she realised that if she bought something, she'd have to make sure she'd be able to take it with her across the pond, else it might sit in storage for some considerable time, if not forever. Of course, she would take any special items with her, and that was something else she'd have to look into. She could hardly pack her kiln into a suitcase, could she? Would she even want to take it? It would probably be cheaper and easier to buy a kiln once she was there – in fact, she might be able to stipulate that having a fully equipped studio was part of the contract.

Gosh, there was so much to think about, it was making her head spin. Time for a break.

After promising Jinny she'd be back, though not necessarily to buy something, she went to the cafe for a slice of cake and a restorative coffee, and tried not to think about anything other than the immediate future.

But the immediate future didn't involve Mack, so why on earth did an image of him pop into her head and her heart miss a beat?

Chapter 19

Freya swallowed hard and tried to ignore the unmistakable smell that all hospitals seemed to have. For weeks after her mother's death, she'd imagined she could still smell it in her hair, no matter how often she showered or what products she used.

'Stop fidgeting,' her dad hissed, and Freya realised her foot was tapping a staccato tattoo on the grey-tiled floor. She willed herself to keep still, and stared at the notices dotted around the walls, and then at a muted screen playing an NHS information video on a loop.

Her foot tapped again, and her dad elbowed her.

'Anyone would think you're the one who's about to be prodded and poked, not me,' he grumbled.

She prayed he'd get a good report. Despite being hopeful that her dad was making good progress, Freya didn't have any measure to compare it to. She didn't know anyone who'd broken their hip, and Dr Google had so much conflicting advice and information that she didn't know what to believe.

Just then his name was called and as he struggled carefully to his feet, Freya leapt up to help him.

He shook her off. 'I can manage.' It had become something of a refrain, and one that she tended to ignore.

Hovering by his side, she was matching her pace to his as he made his way to the consultation room, when he stopped abruptly.

'Where do you think you're going?' he demanded.

'With you,' she replied, bewildered.

'There's no need. I'm perfectly capable of seeing the doctor on my own.'

Hurt, she asked, 'Don't you want me to come in with you?'

'I've got to do things for myself. When you go back to London, I won't have anyone with me.'

'But that's a long way off.'

'Hmm, we'll see.'

'And you still can't walk properly,' she pointed out.

'No, but I can *hear* properly, so I can listen to what the doctor has to say without you being there. Stay here, I won't be long.'

Freya remained where she was, feeling rejected. Her dad was taking being independent too far. If he were fit and well, she could have understood his reluctance to have her there, but he wasn't. Then again, if he had been fit and well, he wouldn't be here in the first place.

She watched as he went inside, then she returned to her seat, eyeing the door anxiously and wondering how long he would be.

When a nurse came out a moment later and headed in her direction, Freya didn't take any notice, but when the woman came to a halt in front of her, she snapped to attention.

The nurse said, 'Your dad says you can go in with him, if you want.'

Freya *did* want. Happy that the miserable old so-and-so had seen sense, she went into the consultation room. If there was anything wrong, or anything more that her dad could be doing, she wanted to hear it first-hand from the doctor, and not second-hand from her father.

'This is nice,' Vinnie said, looking around the restaurant. 'It makes a change to be somewhere different. I thought I'd go mad if I had to stare at those four walls for much longer. I was going stir-crazy.'

'If you wanted to go out, you should have said,' Freya replied, before it occurred to her that maybe she should have thought to offer to take him out. He'd been home from hospital for over two weeks, yet he hadn't left the house once, except for today.

After the consultant said she was pleased with his progress, Freya had suggested that they stop off for a bite to eat on their way home. There was a pub where she'd eaten once, after she'd visited him in Broadford Hospital and hadn't been able to face cooking. The food was good, the portion sizes were generous, it was on the outskirts of the town, and she felt that they both deserved lunch out to celebrate. Her dad wasn't out of the woods yet, but the edge of the treeline was in sight and he seemed happier in himself.

So was she. Some of the anxiety and tension she'd been carrying for the past month had eased now that she knew the wound had healed well, and he was regaining some flexibility in the joint. She had to admire her dad's determination; he did his exercises religiously twice a day, every day, and made sure he got up out of his chair regularly to walk around the house.

'Did you hear the doctor say that as long as I'm careful, there's no reason for me not to use the stairs?' he said.

'I did.'

'I'm to ask the physio to show me the best way to go up and down them, the next time she comes. Oh, and did I tell you that it'll be her last home visit? I'm to go to the hospital for future appointments.'

'Yes, you did.'

'You'll have to ask Mack if he can take my bed back up. I never wanted it in the sitting room in the first place.'

'I know you didn't, but it was safer and more practical, with the bathroom being downstairs.'

'It'll be nice to sleep in my own bedroom again, and to put the sitting room straight.'

She smiled. This was the liveliest she'd seen him since she'd returned to Skye, but when she said, 'I think you should keep the riser chair for a while,' his face clouded over.

She thought he was going to argue, but all he did was nod, and she guessed he would keep it to humour her then get rid of it as soon as she was gone.

If that's what he wanted to do, that was his prerogative, but for now he still needed it. The armchairs were too low and too soft. Not only were they difficult for him to get in and out of, but they also put unnecessary strain on his healing joint, and having his leg at the wrong angle to his hip was a definite no-no.

Conversation dried up for a moment, as they perused the menu, but resumed again once they'd chosen.

'This is nice,' he repeated. 'I haven't been somewhere different for ages.'

A flicker of concern flitted through her: hadn't he said the very same thing a couple of minutes ago? Then she remembered friends and colleagues mentioning how repetitive their elderly relatives had become, and she let the worry go, especially when he said, 'The pub in

Duncoorie is the furthest I get these days, but I can't manage even that now.'

'I'll drive you there whenever you want,' she told him. Then added, with a smile, 'I'll even bring you home again if you're not too drunk.'

'And what if I am?'

'I'll leave you there until the morning. You'll have sobered up by then,' she teased, then became more serious. 'Promise me you'll be more careful. I don't think either of us can take you having another fall.'

'I'll try, but sometimes it just happens.'

She narrowed her eyes. 'Are you telling me that you've fallen before this?'

'I'm not saying anything of the sort. All I meant was…' He exhaled slowly. 'I wasn't exactly cavorting around the kitchen when I fell, and neither was I up a ladder. It just happened. One minute I was thinking about making a mug of cocoa in the hope it would send me off to sleep, the next I was on the lino and couldn't get up again.'

Freya's eyes filled with tears. 'Oh, Dad, I should have—'

'Hush, I know what you're thinking. Even if you'd been here, it wouldn't have made any difference. I would still have fallen.'

'But I'd have heard you calling and you wouldn't have been lying on the kitchen floor all night.'

'Aye, well, that's as may be, but you weren't and you're not going to be. I've said it before, and I'll say it again – you've got your own life to lead.'

She knew she wouldn't have been able to prevent him falling, but the guilt continued to linger, regardless.

'Could you have one of those alarms—' she began, but her dad cut her off.

'Pfft! I am *not* wearing one of those. I'm not old or—' Glowering, he broke off, repeating, 'I'm not old.'

The alarms weren't just for old people, but there was no point in arguing with him. When he got something in his head, there was no budging him.

'I've got an idea,' she said slowly, fully anticipating him to refuse to even entertain it. 'Why don't you keep your mobile phone on you? Just think, if you'd had it with you when you went downstairs to make a cup of cocoa, you'd have been able to phone for help.'

He scoffed. 'You'll have me taking it to the toilet next.'

'What's wrong with that? You could have an accident in the bathroom just as easily as in the kitchen.'

'I'll never remember it.'

'You will,' she insisted, warming to her theme. 'Just keep it in your pyjama or trouser pocket. Before you know, it'll be second nature to carry it with you.'

'Or an addiction,' he grumbled.

She laughed. 'I can't see *you* being addicted to your phone.'

'That reminds me,' he said. 'Are you feeling all right? I haven't seen you playing with yours all morning.'

'I put it on airplane mode before we set out for the hospital, as I didn't want it going off in the middle of your appointment and I knew I'd forget if I didn't do it when I thought about it.' She often put it on airplane mode when she was working, or at the very least she switched it to silent.

Wondering whether she'd had any calls or messages this morning, she was about to reach into her bag to check, when her dad squeezed her hand.

'You're a good daughter.'

Freya knew that wasn't true. She should have visited more often, phoned him more frequently. And she definitely shouldn't have felt as irritated with him as she had over these past couple of weeks. She'd had to keep reminding herself that he was set in his ways and that however much he loved her and she him, it couldn't be easy having her invade his space.

'I'll give it a go,' he said, patting his shirt pocket and bringing out his tablets. 'But you'll have to keep reminding me.'

'Don't worry, I will!'

The peace of mind it would give her would far outweigh the amount of nagging she was going to have to do.

—

Mack knew a bawbag when he saw one, and the guy wearing an obviously brand-new and expensive Barbour jacket, and carrying a camera with a telescopic lens that was big enough to see a speck of dust on the moon, was clearly it.

'We've got a right one here,' Angus muttered in Mack's ear as he walked into the cockpit. 'He's just told me he wants to sit up top.'

Mack flicked a couple of switches and grunted. 'You might want to ask him whether he can read the sonar while he's there. He might be better at it than you.'

'Cheeky blighter! I told him he has to sit on the deck with the rest of them. Up top, my hairy... And have you seen the size of his camera? I reckon he has to have a big one to compensate for the size of his willy.'

Mack barked out a laugh. 'I won't argue with you, but he's one of the castle's guests and we need to treat him with the same respect we treat all our passengers, small willies notwithstanding.'

'Aye, aye, Skip.' Angus sprang to attention and gave him a mock salute. 'I didn't mean anything by it.'

'I know. Are we ready to cast off?'

'I'll go take a look.'

Mack grinned. Angus was as down-to-earth as it got. He called a spade a spade, but Mack knew that he'd be professional in front of the passengers, even if one of them appeared to be a dick. Mhairi's trips paid well, and it wasn't as though they'd never had difficult passengers in the past, as they'd had their fair share.

Thinking about Mhairi reminded him that he needed to have a chat with her about booking a table for dinner. He'd pop in this evening and have a word.

Angus was back. 'All aboard, so we can set sail.'

'You're not on a yacht.' Mack chuckled.

'I wish I was. I wouldn't say no to a trip around the Med.'

'You're having a trip around Loch Duncoorie instead, and you're going to enjoy it.'

'Is that a threat or a warning?'

'It's an observation.' Mack pressed a couple more buttons. 'Go on, admit it, you wouldn't want to be anywhere else. You love it here.'

'That's true enough, but a wee holiday on a white coral beach wouldn't go amiss.'

As Mack steered the boat away from the quay, Angus's words lingered in his mind.

A holiday would be nice. He hadn't had one of those in years, too busy building up the business and renovating his house. Not to mention the cost. If he was going to have a holiday, though, he wanted it to be somewhere warm, where sun was guaranteed and not the hit-and-miss affair it was in the UK. And he didn't want kiss-me-quick hats and an arcade at the end of a pier. He wanted palm trees and a hammock. He didn't want fish and chips on a windy promenade, or a pint and a bag of crisps in a beer garden, either. What he wanted was cocktails on a sun-drenched beach and a bowl of olives to nibble on. And tanned women in skimpy bikinis, with long legs and… *auburn hair and freckles?*

His brain provided him with an image of Freya, and he sucked in a breath.

Now, why would it be doing that? He really must stop thinking about her. She was taking up more space in his head than anyone he'd ever met. Trust him to have developed feelings for a woman who would be out of his life in a matter of weeks. Karma must be having a right laugh at his expense.

–

Hoping there was something important in her inbox, Freya took her mobile out of her bag, but not before she'd hunted for her dad's phone and made sure he put it in his trouser pocket. He gave her a resigned look and she chalked it up as a win, relieved that no nagging had been required. *This* time, at least.

After filling the kettle and plugging it in, she took her phone off airplane mode and… Dear God! She had three missed calls from Hadrian, but he hadn't left a voicemail or sent her a message.

With a hand to her heart, she called him back, her mind filled with worry. This was so unlike him; something must be very, very wrong, and she prayed he was OK. She mightn't love him, but she did still care for him, and the thought of him being ill or injured made her feel sick.

'Hadrian!' she cried, when he answered. 'What's wrong?'

'Guess where I am!' he cried chirpily, and she let out a sigh of relief.

'I've no idea.' Wherever he was, it was windy, and she could hear the sound of an engine and voices and... was that a seagull?

'I'll give you a clue – water.'

'Somewhere near the Thames?' she guessed, despite not being in the mood for games. Her heart hadn't returned to its normal rhythm yet.

'Not even close,' he crowed.

'Where, then?' Frustrated and rather irritated, she put him on speaker and checked her emails. There were several new ones, but nothing from Jocasta Black.

'Skye.'

Freya froze. '*Where?*'

'Skye. Duncoorie, to be exact. I flew in this morning and was hoping you could pick me up from the airport, but you weren't answering your phone. I had to hire a car.'

'You're in *Duncoorie*?'

'I'm on a boat in the loch, to be precise, but I'm staying at the castle. *Quelle surprise*, eh? I've booked dinner for seven thirty.' He uttered a lascivious laugh. 'But if you get there sooner, we can have a quick catch-up before dinner. I hope the food is as good as you say it is. By the way, my room has a four-poster. Got any ribbon?'

Freya didn't know which to reply to first, so she went with the last thing he said. 'Why do you want ribbon?'

'To tie you to the bed with, silly. Isn't that what four-posters are for? Oops, gotta go. See you later, babe.'

Freya stared at the screen. He'd hung up.

Feeling bulldozed, she sank onto a kitchen chair, her mind whirling.

Why was Hadrian in Duncoorie? Not for one second did she presume to think he was here because he was missing *her*.

Or *was* he?

Oh, God, please don't let it be that, not when she had every intention of telling him they were over, and this would be the perfect opportunity to speak to him face-to-face. It had to be done, but sodding hell, she felt like a total cow.

She would be early, she decided, but there wouldn't be any bedroom antics, and neither would she be having dinner with him. The sooner this was over, the better.

She was still reeling from the news that Hadrian had turned up out of the blue, when her dad appeared.

'I thought you were making tea?' He peered at her face and his eyes filled with concern. 'What's wrong?'

'Hadrian is at the castle.'

It took him a moment. '*Your* Hadrian?'

'Yes.' Although he wasn't going to be hers for much longer.

'Did you know he was coming?'

'No. It's a total surprise.'

'That's nice, isn't it?'

She shrugged, and he shook his head. 'You never did like surprises, not even when you were little. He should know that.'

He probably did, but because it hadn't fitted in with his agenda, he'd ignored it.

Vinnie asked, 'When you say "at the castle", do you mean he's staying there?'

She nodded. 'Don't worry, I'm not going to stay there with him.'

'I'm not worried. I keep telling you I can manage.' He sat down opposite. 'You've seen me over the worst, so why don't you spend a few days with him, or however long he's there for, then go back to London when he does?'

Freya smiled weakly. 'Are you trying to get rid of me?'

He ignored her comment. 'Promise me something?'

'What?'

'That you won't let him talk you out of going to America. It's the opportunity of a lifetime.'

That was an easy one. 'I won't, Dad, I promise.'

He stared at her, his gaze keen, then he nodded. 'Good. I'll make my own tea. You go have fun!'

If only he knew…

She'd tell him later, but it was only fair that Hadrian heard the news that she was breaking up with him first, before she told anyone else.

Chapter 20

Mack blew out his cheeks as he watched his passengers disembark, while Angus was giving anyone who needed it a helping hand. He was glad to see the back of this lot, if he was honest, and one person in particular. The flashy git with the exaggerated air of self-importance had spent half the trip on his phone, and the other half exclaiming loudly about composition and light, line and form, and generally bigging himself up.

Mack had no idea who this guy was, and he didn't care. The chap could be the next Picasso for all he knew, but Mack wasn't interested. He just wished the man would shut his gob for a few minutes, because he sure did like the sound of his own voice.

'Got any plans for this evening?' Angus asked as they were going through the end-of-day routine.

'Just some paperwork,' Mack replied. He'd get that done first, then nip into the village for a couple of bits from the shop and call at the castle on the way back. 'You?'

'Taking the kids to the cinema to see the latest Disney film.' He rolled his eyes, but Mack knew that Angus secretly loved kids' films. Comics, too.

'Get away, you'll have a great time,' Mack said.

Angus grinned. 'Aye, I know. Having kids is a great excuse for doing things you used to like doing when you were a nipper.'

Mack knew what Angus meant. He loved nothing better than messing about with his niece and nephew, although Katie was more into pink, sparkly things than Mack was comfortable with, especially when she insisted on using face paints on him and he ended up with a pink beard and purple face, and looking like a character in a Disney film himself. Ted, his nephew, was far easier; give the boy a football and he'd happily kick it around all day.

'What time does the film start?' Mack asked.

'Five thirty.'

'Get off home now,' he told him. 'I'll finish up here. You too, Graham.'

'Cheers, Skip.'

After they'd left, Mack methodically worked through the tasks, not minding doing them on his own. He found it quite relaxing to potter around on the boat and he took pride in his work.

Finally satisfied that everything was as it should be, he made sure the dock lines were secure, then headed to his makeshift office in the lock-up to catch up on his paperwork. It wasn't something he enjoyed doing, but it was a necessary evil and he got stuck in with grim determination.

An hour later, he'd caught up on what he could, had made notes on the calendar for anything he couldn't, and was ready to knock work on the head for the day.

He had two more jobs to do before he could go home but they shouldn't take long. The first was to call into the shop, because he was running low on some essentials like milk and eggs, and the second was to pay the castle a quick visit.

Shopping didn't take long – he was in and out in minutes – and he was soon heading back along the road towards the castle.

He parked around the rear, near the delivery entrance, then made his way around to the front. The craft centre was closed for the day, but seeing it brought Freya to mind. Not that she was out of it much – he'd been thinking about her most of the day, and as he sauntered towards the castle's incredibly impressive main entrance, he wondered what she was doing and whether she'd been to the byre today.

As he approached the reception desk, Avril, who was manning it this evening, gave him a smile. 'Did you want Cal?'

'I was hoping to have a quick word with Mhairi,' he said. 'I promise I won't keep her long.'

'I'll see if she's free.' She picked up the phone and spoke softly into it, before turning her attention back to him. 'She's in the kitchen, checking on dinner, if you want to pop along and see her. Will five minutes be enough?'

'It will. Thanks, Avril.'

The route to the kitchen took him past the residents' lounge, and a cursory glance inside revealed several guests enjoying pre-dinner drinks. One of them was the loud chap from earlier, and Mack grimaced, hoping that the man would check out before he and Freya ate there – assuming Mhairi agreed to bend the rules for him, of course. There was no guarantee that she would.

Reaching the kitchen, he pushed the swing door open and a glorious wall of delicious smells hit him.

Remaining where he was (he didn't want to risk sullying the pristine cooking areas), he waited for Mhairi to notice him. When she did, she ushered him back out into the corridor with a regal waft of her hand.

'You wanted to see me?' she said.

'I did.' He shuffled nervously, wondering where to begin.

'Out with it, Mack, I have guests to see to.'

'Of course, yes, sorry. The thing is, Freya wants to take me to dinner to thank me for letting her use my byre. She's trying to work while she's here and she can't do it at home, so I said—' He stopped. 'I'm waffling.'

'You are.'

'I know it's your policy to only allow guests to eat here, but do you think you can make an exception?'

'I can. When?'

'Whenever is convenient for you. Oh, and there's something else; she's expecting to pay but I don't want her to, so could I pay for it without her knowing?'

'I think that can be arranged,' the old lady said with a twinkle in her eye. 'Speak to Avril.'

'Thanks, I really appreciate it.'

Buoyed up by the success of his mission, Mack had a bounce in his step as he made his way towards the grand entrance hall. Once more, the route took him past the lounge, and once more he glanced inside, thinking that before long he would be there with Freya and they would be enjoying a pre-dinner drink of their own.

Abruptly he halted, his eye caught by a familiar figure.

It was Freya, and she was standing at the bar with the obnoxious guy from the boat.

Unable to take his eyes off the pair, he saw the man put his arms around her and draw her into his embrace. Then the spell was broken by the sound of laughter from a group of ladies as they raised their glasses.

Anxious not to be seen, Mack hurried off, dismay filling him.

But before he left, there was something he had to do – and it wasn't booking a table. That was the last thing he wanted to do right now.

Cringing at his subterfuge, but knowing he had no other choice, as Avril wouldn't be able to give out information about the castle's guests, Mack said to her, 'Did I just see Hadrian Thingamajig in the lounge?' He tapped his forehead with his open palm. 'I've forgotten his surname. My memory is like a sieve these days.'

Avril glanced at the computer screen. 'Yes, you're right. Hadrian Godley.'

'That's it! I thought it was him.'

'Do you want to go in?' Avril was staring doubtfully at his customary T-shirt and shorts.

'I would, but I'm not dressed for it. Mhairi would throw me out on my ear,' he said, and Avril giggled.

'Shall I let Mr Godley know you want to see him?'

'No need. I'll catch up with him another time.'

Mack drove home on autopilot. So *that* was Hadrian.

He didn't know what he was more disappointed about: Freya having such appalling taste in men, or Jinny getting it wrong about Freya's feelings for her boyfriend. Because from the way Freya had sunk into the man's arms, their relationship appeared serious enough to Mack.

—

Freya didn't want to cause Hadrian any embarrassment, so when he saw her enter the lounge and opened his arms, she walked into his embrace, quickly pulling back before he could kiss her. She felt awful rejecting him, but she couldn't pretend.

Keeping an arm around her waist, he whispered, 'I'm glad you're here early. Let's go to my room. Dinner can wait. It won't matter if we're late. I've missed you, babe.'

She wriggled free. 'I'll go upstairs, but to talk, not to…'

'Talk? What do you want to talk about?'

'Not here.'

Realisation spread across his face, and his expression hardened. 'You're *dumping* me?'

Freya said, 'It's not working, Hadrian. Surely even you can see that.'

'*Even me?*'

'Wrong turn of phrase,' she backtracked hastily.

'It damn well is. *Even me*, indeed!'

'Keep your voice down.' She glanced around the lounge, hoping no one was paying any attention to their fraught conversation.

'Had a better offer, have you? A brawny Scotsman in a kilt?'

'No! I keep telling you, I'm here because my dad needs me. I'm not here for fun.'

His eyes were hard, as he slowly said, 'You *have* had a better offer. You're going to New York.' He shook his head, his lips a thin line. 'I thought it was just a rumour, but no smoke without a fire, eh, Freya?'

'It's not that—'

'Of course it is! Don't insult me.'

'It's not!' she insisted.

'Bullshit. And I bet that's what that stupid boat trip was about. I bet you've started working on new pieces to impress your new boss.' His look of disgust made her flinch. He hissed, 'I've supported you and championed you for the past two years, and this is the thanks I get?' In a tone of pure dislike, he added, 'I wouldn't be surprised if your precious father isn't ill at all, and you lied to me so you could throw me off the scent. Good luck in New York – you're going to need it.' He turned away from her and snapped his fingers at the bar staff. 'A double vodka. Now!'

Near to tears, Freya whispered, 'I'm sorry,' but Hadrian refused to acknowledge her, and after a second or two she slunk out of the lounge, utterly ashamed. Not because she'd ended it with Hadrian, but because she *had* been working on new pieces when she really should have been giving her poor dad her full attention.

—

The whisky was smooth, with an earthy undertone, and it was slipping down Mack's throat far too easily. He guessed he might regret it come the morning, but right now he simply didn't care, so he poured himself another dram and turned up the volume.

'Angie' by The Rolling Stones blasted out of the speakers, and he rested his head on the back of the old wooden chair, letting the sound wash over him.

He was sitting on the lawn to the rear of the house, the evening sun on his face, and since there were no neighbours within disturbing-distance, he could play his music as loud as he wanted. Unfortunately, though, it failed to drown out his thoughts.

Staring vacantly across the loch, he tried to work out why he was feeling so damned miserable. It wasn't as though he didn't know that Freya had a boyfriend. He'd known all along. So why had seeing them together disturbed him so much?

Was it because he was disappointed that she didn't have better taste in men? No – although he was, and she should have. The guy was a dick, but why should that make any difference?

Unless... Cal's words floated through Mack's mind, and he finally acknowledged that they'd hit their mark. What Mack felt for Freya was more than lust, desire and attraction.

He *liked* her, damn it. He liked her one hell of a lot. He liked her so much that if she wasn't buggering off soon, he would have made a serious play for her. The kind of play that he'd never made for any woman. The playing-for-keeps kind of play. He liked her that much.

He would have had to get rid of the boyfriend first – which mightn't have been too much of a problem, since Mack was here and the boyfriend was six hundred miles away. But what happened to his rule of staying clear of attached women?

Aware that if Freya hadn't been leaving soon, he would have broken that rule, Mack didn't like himself right now.

How could he be this miserable over a woman he hardly knew and hadn't even kissed – although those two things weren't mutually exclusive, as he'd kissed quite a few women whom he'd hardly known and had thoroughly enjoyed it.

He should eat something before he drank any more whisky. He wasn't hungry, but he could feel the effects of the single malt on an empty stomach, and knew he'd be three sheets to the wind if he wasn't careful.

Oh, who cared? If he wanted to get drunk, he would. The upside of being single and living alone was having no one to answer to. No one would give him the look he'd seen Angus's missus give to Angus when he'd had one too many. No one would tell him he'd had enough. He could get absolutely bladdered if he wanted, and no one would say a word. The downside of not having anyone to ply him with painkillers, tea and sympathy in the morning was a small price to pay.

There was no point in being miserable, since he didn't want to be tied down anyway. He'd hate it. He liked his life fine, just the way it was, so why was he busy drowning sorrows he didn't want? Married life wasn't for him, so there was no need to cry over spilt milk when he had no intention of drinking the stuff anyway.

He needed food. And he needed to pour the rest of this glass of whisky down the sink and not down his throat. He wasn't drunk yet but he soon would be, and although he didn't mind getting plastered once in a while, he preferred to do it in good company and for a good reason. Getting pissed over a woman wasn't reason enough.

Maybe he wouldn't dispose of the whisky just yet, though. It would be a shame to waste it. He'd eat first, give himself time to sober up, then finish it later.

Irritated by the music, he switched it off and the sudden silence was deafening: not even a bird tweeted. Perhaps his feathery friends didn't like The Stones?

Going inside, he put the tumbler on the counter in the kitchen and made his way a tad unsteadily towards the bathroom.

As he did so, a flash of red outside the front of the house stopped him in his tracks.

Freya's little red van was parked beside his truck, and Mack's heart lurched.

Suddenly, he didn't feel quite as tipsy, and questions danced through his mind. Why was she here? Had she brought Dickwad with her? Was she currently packing up her stuff?

There was only one way to find out… And if Hadrian Loud-Mouth was with her, Mack might be tempted to order the bastard off his property.

However, Freya was alone.

She was seated on the stool at the workbench with a ball of clay in her hands. She was working it, turning and pinching the material, absorbed in her task.

He didn't think she was aware of his presence until she said, 'Do you always play music that loud?'

Mack stepped inside. She didn't look up when he replied, 'No.'

'"Angie", eh?'

'It suited my mood.' He moved closer. 'You're not normally here in the evenings.'

'No, I'm not.' There was a hitch in her voice. Could she be upset? Might she have had a row with her boyfriend? Probably not; from where Mack had been standing, they'd looked pretty cosy.

He said, 'You're busy. I'll get out of your hair.'

She didn't say anything, but when her shoulders began to shake, he realised she was crying.

In three strides, he was at her side. Crouching, he peered up at her. She had her face in her hands.

'Has he hurt you?' Mack demanded.

'Who?'

'Your boyfriend. Freya, look at me – has he hurt you?'

Head bowed, she let her hands drop. Her cheeks were damp and her eyes brimmed with tears.

Mack had never felt such rage. The sight of her distress made him want to tear the bastard limb from limb and feed the wee gobshite to the fishes.

'I'll kill him,' he muttered.

'He hasn't hurt me.'

'So what's wrong? Is it your dad? Please don't tell me he's had another fall.'

'He's fine. It's just...' Her chin wobbled and she bit her lip. 'Hadrian accused me of lying about Dad's fall so I could come up here and work on new pieces.'

'That's not fair. He only has to take one look at him to know you're not making it up.'

She drew in a juddering breath. 'It's kind of true, though. Look at me; I'm here having fun when I should be at home looking after my dad!'

'Vinnie wouldn't want you fussing around him all day. It would drive him mad. And it's not as though you *haven't* been looking after him, because you *have*.'

'But there's more. You see, Hadrian didn't know about the offer from New York. He'd heard a rumour, but I don't think he believed it until I told him we were over.'

'What?'

'I broke up with him this evening. That's why he said those things.'

Mack reeled at the news. His heart thumped and a treacherous glimmer of hope flared in his chest. She was free, which meant—

Realisation doused his hope. She was still going to New York, whether she had a boyfriend or not.

Pulling himself together, he said, 'He's hurting. Love can make people do or say things they don't really mean.'

'He doesn't love me.'

It was a bald statement, and his heart went out to her.

He cast around for something to say, but all he could come up with was, 'I'm sorry, Freya. No wonder you broke up with him.'

Her lips twitched into the smallest of smiles. 'I didn't break up with him because he doesn't love me. I broke up with him because *I* didn't love *him*.'

It took Mack a second to process it. 'You don't love him?'

'No. I feel awful, because we've been together two years, but I don't love him. I'm not sure I even like him.'

Mack was utterly positive that *he* didn't. 'You're not crying because you split up?' he clarified. 'You're upset because you think you're not taking good care of your dad?'

She nodded.

'You muppet.'

'Excuse me?'

'You're working yourself into a tizzy because some wee gobshite who doesn't know his arse from his elbow has made you doubt that you're taking good care of your father? What does he know?'

'It's what *I* know.' She tapped her chest.

Mack threw his hands up. 'Shall we go ask Vinnie what he thinks?'

'Definitely not!'

'Because you know he'll tell you that you're making Ben Nevis out of a bloody molehill. So what if you take an hour or two for yourself now and again? So what if being back on Skye has fired your imagination? It's not an either/or thing, Freya. You can look after your dad and still have ideas, and work on them if the opportunity allows.'

Freya was staring at him, her mouth open. 'That's some speech.' She sniffed. 'Is that whisky I can smell?'

'It is. If you didn't want me to drink it, you shouldn't have given it to me.'

'Is there any left?'

'I haven't drunk it all.'

She sniffed again. 'You've had a good go.'

'I'm not drunk, if that's what you're hinting at. I've had two.'

'Large ones?'

'If you're gonna have one, have a proper one, not a piddling thimbleful.' He struggled to his feet, his knees stiff and his thigh muscles cramping from crouching for so long. 'Shall I bring a glass out to you?'

'Do you mind if I drink it inside?'

'Not at all. Do you mind if I have one with you?'

'I was hoping you would. Drinking on your own is a bit sad.' Freya pulled a face. 'Oops – I didn't mean to imply that *you're* sad because you're drinking on your own.' Her eyes widened. 'You *are* on your own, aren't you? I haven't interrupted anything?'

Nah, just him trying to drown the sorrow of knowing that Freya Sinclair was out of bounds.

She wasn't out of bounds *now*, though. She was very much *in* bounds. Whether he acted on it depended on whether he wanted to risk being rebuffed. Or being hurt, because he had a suspicion that this woman had the power to hurt him badly.

So maybe it was best to leave things as they were, he told himself, as he poured her a tumbler and topped up his own glass.

Unfortunately, he failed to heed his own advice.

Chapter 21

Whisky, a sunset and an incredibly sexy man didn't mix, Freya concluded, staring at the bottom of her glass. She would dearly like another, but she didn't trust herself. Although she was fairly certain Mack didn't think of her as anything more than a friend, it didn't stop her from fantasising about running her hands over his chest or pressing her body against his.

She'd managed to keep such lascivious thoughts in check until now, but finding herself suddenly single seemed to have set them free, so the last thing she wanted was to have too much to drink and make a fool of herself by throwing herself at him — after all, as well as her lustful thoughts, she also had her heart to consider. Becoming involved with Mack, no matter how fleeting the encounter, would be a serious mistake, as she couldn't shake the suspicion that he would be an easy man to fall in love with.

However, with the likelihood of having any kind of relationship with him being so small, it was pointless even thinking about it.

Or was it?

Once or twice, she could have sworn she'd felt a connection, seen a spark of interest in his eyes. It came and went so quickly that she'd assumed she'd imagined it.

What if she hadn't? What if he did fancy her? What if, what if, what if…

None of the what ifs in the world would make the least bit of difference, because she had no intention of acting on any of them. She'd be better off concentrating her attention on her dad, her work and her new job in the States. The contract had finally come through and she was more than happy with it, so it was all systems go and she was becoming increasingly excited.

Aw, but look at him… Mack was bloody gorgeous. And the nicest thing was that he didn't know it – unlike Hadrian, who was well aware how handsome he was.

The two men couldn't be more different, and she knew which one was responsible for getting her knickers in a twist – and it wasn't the slick, confident, well-dressed, over-styled artist.

Mack broke into her thoughts. 'Do you want a refill?'

'Better not. I should be getting back. Dad will wonder where I am.' Actually, he probably wouldn't be wondering at all. He was fully expecting her to be out all evening and possibly all night, too. As if she'd do that, with him still needing her to keep an eye on him.

'I'll walk you back.'

'Oh, hell, I'd forgotten I'll have to walk.'

'It's not far.'

She glanced down at her feet. Mack followed her gaze. 'Ah,' he said.

While she wasn't wearing ridiculously high heels, they were high enough, and she didn't fancy walking any distance in them. She should have worn her trusty old Doc Martens, posh castle or no posh castle.

'I've got some wellies you can borrow…' Mack began, then trailed off as she stared at his feet. 'Or maybe not.'

His feet were considerably larger than hers. It didn't matter that she'd look like a kid in her mum's boots; the issue was that she wouldn't be able to manage more than a shuffle.

'It might work with four pairs of socks?' he suggested.

'How about ten?'

'You're winding me up.'

'I'm guessing the taxi situation isn't any better than it was when we were kids?'

'Nope. If we phone now, we might get one before midnight and that's assuming a cab will come all the way from Portree.'

'I'll have to take my chances and walk,' she said, hoping her feet wouldn't be rubbed raw by the time she got home.

'No, you won't. I'll phone Cal or Angus.' He pulled a face and Freya guessed he wasn't keen on phoning either. 'Or my mum,' he added. 'She'll come fetch you.'

Freya shook her head firmly. 'I'll walk. It'll sober me up.'

'You're not drunk.'

She wasn't, and neither was he. She'd noticed that he'd been nursing his whisky, not gulping it. Still, it was kind of him to let her intrude on his evening. She hadn't meant to burst into tears, and she wasn't the weepy type, but the stress of the past month had finally caught up with her.

She had to admit that she felt better for having had a little cry, and the restorative whisky had also helped. So had Mack. His calm support had been just what she'd needed to help her see reason and get her back on an even keel.

'We'll take it slow,' Mack said and Freya bit her lip, trapping in the 'Yes, please,' she'd almost let slip, as the thought of an entirely different kind of slow to the one he'd meant popped naughtily into her mind.

Dear God, she shouldn't have drunk that whisky on an empty stomach. Lunch, even though it had been a late one, had been hours ago.

'Do you need anything before we set off?' Mack asked.

Hmm, yeah, *you*. 'Such as?'

'Is there anything in your van you can't live without until tomorrow?'

Oh. 'No, nothing.'

'Hang on, I'll grab some plasters. There's some in the first-aid kit.'

She hovered in the hall while he rummaged through the bathroom cabinet. 'You've got a first-aid kit?'

'Hasn't everyone?'

Not really. Hadrian hadn't.

Mack emerged from the bathroom with several plasters in his hand. 'Do you think these will be enough?'

'Plenty. I hope.' If they weren't, her feet would be in serious trouble.

They set off at a gentle stroll, Freya thinking that this wasn't so bad. The shoes weren't uncomfortable as such, she simply wasn't used to walking any distance in them. That was what her Doc Martens and trainers were for.

'I saw you at the castle,' Mack said. 'You were in the lounge.'

Surprised, Freya gave him a sideways look. 'I didn't see *you*.'

'You were busy.'

'Ah.' She took it to mean that he'd seen her with Hadrian. How embarrassing. 'Did you manage to book a table?' she asked.

'Um, not really. I wasn't sure when you would be free.'

A thought caught her off-guard, coming out of left field, and she stumbled. Mack's arm immediately snapped around her waist, keeping her upright.

'Are you OK?'

Oh, God, that felt so good, and she leant into him. 'I think so.'

'You haven't twisted your ankle or anything?'

She was so tempted to say yes. 'No, I'm fine.'

He released her, and she breathed out slowly, her body tingling. She was left with the impression of arms of steel, a solid, muscular chest, and a woody cologne filling her nostrils.

Reluctantly, she resumed walking, aware that there was still some way to go and that her heel was already rubbing. She'd have to ask him for a plaster soon.

What was it she'd been thinking that had made her stumble? Oh, yes: Mack, the castle, him seeing her with Hadrian, two glasses of whisky, and 'Angie' playing at full volume… She was joining the dots, but the picture didn't make sense.

'Ouch!' Stopping abruptly, she grabbed hold of his arm for balance and reached down, easing off her shoe. A blister the size of a dinner plate had formed on her heel. *Sod it.*

'I'm going to need a plaster,' she said.

He peered at her foot. 'More than one.' He took the plasters out of his pocket while she wobbled precariously on one foot. 'It'll be easier if you sit down,' he suggested.

She lowered herself onto the verge, thinking it was lucky the grass was dry, and grabbed her ankle, trying to get a better look at the offending heel.

'Let me.' Mack sat beside her and took her foot in his hands.

Freya let out a squeak.

'Did that hurt?'

'Ticklish,' she managed. But it wasn't ticklish she felt, it was lust. His touch was soft, almost a caress, and it sent shock waves through her.

He tightened his grip, his hold not as gentle but equally as erotic. 'Is that better?'

'Uh-huh.'

'I think two should do it.'

She watched him peel the backing off the plasters, and almost squeaked again when he stroked them gently into place.

'How is your other foot looking?' he asked.

'Fine, I think.'

'Let's make sure. Take your shoe off.'

Freya did as he instructed.

'Hmm, I think we'd better put a plaster on this one as well.'

Having him fondle her other foot was almost too much, but she kept as still as she could while he ministered to her, and when he finished and stood up, she exhaled slowly.

Stress. That was it – stress. There was no other explanation. And maybe the whisky. Except… she'd never got drunk on a single glass before. She was a Scot, for goodness' sake – she'd grown up with the stuff.

Mack held out his hand. She took it and he hauled her to her feet.

Upright once more and with her shoes on, she wondered whether she'd had some kind of episode, because a reaction like that to something as unglamorous as having a blister tended to wasn't normal. Maybe she was having a breakdown. Or maybe she simply needed a slice of toast, a cup of tea and an early night.

Freya tried her best not to limp, but it was hard not to. Even with the plasters, both heels were sore and getting worse. Damn these blasted shoes. She didn't even like them much. In fact, when she got home, the first thing she was going to do was put them in the bin. If her dad still had an open fire in the sitting room, she would have burnt them.

'We'll cut through the castle grounds,' Mack suggested. 'It'll be quicker than taking the road. It'll be rougher underfoot, though. Unless... You could wait at the castle, and I'll run to yours and fetch you some proper shoes?'

'Ones I can actually walk in, you mean?'

He chuckled. 'Aye.'

Freya thought of Hadrian inside those walls, probably still in the lounge, drinking. 'No, thanks. I'll be OK. It's not far.'

'It's far enough.'

'I'll be fine,' she insisted.

She managed to make it to the start of the path, before she decided that she definitely *wasn't* fine. If she had to walk another step in these bloody shoes, she was going to cry. So Freya did the only sensible thing – she took them off.

Mack was aghast. 'You can't walk home barefoot!'

'Watch me.'

'I'll be damned if I will! Come here.'

Freya wasn't prepared for being scooped off her feet and she let out a shriek as he swept her into his arms.

'Put me down!' she cried, but all he did was tighten his grip.

'It'll be easier if you stop wriggling and put your arms around my neck.'

'You can't carry me, I'm too heavy.'

'Yeah, you do weigh a tonne,' he wheezed, and her mouth dropped open. 'I'm joking,' he said, striding down the path at a steady pace. 'But if you want me to put you down, I will.'

She didn't want, so she wound her arms around his neck and rested her head on his shoulder to show him exactly how much she didn't want him to put her down.

His beard tickled her nose, and she rubbed it against his neck to relieve the itch, then nuzzled her face deeper, breathing in the smell of him.

'If you keep doing that, I won't be responsible for my actions,' he murmured.

'Doing what?'

'Nibbling my neck.'

'I'm not nibbling. *This* is nibbling.' Gently, she nipped the soft skin below his ear.

'Freya, you're going to have to stop doing that.' His voice was hoarse, and it did strange and wondrous things to her insides.

Recklessly, she did it again.

Mack halted. 'I can't— You mustn't—'

'Don't you like it?' She had no idea what had come over her, but she was enjoying the power she had over him, as his breathing deepened and he tightened his grip on her.

He said, 'That's the problem, I like it a lot.'

Her pulse throbbing, she found his earlobe and kissed it, and the groan he uttered turned her insides to liquid.

'I'm warning you,' he growled. 'Stop, or—'

'Or what?' She raised her head and was awed by the hunger in his eyes.

'I'll be forced to kiss you.'

'What are you waiting for?' She was playing with fire, but the thought of being burnt by this man was irresistible.

Slowly, he bent his head to hers and she closed her eyes, her lips parting.

The kiss was sweet, tentative, a mere fluttering. Her heart hammering, her pulse soaring to a roar in her ears, she dug her fingers into his hair. Still kissing her, he gently released her legs and she slowly slid to the ground until she was standing upright, her body pressed against his, his arousal making her weak with longing.

It was Mack who ended it, but not before he'd thoroughly explored her mouth.

Resting his forehead against hers, he murmured, 'We should stop.'

Freya didn't want to stop. She wanted to kiss him and keep kissing him until—

'You're right.' She breathed slowly, gathering her scattered wits and trying to calm herself.

Mack cleared his throat. 'Let's get you home.'

Freya gave him a dubious look. 'I don't think carrying me is a good idea. I'll be fine going barefoot.'

'You won't.' He turned his back on her and she stared at him incredulously. Was he going to walk away and leave her here?

When he crouched down and said, 'Hop on,' she was even more incredulous.

'Are you offering to give me a *piggyback*?'

'Hop on,' he repeated. 'We should have done this from the get-go.'

Dismay swept over her as his meaning became clear: if he had given her a piggyback in the beginning, they wouldn't have kissed. When he'd said, 'We should stop,' he hadn't meant they should stop before they got carried away; he'd meant that the kiss had been a mistake.

Hurt and rejected, she pushed past him and stalked off down the path, ignoring the discomfort. She didn't care if her feet fell off, she had to get away.

Mack strode after her, catching her by the arm before she'd managed more than a handful of steps. 'Where are you going?' he demanded.

'Home.' She shook him off.

'What about your feet?'

'They'll be fine.'

'I don't understand. Have I done something wrong?'

'You kissed me!'

'I thought you wanted me to. *You* started it.'

'I wish I hadn't.'

'I'm sorry. I didn't realise… I misread the situation.'

'It's me who misread it. I thought—' She huffed angrily, but tears lurked behind it. What a bloody awful day. First Hadrian and now Mack.

'What did you think?' he asked.

'It doesn't matter.' She made to stalk off again, but he held her back.

'It matters to me. What did you think?'

She rounded on him. 'That you liked me.'

'I *do* like you.' He seemed genuinely puzzled.

'Not like that.'

'Like what? Freya, you're going to have to spell it out for me, because I don't understand.'

She pressed her lips together, debating whether she should tell him, then thought, *What the hell*. 'I thought you fancied me.'

'I do. I don't kiss women I don't fancy.'

'But you just said that we should have done the piggyback thing from the start.'

'We should have. Carrying you like that was a daft idea.'

'Because it led to us kissing.' Her voice was flat.

'No, you numpty – because it made my arms ache and my back is in bits.' He chuckled. 'Did you think I meant that it was a mistake to kiss you?'

She refused to meet his gaze. 'No,' she replied sulkily.

The chuckle turned into a chortle. 'Yes, you did.'

'It was a logical assumption to make.'

Mack sobered. 'I'm going to be honest with you, Freya. I fancy you rotten. You're beautiful and sexy, and I like you a lot. The problem is, I think I like you *too* much. So yes, I do want to kiss you again.' He leant towards her, his mouth almost touching hers. 'I want to do *much* more than kiss you, but I don't think it's wise.'

He was right, it wasn't wise. Getting involved with him was a bad idea. She should concentrate on her father and her future, not on a quick fling, especially since she'd just come out of a relationship.

'Do you still intend to walk home in your bare feet?' he asked.

Oh, what the hell! 'Giddy-up, Burns,' she said. 'I need a lift home.'

Chapter 22

How are your tootsies? Freya read the message and laughed.

Tootsies fine, she replied.

Her feet were still sore, even though she'd been wearing sliders for the past three days. It would be a while before she wore heels again. Her phone pinged with another message.

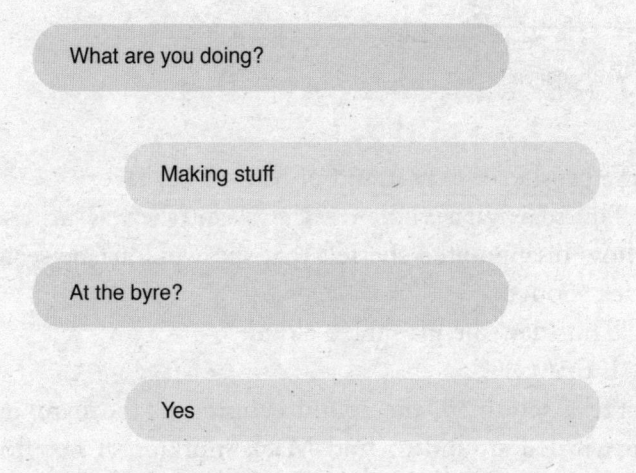

> What are you doing?

> Making stuff

> At the byre?

> Yes

She was pleased with her progress. Seven pieces so far. She was itching to fire them, but they'd have to wait until she got back to her studio. Anyway, they weren't bone dry yet, the clay still holding too much water. Potters learnt early on in their careers that patience was most definitely a virtue. Firing too soon could, and often did, cause pottery to crack or even explode in the kiln.

She examined her most recent piece, studying it critically. The bowl appeared organic: a delicate weaving of sprigs of heather, the stems emerging from the base, and covered in tiny delicate petals. It was intricate and fragile, and it had taken her a long time to make.

With extreme care, she placed it on the shelf to dry, then rinsed her hands. She was done for today. Dad would want his tea soon and he could probably do with some company; she'd been here longer than she'd intended, having become so engrossed that she'd lost track of time.

She'd almost finished clearing everything away, when she noticed another message on her screen.

> Is next Thursday OK for a meal at the castle?

Freya brushed a stray strand of hair off her face.

Thursday was a whole week away and she was surprised at how disappointed she felt that she wouldn't be seeing Mack sooner.

'Thursday,' she grumbled aloud.

'Is that OK?'

Freya screamed, the sound echoing in the byre, and she whirled around to find Mack smirking at her from the doorway.

'I hate you!' she cried. 'You scared me half to death.'

'Sorry, I didn't mean to.' He didn't sound in the least bit sorry.

'Liar.'

'You didn't reply to my message, so I thought I'd ask you in person. And you still haven't answered me.'

'Yes, Thursday is OK.'

He cocked his head to the side. 'I didn't expect you to still be here.'

'I was just about to leave, actually. I lost track of time. Dad will be wondering where I am.' She picked up her keys and as she walked towards the door, she noticed he had dark circles under his eyes. 'Are you all right?'

'Tired, that's all. I've had a busy couple of days.'

Impulsively, she said, 'Dad and I are having chicken and peanut stew. There's plenty, if you don't feel up to cooking this evening.'

Mack ran a hand through his hair and looked away.

She thought he'd refuse, but instead he said, 'That would be great, thanks. I'll need a shower first, though.'

'I'll go on ahead. Be at mine for six thirty?'

He nodded and she hurried off, thinking she could do with a shower herself.

'Mack is joining us,' she told her father when she arrived home. His eyes lit up and she knew she was in for an evening of boats, tides and fishing talk.

As she prepared the stew, he told her about his afternoon.

'Norman came to see me while you were out. He brought me a couple of bars of chocolate. That was nice of him, wasn't it? And Rhona knocked on the door to tell me she was off to the mobile library and ask if she could fetch me something. I told her anything by James Patterson. What are you making?'

'Chicken and peanut stew.'

'What's that?' He pointed at the jar she was holding.

'Peanut butter.'

'You're putting it in a *stew*?'

'I am.'

'I don't like the sound of that.'

'It's really tasty,' she assured him. She put the lid on the pan and turned the heat down to a simmer. 'I'm going to have a quick bath while this is cooking.'

Freya could feel his eyes on her as she walked out of the kitchen, and she hoped he would like the stew. Their tastes in food didn't necessarily align, but she was getting bored with cooking the same old meals.

She was also getting fed up with having to have a bath, and she grumbled to herself as she waited for the tub to fill. There were a great many things she missed about London and one of them was the power shower in her flat. She enjoyed a bath as much as anyone, but only when it involved scented bubbles, candles and soft music. As a quick freshen-up, it left a lot to be desired.

It did the trick, though, and soon she was dressed in a clean pair of jeans and a T-shirt, contemplating the contents of her make-up bag.

She got as far as taking the lid off her eyeliner, before wondering why. Eyeliner wasn't something she usually applied, so why was she thinking about doing so now?

Freya replaced the lid and dropped the eyeliner back in the bag. This wasn't a date. This was a friend coming to tea. Nothing more. But her pulse leapt every time she thought of Mack, and she was thinking about him far more frequently than was good for her.

A knock on the door sent her hurrying downstairs to answer it, and after letting Mack in, Freya ushered him into the sitting room to keep her dad company while she finished cooking.

As she'd predicted, talk around the dinner table was dominated by all things boat-related. Mack did most of the talking, though, her dad content to ask questions and listen.

'Does he seem subdued to you?' she asked Mack when she was cleaning up afterwards. She had sent her father into the sitting room, but Mack had insisted on staying in the kitchen to help.

'A little.'

Keeping her voice low, she said, 'He's lost his sparkle.'

'He's been through a lot,' Mack pointed out, stacking the plates next to the sink.

'I know, but getting him to smile is hard work. Could he be depressed?'

'Maybe.'

'I think he needs to get out more. He really enjoyed lunch out the other day, but he can't walk far, so we're a bit limited. Any ideas?'

'Why don't I take him to the quay? He'll like that. I could even take him out on the boat.'

Freya was shaking her head. 'I don't think that's a good idea.' The boat had a ramp for less able passengers to embark, but how would he cope with the waves? The loch could be choppy, the swell high. Even seated, he might struggle to keep his balance, which would put undue strain on his hip.

'I'll take good care of him, Freya. He can sit in the cabin, and I'll pick a calm day. It'll be just me and him.'

'When? You run three trips a day.'

'Early morning, late evening?' He shrugged.

Vinnie shuffled into the kitchen. 'What are you two whispering about?'

Mack caught her eye, questioningly.

Freya bit her lip, then nodded. Mack would take good care of him, she knew.

'Fancy a boat trip?' he asked Vinnie.

Her dad's expression didn't change, but there was a flicker in his eyes. And when he nodded wordlessly, Freya realised he was holding back tears.

Without thinking, she rose up on tiptoe to give Mack a kiss on the lips, and the flash of surprise and pleasure on his face made her smile.

However, the speculative look on her father's face quickly wiped it off. She didn't want either man to get the wrong idea.

But long after Mack had said good night and her dad had retired to bed, Freya knew that they wouldn't have got the wrong idea at all. They would have hit the mark. Seeing Mack with her father, the thoughtful, gentle way he had with him, had brought it home to her – she was in love with Mack.

She suspected she had been in love with him when she was a teenager, and it had taken her return to Skye to realise that she had never stopped loving him. But however she felt about him, it didn't change anything – she would be leaving the island as soon as her dad regained his health.

Her place in this world wasn't on Skye, even if her heart was.

Mack loved early mornings on the loch. The sea was calm today, low tide exposing glistening rocks and the rippling pools teeming with life. A gentle breeze was blowing away the low mist drifting across the waters and the sun poked through scattered clouds.

Vinnie had said little since Mack had picked him up in the truck, but his eyes were shining and there was a small smile on his face.

Getting him on deck had been tricky, but with care they'd managed it, and Vinnie was now settled at the helm, gazing out to sea with quiet excitement as the boat chugged away from the quayside.

'It's been a while,' he said.

'Five years, six?' Mack estimated.

'Aye, there or thereabout.'

'You miss it, don't you?'

'I do.'

Vinnie could have come out on the *Sea Serpent* any time, but it never occurred to Mack to ask him. He'd assumed that Vinnie was done with boats when he'd sold the trawler and hadn't bought himself a dingy. 'Just say the word, and I'll take you whenever you want.'

'I'm not going to put you out. You've got enough to be getting on with.'

Mack smiled, knowing that the old man was too stubborn and proud to ask. 'If you think you're going to be having your own private trip every time you fancy feeling a wave under your size nines, you're sadly mistaken. If you come out on the boat, you'll be expected to join in with a proper tour. The only difference between you and a punter is that I won't charge you.'

'I can pay my own way,' Vinnie growled. 'I don't need charity.'

It was the response Mack had expected. 'Och, it's not charity I'll be giving you. You'll have to pull your weight, like the rest of the crew.' Mack would make sure that Vinnie didn't do much – just enough so he didn't feel he was getting a free ride.

'We'll see.'

'The offer is there.' Mack thought Vinnie might need a while to come around to the idea.

'I can't do anything with a gammy hip,' Vinnie grumbled.

'You're not going to have a gammy hip forever, so let's see how you feel when it's healed. Are you hungry?'

Vinnie's eyes lit up. 'I could manage a bite.'

'How about we drop anchor off the castle? I've brought us some bacon sandwiches and a flask of tea.'

Mack had hoped Vinnie would approve, and the old man's smile confirmed it. You couldn't beat a piece and a mug of tea on the water. And he'd also brought a packet of oaty nibble biscuits for a bit of sweetness after the salt of the bacon.

Bringing the boat closer to the shore, he dropped the anchor.

'This is a braw breakfast,' Vinnie enthused as he bit into his sandwich. 'It's even got a dollop of brown sauce!'

'I haven't forgotten you like sauce in your bacon butties. I've put sugar in the tea as well.'

'You're a good wee lad.'

Silence ensued as they ate their breakfast, and Vinnie chewed vigorously, polishing his off in a matter of minutes. When he settled back with a mug of tea in one hand and a biscuit in the other, he said, 'Do you mind me asking you a personal question?'

'It depends on what it is. You can ask all you like, but I mightn't give you an answer.'

'Fair enough. I was wondering why you've never settled down.'

Mack sighed and rolled his eyes. 'Not you as well. You're as bad as my mum. Carter's always on my case, too.'

'What do you tell them?'

'That I'm not ready.'

'Will you ever be?'

'I don't know.'

'It took me a while. I was thirty-six when I met my Sandra. You probably haven't met the right woman yet.'

'I thought I had, once. But it was a long time ago. I was barely twenty. She broke my heart when she moved away.'

Vinnie shot him a sharp look and Mack hastened to add, 'Not Freya. Her friend Alice. We got together after Freya went to London. I think she was lonely. And I don't know why I'm telling you this.' He uttered an embarrassed laugh.

'It's mended now, though? According to Jean, you've got a new girl every other week.'

Actually, he hadn't. Not recently. 'Yeah, I guess it's mended.'

'Then I'll say it again: you haven't met the right one yet.'

Actually, Mack feared he had, but she wasn't here to stay.

Vinnie continued, 'I never regretted settling down, not even after Sandra passed away and all the hurt that came with it. And without her, I wouldn't have Freya. But if we'd never had children, I wouldn't have any regrets. She was the love of my life and I miss her every single day. She would have been so proud of our girl. I wish she was here to see it. New York, eh? Who'd have thought it?' Then he chuckled. '*Sandra* thought it – she always said Freya would go far.'

Mack remained silent because he was imagining what his life would be like with Freya no longer in it – and he didn't like the look of it one bit. Soon she would be on the other side of the world, and he really didn't want her to go.

When she left, she would be taking a piece of him with her.

Mackenzie Burns had finally found the right woman, but he'd lost his heart in the process.

—

Freya had always loved Portree, with its quaint charm and its pastel painted houses, and it was also the nearest town with any decent clothes shops. It didn't have many, but she was hopeful she could find *something* to wear to dinner at the castle. And shoes. She needed shoes. Flat ones. Despite having no intention of walking anywhere afterwards, she wasn't taking the chance.

Negotiating the one-way system, she drove along Wentworth Street, searching for a place to pull over, and was pleased when she spied a space up ahead.

'Will you get the van in there?' her dad asked doubtfully, peering into the passenger side-mirror as she pulled alongside the space.

'I mightn't be the best driver in the world, but I'm ace at parallel parking,' she said, hauling on the wheel. 'You'd be surprised at the places I can get into with this.' A small adjustment to tuck the van as close as possible to the kerb, and it was done. 'I'll walk you to the cafe and have a quick coffee with you first,' she told him. 'Are you sure you'll be all right on your own for an hour?'

She helped him out of the van, and when he was upright with his walking stick firmly planted on the pavement, he gave her the side-eye. Freya took the hint and stopped fussing. Of course he would be all right. He'd read his newspaper, people-watch and drink tea.

It took them a while to make it to the cafe, their progress slow, her father understandably nervous with so many people around. She could tell he was worried about being jostled and was scared he might lose his balance, but she had a firm grip on his arm and acted as a buffer between him and the other pedestrians.

When they finally got there, the cafe was full and there didn't appear to be any free tables.

Freya was beginning to worry, because he couldn't stand for long to wait for one to become available, when she spied a middle-aged woman with two young children getting ready to leave. Telling him to wait by the door, she hurried over to nab it, but as she reached it, she happened to glance over her shoulder and saw him trying to shuffle between two tables. His face was set in its customary grim and determined expression.

'Stay there, Dad,' she called, then she turned back to the woman and said, 'Do you mind if…' The rest of the sentence died on her lips. 'Mrs Henderson?'

'Do I know you?'

'I'm Freya Sinclair, Sandra and Vinnie's daughter. Alice and I used to be friends.'

'*Freya?* Well, I never! I should have realised – you're the spit of your mother.'

Was she? Freya didn't think so. Her mother had been beautiful.

Mrs Henderson continued, 'How lovely to see you after all these years. And is that your father? I can't see too well without my glasses.'

'It is. Do you mind hanging on to the table for a minute while I go rescue him?' He had once again ignored her and was carrying on trying to forge an unsteady path towards her.

She hurried over to him. 'Why didn't you wait by the door?' she demanded, taking his arm.

He shook her off. 'I can manage. Isn't that Pearl Henderson?'

Mrs Henderson was busy gathering up her shopping, as she minded the table for them.

'Pearl, is that you?' he asked when he reached her. He was a little pale and his jaw was tense, but there was a smile on his face. Freya pulled out a chair for him and he lowered himself awkwardly into it, breathing hard.

'You look like you've been in the wars.' Mrs Henderson tilted her head in concern.

'I broke my hip a month ago, but I'm on the mend.'

'Should you be out?' she asked.

'They tell you to keep moving.'

Freya said, 'He thinks he should be better by now.' She patted him on the shoulder. Hopefully, a sit-down and a cup of tea would put him right.

'Are these your grandchildren?' he asked.

Mrs Henderson's face glowed with pride. 'They are. Rosie is six and Reba is eight.'

'Do you want a sweet?' the younger of the two children asked. She was holding out a packet of Haribo.

'No, thank you, but it's nice of you to offer.' He said to Mrs Henderson, 'Aren't they bonnie!'

'They're a pair of little terrors,' she said, but Freya could tell that the woman didn't mean it. 'How about you, Freya, are you married? Got any children? The last time I saw you was at—' She stopped and bit her lip.

'At Mum's funeral,' Freya finished for her. An image of that awful day flashed into her mind and tears pricked at the back of her eyes. She had been coping so well up to now, living back in her childhood home surrounded by so many reminders of her mother, that this abrupt unfurling of the coiled grief she would always carry with her, but usually managed to corral, was an unwelcome surprise.

Moments like these, caught off guard by emotions she had little control over, was the reason she had always been so reluctant to return to the island, and the reason she never stayed long. In London, she could bury the grief deep and ignore it for the most part. Here, she was ambushed by it when she least expected it.

She forced a smile to her lips. 'No, I'm not married and I don't have children.'

'She's got a career,' her dad said grandly. 'She's a professor in London. Just got a promotion, she has.'

'Ooh, how wonderful. Sandra would have been so proud.'

Vinnie nodded. 'She would. She always said Freya would make a name for herself. She works in the top art college in the world, and she's been offered a job in New York.'

'Not quite, Dad.'

'It's in the top five, then. And she had an exhibition of her own work a few weeks ago.'

Pearl turned her gaze on her. 'An exhibition? What of?'

'Ceramics. That's what I lecture in.'

'Och, now I remember! You and Alice used to make wee clay pots from the mud in the burn when you were bairns. So, you made a career out of it, did you? As I said, your mum would have been proud. New York, eh?'

Freya asked, 'How is Alice? We lost touch when I went to university.' The truth was, Freya hadn't been able to face her friend's sympathy and pity.

'Doing well. She still lives in Aberdeen and is married to a nice chappie who's got his own plumbing business. These two are hers. We're here for a wee visit for a few days. I'll tell her you were asking after her. Anyway, I must get off. It was nice seeing you again, Vinnie. You too, Freya. Come on, girls, your mother will be wondering where we've got to.'

Pearl gathered her grandchildren, ushering them ahead of her, and when she reached the door, she looked back and waved.

Vinnie waved back thoughtfully. 'I haven't seen her for years. It's strange to think your mum would have been her age now. But Pearl's right, she'd have been cock-a-hoop about your new job. And so am I. I know I keep saying it, but it's true. I wish she could have seen that exhibition of yours.'

So did Freya. Her mum would have loved how the colours, textures and shapes of her homeland had such an influence on her work. Without Skye, Freya wouldn't be the potter she was now, and although she'd run away from the island and from the memories that even now were so hard to bear, Freya understood that wherever she went in the world, Skye would always be in her heart.

Chapter 23

This isn't a date, this isn't a date, this isn't a date. Freya kept having to repeat the mantra over and over in her head, because it certainly felt like it. Here she was, in the most glorious of settings, about to eat a fantastic meal, sitting opposite a simply gorgeous man – tonight was the most date-like non-date she'd ever experienced.

Mack had also made an effort with his appearance. No shorts and no T-shirt. Instead, he was wearing a navy suit with a navy shirt. The shirt had a tiny pattern of white leaves, almost too small to see. His golden hair was tied neatly into a bun and he'd trimmed his beard. He was a cross between a surfer-dude and James Bond.

The delicious smells emanating from the hotel's kitchen weren't the only thing making her drool. Mack had taken her hand when they'd entered the bar, and his touch had sent her into a tailspin.

'You look beautiful,' he said, as they sipped their drinks.

His was non-alcoholic, which she felt bad about. He'd insisted on driving this evening, despite her argument that since she was taking him to dinner, she should drive so he'd be able to enjoy a couple of glasses of wine or whatever he fancied. Mack Burns could be as stubborn as her dad when he wanted to be, she was discovering.

'I love the dress,' he added.

She'd found it in a second-hand shop, the last place she'd tried before she'd been about to give up and return to the cafe and her patient dad.

Her dress-buying mood had evaporated after meeting Mrs Henderson. Freya would have given anything to have had her mother go shopping with her and help her pick out a dress for this evening. She was reminded yet again that her mum hadn't been there to witness many other milestones in her life – her twenty-first birthday, graduation, first job, attaining her PhD... And she wouldn't be there if she ever got married or had children. Freya hoped Alice Henderson knew how lucky she was.

'Did I say something wrong?' Mack asked.

'Huh?'

'You've gone very quiet.'

'Have I? Sorry, I didn't mean to.'

He reached for her hand again. 'Would you like to go somewhere else? We could go to Portree.'

'The castle is fine.'

He glanced around the room. 'No, it's not, if it reminds you of Hadrian.'

Surprised, she said, 'Actually, it doesn't. I wasn't thinking about him. I was thinking about when I went into Portree. Dad came with me and had a cup of tea in a cafe while I had a mooch around the shops, and while we were there, we bumped into Mrs Henderson, Alice's mother.'

'Oh, right. Has she moved back to Skye?' He let go of her hand and reached for his drink.

'Only for a few days; she's here for a visit. She said she hadn't seen me since Mum's funeral.' Her eyes filled with tears. 'I'm sorry. I don't know why I'm like this. You'd think that after all these years...' She blinked furiously, looking at the ceiling, willing herself not to cry. 'I'm not like this normally. In London I—' She stopped, swallowed and tried again. 'That's why I had to escape – to get away from everyone's pity, from Dad's grief. From *me*.'

'So you went where no one knew you and you could reinvent yourself?'

'I suppose.'

'You've done a damned fine job of it. Alice always said you had the talent, the vision and the drive.'

'Alice?'

'We dated for a while, before she moved away.'

There was something about the way he said it – regret, maybe? A little spike of jealousy prodded her in the stomach.

She said, 'Mrs Henderson reckons I'm the spit of my mother, but I don't think I look like her at all.' Freya certainly didn't see any resemblance when she looked in the mirror. 'She was so pretty.'

'So are you.'

'Huh! I've got red hair and freckles, and I usually smell of clay and paint.'

Mack leant close and sniffed. 'So you do.'

'Oi! I'll have you know I'm wearing Paco Rabanne.'

'I like the smell of clay and paint.'

'You like the smell of diesel and engine oil, with a hint of fish thrown in,' she shot back.

'True.' He paused. 'We can leave, if you want.'

'Oh, hell, I've really killed the mood, haven't I? This is supposed to be a thank-you dinner, and it's turning into a Freya pity-party. I'm fine, honestly. Bumping into Mrs Henderson just brought it all back for a moment: Mum being ill, and then dying. I…' She shrugged, unable to put her feelings into words.

'It can't have been easy for you.' His face was full of sympathy and understanding, and Freya felt comforted.

She liked that Mack had understood why she'd felt the need to run away and not come back, without her having to spell it out to him. She couldn't imagine ever having this conversation with Hadrian. In hindsight, she realised she'd never entrusted her ex with her innermost thoughts or feelings. Mack, she felt, she could trust with her life. But probably not her heart.

Freya pulled her shoulders back and gave herself a mental shake – enough of this wallowing. 'Shall we go eat? My stomach thinks my throat has been cut.' She was telling a little white lie, since she wasn't in the least bit hungry, but she hoped her appetite would return when she saw the menu.

'That dress *is* lovely on you, by the way,' Mack reiterated, as they rose to go to the dining room. 'It brings out the colour of your eyes.'

'Muddy brown?' Was he flirting?

He arched an eyebrow. 'Are you fishing for compliments, Ms Sinclair?'

'Absolutely!'

'They aren't muddy brown. They're hazel with flecks of amber and gold.'

'Poetic.'

'I'm not just brawn and muscle. I have a touch of the Rabbie Burns about me – he's a direct ancestor, you know.'

'No, he's not!'

'OK, he isn't. But he *could* be. We've got the same surname.'

Freya rolled her eyes as he pulled out a chair for her. She shook out the linen napkin and draped it over her lap. 'Has anyone ever told you that you're daft?'

'Many times. I try not to take any notice.'

'My dad thinks you're fab,' she blurted, her eyes on the menu.

Mack smirked and said, 'That's because I am.' Then he grew serious. 'I've got a lot of time for Vinnie. Would you mind if I took him out in the boat again?'

'I wouldn't mind in the slightest, and I know he'd love it. He really misses being at sea. When he sold the trawler, I thought he would have bought himself a RIB just to keep his hand in and potter around on the loch, but he lost all interest. Going out on the *Sea Serpent* may spark his interest again, although if he did decide to buy a small boat now, I'd be worried sick – he's getting too old to go out on his own. It wouldn't be so bad if Loch Duncoorie was a freshwater loch, but with the currents and tides...'

'Don't worry, I'll keep an eye on him for you after you leave, and if he shows any sign of buying a boat, I'll let you know.'

She smiled. 'You're a good friend, Mackenzie.'

'Och, don't call me that! Only my mum calls me Mackenzie and even then, only if I've annoyed her.'

Freya held back a sigh. From his reaction, it was clear Mack thought of her as just a friend. He hadn't been flirting, and he'd held her hand in the lounge for no other reason than he thought she might have been fretting about the last time she'd been there, when she'd broken up with Hadrian.

She told herself once more that it was for the best that he didn't want to take their friendship to another level. The kiss had been an anomaly, her fault for having started it. But she hadn't been able to resist, clasped in his arms, his heart beating against hers. Thank goodness he'd seen sense, otherwise she would have had her wicked way with him and would be in even deeper trouble than she already was.

—

Mack couldn't blame the alcohol this time, because he was stone-cold sober and fully in charge of his actions. It was his thoughts and feelings that he was having trouble keeping in line.

All through the meal (which was delicious), he'd wanted nothing more than to tell her how he felt. He kept having to bite his tongue and avert his eyes, because he was scared she would see the longing in them and guess how he felt about her.

But when it came to the end of the evening, he blew it.

'I've had a lovely time,' he said, as the truck coasted to a stop outside her house.

'Me too, right up until I asked for the bill and found you'd already paid it.'

'My bad.' He smirked.

'This was supposed to be my treat.'

He turned his head away to stare out of the side window. 'I'm not listening.'

Freya scooted to the edge of the seat, grabbed hold of his beard and gave it a tug.

'Ow!'

'That'll teach you not to listen. If you think you've got away with it, you haven't. We'll go out for another meal and this time *I'll* pay.'

'I'll tell Mhairi to say no.'

'I'm not going to ask Mhairi. She's as sneaky as you. I'll book somewhere else.'

'I'll refuse to go.'

'Will you now? In that case, I'll order the biggest takeaway ever and have it delivered to your house. You'll be eating Chinese food for a week.'

'You don't take no for an answer, do you?'

She smiled sweetly at him and pulled his beard again. 'Say yes.'

He gritted his teeth. Not because she was yanking on his beard, but because her smile melted his heart. It did some other stuff to him as well, but he was trying not to think about that too closely.

'Yes. Happy?'

'Blissfully.'

'You can stop trying to tear my beard off now. Or have you got any other demands?'

Her grip loosened and she stroked his cheek instead. Her face was too close for comfort and he swallowed hard, averting his gaze. He didn't trust himself to speak. Or move.

'Thank you, Mack, for everything. I don't know what I would have done without you.'

'You'd have managed.' His voice sounded strangled.

She didn't seem to have noticed. 'Pick a day.'

'I'll have to check my diary.'

'Mack…' she warned.

'Saturday?' It was only two days away. He could last until then without seeing her. Couldn't he?

Her hand continued to rest on his cheek, and he closed his eyes. He didn't think he could take much more. Her touch inflamed him, but despite wanting her to stop, he put his hand over hers, holding it in place.

Then he lifted it to his lips and kissed her palm. And when she didn't snatch her hand away, he risked looking at her.

Her eyes were closed, her lips parted just enough to show a glimpse of teeth.

It was his undoing.

His arm snapped around her, pulling her to him, and his mouth found hers. He kissed her deeply as she melted into him, exploring her with his tongue, tasting the wine she had drunk.

Mack lost himself in her, was aware of her and nothing but her. His world shrunk to this one exquisite moment, where nothing else mattered but the way he felt about her, and the way she made him feel.

And he suddenly realised he was in love, totally and utterly. It was both beautiful and devastating.

He would have happily kissed her until his heart gave out, and when she gently pulled away, he was desolate.

'You said this wasn't wise,' she murmured. Her lips were swollen, her eyes a dark Highland pool.

'It's not.' He hid his pain well. There was no hint of it in his voice.

'I'd better go.' She reached for the door handle.

'Yes.'

'See you Saturday.'

He nodded. He didn't want to see her Saturday. He didn't want to see her at all. It would hurt too much. But he would keep up the pretence of being friends who happened to fancy each other, because that was what she expected, how she herself felt.

It would kill him, but he'd do it – because not seeing her would kill him even more.

Chapter 24

'Freya? *Freya!*'

'All right, Dad, keep your hair on,' Freya mumbled as she plumped up the pillows on her bed. She'd been thinking about Mack – but when didn't she? He was constantly on her mind.

If she closed her eyes, she could still feel his mouth on hers. He'd kissed her with tenderness and passion, and the combination had been electric.

She was in imminent danger of falling in love with him – if she hadn't already – and that would never do.

'Freya!' her dad yelled again.

That man could shout louder than a foghorn. It was a wonder the neighbours didn't hear.

'I'm coming, Dad. Let me put my dressing gown on.' She'd woken up a mere five minutes earlier and hadn't even had a chance to wash and dress yet, and her father was already yelling for her.

He sounded cross, and when she walked into the sitting room and saw the state of it, she felt cross too. 'What's going on?' she demanded, frowning as he jabbed his walking stick under his chair, sweeping it from side to side.

'I can't find my tablets!' he snapped.

'You know you're not supposed to be bending over like that,' she scolded, and he straightened up reluctantly. 'Let me see.'

Freya knelt on the floor and peered underneath. 'They're not here, but I've found the pen you lost.'

'I don't care about the ruddy pen. I need my tablets.' His face was thunderous.

'They'll be around here somewhere. I'll put the kettle on and make a cup of tea, then I'll have a proper look.'

He let out a snort. 'Don't bother, I'll find them myself.'

Freya gave up. When he was in this mood, there was no reasoning with him and she knew he wouldn't settle until they were found.

'Sit down, Dad. I'll look for them now: the tea can wait.' She scanned the disordered room, thinking that she'd have to tidy up first, before she could begin looking.

As she moved around it, picking things up and putting them in their rightful places, she asked, 'Where did you last have them?'

'I don't know, do I?' His tone was petulant, like a small child or a whiny teenager.

She tried again. 'You took them last night, didn't you?'

'Of course I bloody did!'

While Freya appreciated that her dad was frustrated, she didn't appreciate being spoken to in that manner, especially since she was only trying to help.

Putting her hands on her hips, she turned to face him. 'We've got a while to go yet before I'm out of your hair, so I suggest we do our best to be civil to each other.'

'What you mean is, *you're* being civil but *I'm* not.'

She gave him a pointed look. That was precisely what she'd meant.

Sullenly, he said, 'You can go back to London whenever you want. Don't think you've got to stay here on my account. I've been managing without you fine.'

'Yes, but that was before you fractured your hip.'

'Pah! You're hardly here these days.'

Freya gasped. 'That's so unfair! I *always* put you first. I clean the house, cook your meals, do your laundry, your shopping... How much more do I have to do?'

His face mutinous, he turned his head away and refused to look at her.

Because he knows I'm right, she grumbled silently to herself. She'd find his flipping tablets, then make him his breakfast.

'Someone got out of the wrong side of the bed this morning,' she muttered, then wished she hadn't been so snide, when his defiant expression turned to worry.

'I just want my tablets, that's all,' he said, his voice quivering.

Instantly contrite, Freya crouched by his chair. 'I'm sorry. I'll knock my visits to Mack's place on the head.'

Vinnie put a hand on her shoulder. 'You'll do no such thing. You need to keep working.'

Her eyes filling with tears, she said, 'I don't, Dad. I'm doing it because I want to; and I'm being incredibly selfish.'

'I didn't have to go to sea, you know. I could have got a shoreside job – it's what your mother wanted me to do – but the sea called to me. Clay calls to you the same way. You know what they say: if you find a job you love doing, you'll never work a day in your life. We've both been blessed.'

So has Mack, she thought – and Cal and Tara, and Mhairi, and the other crafters she'd met.

Freya covered her dad's hand with hers. 'Shall we start today again? I'll find your tablets while you put the kettle on.'

'Deal!'

But when she found the box and looked inside, she realised there were none left in the blister pack. He'd taken his last tablet, and he wasn't going to be happy.

Freya smiled at the pharmacist. 'Hi, I've come to pick up a prescription for Vincent Sinclair? It's a repeat one.'

'Vinnie? How is he? I was sorry to hear about his fall.' The woman turned away to look through the stack of bags on the shelf behind her.

'He's getting there, slowly.'

'I bet you're giving him lots of TLC.'

'I try, but he accuses me of fussing.'

The pharmacist glanced over her shoulder at her. She was frowning. 'I don't appear to have anything here for him. Let me check.' She walked across to a computer screen and tapped something in. 'No, sorry, we've had nothing through from the surgery.'

Freya's face fell. 'Oh dear, he's not going to be happy when I tell him.'

'Ask at the surgery first. They might have forgotten to send it through.'

'Good idea. I'll go there now.' With any luck that was what had happened, and she could pop straight back to the pharmacy with the prescription.

There was a small queue at the surgery, and as Freya waited in line to speak to the receptionist, she glanced around curiously. She hadn't been here since she was a teenager and was intrigued to see that it had gone hi-tech, with an automated signing-in system and another screen directing patients to the various appointment rooms.

It took a while, but she eventually reached the head of the queue. 'I wonder if you could help?' she began. 'My father asked me to collect his prescription from the pharmacy, but it isn't there. Would you have any idea what's happened to it?'

'I'll take a look for you now. What's his name?'

Freya told her, along with his address and date of birth, then waited anxiously.

The receptionist studied her computer for a moment, the mouse clicking as she moved around the screen. 'Is it for his Parkinson's meds?' she asked, without looking up.

'Sorry, his what?'

'Tablets for his Parkinson's. There's a note on here to say that the doctor wants to see him to review his meds since his fall.'

'Parkinson's?' Freya was confused.

This time the woman did look up, speaking slowly, her voice raised as though Freya was hard of hearing. 'Parkinson's disease? The doctor wants to see him before he'll issue another prescription. Would you like to make an appointment now?'

Freya's brain had gone numb. She'd heard what the receptionist had said, but she was unable to process it.

'Parkinson's disease?' she asked again.

'Yes, your father— *Oh!*' The woman's eyes widened and her face paled. 'You didn't *know*?'

Mutely, Freya shook her head.

'Oh, God, I'm so sorry. I don't know what to say.' She looked distraught as she eased herself out of her seat. 'I'd better fetch the practice manager.' She took a few steps, then looked back. 'I really am sorry. I should never— Oh, God.'

Freya waited, in a daze. Her mouth was dry, but her palms were damp, and there was an ache in her chest.

Parkinson's disease?

Snippets, like short videos and snapshots, kaleidoscoped across her mind's eye: the way he'd glossed over the fall; the way he was visibly uncomfortable whenever she spoke to a member of the medical profession; his continual insistence that she should return to London and that he could manage on his own. Her father hadn't wanted her to know. *He'd deliberately kept it from her.*

But other people knew. The medical staff at the surgery and the hospital, obviously. The pharmacist knew and probably the rest of the staff there. And the people from social services; did they also know? Is that why they'd been so insistent on her dad having a stairlift? But who else? Was her father's condition common knowledge in Duncoorie? Did *everyone* apart from her know that he had Parkinson's?

'Ms Sinclair?' A woman in her forties with a severe bob and horn-rimmed glasses emerged from a side door. Behind the counter, the receptionist hovered, wringing her hands and biting her lip.

'I'm Helen Barclay, the practice manager. Would you like to follow me? We can have a chat in private.' She led Freya into a treatment room and closed the door.

Freya stared at her wordlessly.

'I understand you weren't aware of your father's condition,' Ms Barclay said, sitting down at the desk. 'Please, take a seat.'

Freya remained standing.

The woman nodded to herself and pursed her lips. 'I'm sorry you found out this way. It must be a shock.'

'You could say that.'

'Kayleigh should never have disclosed that to you. Patient confidentiality is a major concern. On behalf of her and the practice, please accept our apologies. She is distraught, as you can imagine. Of course, if you feel you're not able to accept our apologies and wish to take matters further, you have the right to complain to the—'

'How long has he had it?' Freya broke in. She didn't give a toss about Helen Barclay's concern that the practice had disclosed confidential information, or that she might put in a formal complaint. Freya's only concern was her father.

The practice manager took a deep breath. 'I'm sorry, but I can't tell you that. Patient confidentiality—'

Freya barked out an incredulous laugh. 'You've got to be kidding!'

'I really *am* sorry, but two wrongs won't make a right. You need to discuss this with Mr Sinclair.'

Without another word, Freya turned on her heel and left. She heard her name being called but didn't stop. She had to get out of there now, before she broke down.

She began walking, not caring where her feet took her; all she knew was that she couldn't go home. Not yet.

Freya eventually found herself at the loch, at the very spot where she and her father had scattered her mother's ashes. It seemed fitting.

Perching on a rock, she sat staring out across the water. While she didn't know much about Parkinson's disease, she knew it was serious. She also knew that she needed to learn about it fast, before she confronted her father.

Freya took out her phone and after finding a reputable website, she began to read. What she learnt rocked her to the core. Phrases circled in her head like crows over carrion: 'progressive disorder of the nervous system…';

'causes parts of the brain to weaken and die…'; 'gets worse over time…'

The list of symptoms was long and varied, but she began to pick out the ones her father was displaying and that she'd ignored or had put down to other things, such as the tremor in his hand, and the way he'd slowed down significantly, his frequently blank expression, his sleep issues, the tendency to lean forward as he walked, and his small, hurrying steps that she'd attributed to his fractured hip. His occasional memory lapses and irritability, she had assumed to be a result of frustration at being incapacitated, and resentment that he was dependent on her. And there was the fall itself. People with Parkinson's disease had a higher risk of falling.

The realisation that he'd probably suffered falls previously, although less serious, hit her. The realisation that he would undoubtedly suffer more falls in the future made her want to cry.

The hope she'd had that he would regain his mobility in a matter of weeks was dashed against the rocks of her newfound knowledge. His fractured hip was mending well, but his world was falling apart and had been for some time. Parkinson's wasn't something that developed suddenly. He'd had it for a while and he'd kept it from her.

Her stomach clenched, bile rising into her throat, and she leant to the side and vomited, the spasms tearing through her until she was completely empty.

Weak and drained, she stared bleakly at the mess and began to cry.

Burying her face in her hands, great heaving sobs burst out of her, grief twisting her gut and stabbing her in the heart. But her grief for her father was soiled and stained by grief for herself – because she knew now that she could never leave him, could never leave Skye. She'd be stuck here looking after him, and her selfishness in thinking of her own needs and wants, when her father had been prepared to face this awful disease alone, appalled and shamed her.

Her dad had kept it from her because he knew she'd sacrifice her own dreams to care for him – *and he hadn't wanted her to.*

Freya pulled her knees up to her chest, wrapped her arms around her legs, and with tears pouring down her face, she howled her anguish to the uncaring sea.

She cried until she didn't think she had any tears left, then she cried some more.

Chapter 25

Millpond days, when the waters of the loch were glass-smooth and mirror-clear, happened only occasionally, and today was one of them. With no wind, and the tide in that brief hiatus between being fully in and before it began to turn again, there was hardly a ripple.

Mack slowed the boat as he steered it nearer to the shore and when he deemed it to be close enough, he cut the engine. It would soon start to drift, but for a minute or two they could enjoy the peace. There was at least ten metres of water beneath the *Sea Serpent*'s keel, yet the pebbly seabed was clearly visible, and the reflections of the hillsides above the loch could have been painted on its still surface.

It was a perfect day for being out on the boat, and Mack's passengers were loving it.

The calm of the water was echoed in their hushed tones, only broken by the calls of glaucous gulls overhead, and the unexpected snort of a seal as it blew out water from its nostrils after it poked its sleek head above the surface to stare at them.

Mack leant casually against the cabin door, his arms folded, his eyes resting briefly on the faces of his passengers as they snapped away furiously, before automatically scanning his surroundings to check for other craft, the sky, the tide and the location of his vessel in relation to the shore.

A figure caught his attention.

A woman was sitting hunched on the rocks. Straightening, he moved to the port side and gripped the gunwale as he leant forward and squinted, trying to make out her out.

It was Freya, he was certain of it.

Tempted as he was to shout and wave to attract her attention, he held himself in check. His passengers didn't need him shattering their peace, and since the excursion was for their benefit…

What was she doing? She had her face in her hands and was rocking gently back and forth. Or was the slight roll of the boat making it seem that way?

The seal slipped below the surface and Mack sensed his passengers becoming restless. Nevertheless, he didn't move. Although he couldn't put his finger on it, he had a feeling something was wrong.

A flurry of exclamations distracted him and he glanced around to see all nine of the passengers peering over the starboard side.

Mack gave Angus a questioning look.

'Sea eagle,' Angus told him, and the boat fell silent once more as the bird's unmistakable cry pierced the air, panicking the gulls.

Mack understood why. The eagles were magnificent, truly awe-inspiring. Indiscriminate and opportunistic hunters, they would take whatever they could get, whether it be fish, eels, small mammals or birds. No wonder the gulls were alarmed, although their cries sounded more like a human cry of anguish than an alarm call.

The realisation that the gulls had fled and that the cry was actually coming from the woman on the shore struck him simultaneously.

Without stopping to think, Mack untied his boots and pulled his T-shirt over his head.

'Skip, what are you doing?'

Taking his wallet, phone and keys out of his pockets, he shoved them at his second-in-command, and climbed onto the gunwale, saying, 'Freya's in trouble. Take the helm and finish the trip. I'll see you back at the quay.'

'Mack, you can't—'

The rest of Angus's sentence was lost as Mack hit the water, diving in head first, his arms outstretched. When he broke the surface, he began to swim, cutting through the water with strong, clean strokes as he kicked for the shore.

It wasn't too far, no more than a football pitch away, but he was breathing hard by the time he felt pebbles beneath his feet. Quickly he waded out, splashing through the shallows, ignoring the sharp rocks, his focus on Freya. He could hear her crying, her sobs cutting him to the quick, shredding his heart. He'd do anything, *anything*, to make them stop, to take away whatever was causing her so much distress.

Praying that nothing had happened to Vinnie, Mack hurried towards her, calling, 'Freya! Freya!' and when she looked up, the pain in her eyes and the expression on her face tore him in two.

'What's wrong?' he demanded. 'Is it your dad?'

'What?' She was gazing at him blankly, her eyes brimming with tears, her cheeks and nose red from crying. Never had she looked more beautiful. And never had he wanted to take someone else's pain away as much as he wanted to shoulder hers.

He was desperate to hold her in his arms, but she continued to stare at him as though he were a stranger.

Inexplicably, her gaze hardened. 'Did *you* know?'

'Did I know what?' He lowered himself gingerly down beside her, then flinched as she edged away.

'About my dad?'

She wasn't making sense. 'Freya, I don't know what you're talking about.'

'His Parkinson's,' she spat. 'Did you know?'

'Parkinson's?'

'He's got Parkinson's disease and he didn't bloody tell me.'

Mack shook his head slowly. 'No, I didn't know. How long has he—?'

'No bloody idea. The damned GP surgery wouldn't tell me anything.' She barked out a bitter laugh. 'They should have, considering I only found out because the receptionist slipped up big time.'

'What does your dad say?'

Another laugh. It ended on a sob.

He inched closer, and this time she didn't move away. He desperately wanted to comfort her but feared she might reject him.

'I haven't spoken to him,' she muttered.

At the risk of getting his head bitten off, he said gently, 'Don't you think you should?'

Freya rounded on him, her eyes flashing fury. 'Don't you think he should have told me? I shouldn't have had to find out like this.'

Mack took a deep breath. 'I expect he didn't want to worry you.'

'Do you know anything about Parkinson's?'

'Not a lot,' he admitted.

Freya stared up at the sky, blinking hard. 'It's a progressive, degenerative disease and it's probably why he fell.' Tears trickled down her face. 'He isn't going to get better; he's going to get worse. And the stupid old bugger didn't tell me because he knew what I would do. What I'm going to do.'

'Which is?'

'Stay here and look after him. For however long it takes, no matter what it takes.' Her tears turned into noisy sobs, her body shaking with the force of them, and Mack gathered her to him.

It was as he held her tight, her damp face on his shoulder, that he understood that she wasn't going to leave Skye after all. She was going to stay in Duncoorie.

And to his shame, his heart soared with the hope that maybe, given time, she might come to love him the way he loved her.

—

Freya paused outside Jean's door as Mack was about to go inside. After her crying jag had eased, he'd walked back home with her, and she hoped his mother had some dry clothes he could fit into.

'I'm sorry I snapped at you,' she said, noticing the goosebumps speckling his arms and chest. His hair was still wet, and she could see a faint dusting of salt on his skin. He must be freezing.

'It's OK.'

'You didn't have to jump in. I wasn't in any danger.'

'You were sobbing your heart out,' he replied. 'Was I supposed to ignore it?'

'Are you sure you won't let me drive you home?'

'I'm sure. Mum won't mind taking me, although she will be asking loads of questions. What should I tell her?'

'The truth. There's been enough of a cover-up already.'

'Don't be too hard on your dad. He did it for the best of reasons.'

That was what Freya was finding so difficult to take: the knowledge that her father would have struggled on so that she could have sailed off into the sunset, blissfully unaware that he was so ill.

She placed a hand on Mack's chest and reached up to kiss his cheek. 'Thank you.'

'I didn't do anything.'

'You did. I'd probably still be sitting on that rock and feeling sorry for myself, when it's my dad I should feel sorry for.'

He stroked her face, his finger wiping away a stray tear. 'If you need me, call. Day or night.'

She pressed her lips together and nodded, then turned to leave. It was time she faced her father.

He was in the sitting room. The TV was off and so was the radio. The air was thick with silence, and she didn't know how to break it.

He didn't look at her, but his face told her that he knew what had happened. He'd aged ten years in the couple of hours that she'd been out, and it broke her heart.

Moving slowly, she sat on the arm of the chair opposite. He shot her a glance, then hastily looked away. He looked cowed, defeated, and the tremor in his hand was worse than ever.

The silence stretched between them, a physical thing, a barrier that neither appeared to want to cross. But one of them had to make the first move.

'I didn't manage to pick up your tablets,' she said.

'I know. The surgery phoned.'

'They said you need to make an appointment for a review, before they'll issue you with another prescription.'

'I've got an appointment this afternoon. Five fifteen.' The tremor intensified, and he clasped that hand with his good one. Although it mightn't be good for much longer, from what she'd read.

'I'm coming with you,' she said.

He hung his head. 'I thought you might.'

'I've got so many questions.'

'I expect you have.'

'I understand why you didn't tell me, Dad, but you must have known I'd find out sooner or later.' Her voice shook.

'If I hadn't fallen—'

'But you did,' she interrupted. 'Almost definitely because of the Parkinson's.'

There was a hint of belligerence as he retorted, 'That doesn't mean I'll have another.'

'It probably does. You know that as well as I do.'

'Since when did you become an expert?'

'Since the receptionist at my doctor's surgery let slip that my dad has a disease he's been keeping secret from me,' she retorted sharply.

He swallowed, his Adam's apple bobbing up and down, and she suspected he was trying not to cry.

Freya slid off the arm of the chair and sank to the floor by his feet. 'I'm so sorry, Dad. I don't mean to be sharp with you, but it's been a bit of a shock. It'll take a while for it to sink in.' She laid her head on his lap. 'We'll get through this. I'm not going anywhere, I promise.'

'I didn't tell you because I didn't want you to waste your life. I still don't. Look at me, Freya.'

She lifted her head, her heart in tatters as she saw the tears running down his cheeks.

He said, 'You can't let me hold you back. You've been given a wonderful opportunity; you can't give it up for me. I won't let you.'

Of course she had to give it up. What else could she do? There was no other option. He was her father and she loved him, and that was that.

—

'You silly, silly boy!' Mack's mother scolded as she handed him two warm fluffy towels. 'Take those shorts off and I'll put them in the wash.'

'I haven't got time for that. I've got to get to the quay.'

'You won't be going anywhere if you catch your death of cold.'

Mack rolled his eyes. 'I'm used to getting wet. A drop of sea water isn't going to kill me!'

Jean tutted. 'Diving over the side into the loch might have.'

'I'm a good swimmer,' he replied, placing one towel on the kitchen chair to sit on and rubbing his hair with the other.

'It was still a silly thing to do. Parkinson's, you say?'

'That's right.'

'And his daughter didn't know anything about it?'

'Not a thing.'

'I can't make up my mind whether he's mad or a martyr. How did he think he'd get away with it?'

Mack shrugged. It had been a gutsy thing to do, even if the old fella hadn't had a hope in hell of carrying it off. And Mack couldn't help thinking that Vinnie was incredibly selfless.

'It was sheer bad luck that he didn't,' he said.

'Humph. She would have found out eventually.'

'But maybe not for months.'

'True. You just can't tell with that disease,' Jean said. 'Maxine Morris's brother has it, but you'd never guess unless you knew him, yet Mrs Semple who used be in my knitting club went downhill fast. Pneumonia killed her in the end, but don't tell me that Parkinson's didn't have a lot to do with it.' She sighed loudly. 'I'm guessing Freya won't be going to New York now. She can hardly take him with her – she'll never be able to afford the medical bills. It's such a shame. He's so proud of her. Will he go to London to live, do you think?'

'She intends to stay here, in Duncoorie.'

Jean sighed again. 'That might be for the best. Vinnie would hate London, and what with her job at the university and such, I get the impression she doesn't have a lot of time. He's forever telling me how busy she is. I suppose she could try to get carers in, for when she's at work, but it wouldn't be cheap. Here, put this on.' She handed Mack one of her dressing gowns.

He eyed it doubtfully. 'I'll give it a miss, thanks.' It wouldn't fit, for one thing, and for another, he'd look ridiculous. He'd be OK in the car for the short drive from her house to his.

She said, 'The other option would be to try to organise care for him here, so she can go back to London. Personally, I wouldn't, because you could have all and sundry in and out, and the list of things they *won't do* is four times as long as what they *will do*. Just ask Maxine, she's forever complaining about them. I'm sure they do their best, but…' She trailed off, before adding, 'It's probably better if Freya stays here to look after him.'

For Vinnie, maybe, but not for Freya. Her distress hadn't been solely for her father. Mack suspected some of it had been for herself. She was devastated for Vinnie, but she was also crushed that her chance of going to New York was scuppered. Not only that – she couldn't return to her life in London either. And what about her ceramics? He'd witnessed her quiet excitement as she'd worked, her satisfaction when she completed a piece. Without a studio and a kiln of her own, she was going to struggle and his heart ached for her.

His mother gave him a knowing look. 'How do you feel about Freya staying on Skye?'

Mack didn't answer. He was too busy thinking about studios, kilns and what he could do to help the woman he loved.

—

Freya sat on her bed in the dark, a sliver of moon visible through the skylight. She was weary to the bone, in both body and mind. Her emotions were fractured: one second she was calm, the next she wanted to scream. She'd managed to keep herself together for her father's sake, but now that he was in bed and she was on her own, she let her tears fall once more.

She cried until her throat was sore and her head ached, but eventually she calmed, and when she did, she opened her laptop and did what she had to do.

The email she sent to Jocasta Black was the hardest thing she'd ever had to write. The second email to the chancellor of the college, tendering her resignation effective from today, was the next.

All the things she needed to do flitted through her mind, but she had trouble grasping them and pinning them down, and even more difficulty summoning the energy to actually do them. The main thing was to pack up her apartment and decide whether to keep the flat on.

Would she go back to London one day, after her dad—

A sob caught in her throat. She didn't want to think about that. It would be years away, decades. Those years stretched ahead of her, the shape of them indistinct. She had to fill them in the only way she knew – she had to make her ceramics.

But what would she do for a studio? She could hardly expect to keep using Mack's byre, and neither could she impose on Rob at the castle. She would have to find somewhere to rent, somewhere either in Duncoorie or a short distance away. But that was easier said than done. There weren't many commercial properties around. And she couldn't pack up her studio in London until she had somewhere suitable for her wheel and kiln.

Dear God, this was going to be a logistical nightmare.

There was *one* thing she could do, though – she could start the ball rolling and look into how to go about having a stairlift installed, because before too long her poor old dad was going to need it.

Chapter 26

The gusty wind caught Freya's hair, tugging and snapping at it until it streamed out behind her like a pennant. She wished she'd thought to tie it up, but when Mack had messaged her to ask whether she fancied a walk to blow away the cobwebs – and told her that if she did, he'd be there in ten minutes – she'd only had time to change and make sure Dad didn't need anything.

Since Freya had discovered his secret, nearly a week ago, her father had been much less argumentative (though he still had his moments). He seemed to have resigned himself to the inevitability of her being there.

After a few more attempts at trying to persuade her that he could manage on his own if he had a bit of help with his shopping and maybe a cleaner to come in once a week, he'd finally stopped trying. Freya had made it clear that she wasn't going anywhere, and that nothing he could do or say would make her change her mind.

She'd continued to stand resolute, even when he'd threatened to go into a nursing home. As if she'd let *that* happen!

It wasn't a day for being out on the loch. The wind whipped the sea, churning the surface into racing white horses, as wave after white-topped wave battered the shore. Mack, understandably, had decided to cancel today's excursions.

He asked, 'How have you been? I haven't seen you all week.'

'Oh, you know… Taking one day at a time. Dad's improving slowly.'

'Not Vinnie. You. How are *you*?'

'Fine.' It was her stock response these days whenever anyone asked.

'I don't think you are,' he observed.

Freya squinted into the distance, ignoring the breathtaking view as she struggled to hold back unexpected and unwelcome tears. 'I will be,' she said eventually.

'I know you will.' Mack stopped walking and turned to face her. She stopped too and when he took hold of her hands, his touch sent tingles up her arms.

He was the one – the *only* – light in the twilight that her life had suddenly become, and even that glow was dim. Just because they'd shared some passionate kisses didn't mean he loved her. He liked her and he certainly fancied her, or he wouldn't have kissed her the way he had, but lust didn't equate to a relationship.

However, it was the quiet hope that love might blossom one day which had kept her going these past few days, that something positive might rise out of the ashes of her hopes and dreams for the future.

Mack was studying her intently, and she blushed under his scrutiny.

'Can I ask you something?' he said. 'If your dad didn't have Parkinson's, would you have definitely gone to America?'

'Yes.' She didn't hesitate. There was no question that she would. 'But he has and I'm not, so I don't want to dwell on what might have been. I can't afford the headspace. I've got too many other things to think about.'

'Such as?'

'How I'm going to earn a living, for a start. I need to work, but there's not much call for a ceramics professor on Skye, and the craft centre already has a resident potter.'

'I've seen your website – you sell things on there, don't you?'

'Yes, but I'm not sure as to its sustainability. I've always had a day job alongside.'

'Maybe it's time to take the plunge? Those pieces in the byre... They're beautiful, Freya.'

She hesitated. 'I could, I suppose, but I can't do it without a studio, and there's nothing suitable nearby. I thought about begging for some kiln time from Rob, but that wouldn't be fair on either of us. And even if I do manage to find a studio, I keep asking myself whether there'd be any point. All my contacts are in London, as are all the galleries.'

'Are you saying that you're thinking of giving up ceramics?'

'Maybe. I don't know. To be honest, I can't think straight at the minute.'

He was gazing intently at her, his eyes searching hers, and she wished she knew what he was looking for.

'I've got a proposition for you,' he said, his voice low, his tone urgent. 'Don't say anything until you've heard me out. Promise?'

'OK, I won't say anything,' she promised.

But when he said, 'Angus, Graham and the others are a good bunch,' she nearly changed her mind. Where was he going with this?

Mack gave her a warning look, and she subsided.

'They took another excursion out on their own yesterday,' he continued. 'That's the fifth one this week – and you're wondering why I'm telling you this.'

Mindful of her promise, she merely nodded.

'I wanted to make sure the guys could manage without me most of the time.' He gave a wry chuckle. 'To be honest, they can manage without me *all* of the time, which is rather disappointing, because I thought I was indispensable.'

Freya couldn't resist. 'Why would you want them to manage without you?'

His eyes darkened, the blue turning to navy as he blurted, 'You've *got* to go to New York, Freya. If you don't, you'll be forever wondering what it might have led to. I'll look after your dad. That's what I'm trying to say. This is *your* time, Freya. I won't be putting my life on hold. I'll be doing much the same as I always do, just a bit less of it, that's all. I've been reading up on Parkinson's: it could be years before he needs full-time care. When his hip has healed, he probably won't be as mobile as he was before, and he mightn't be able to do all the things he once did, but that's where I'd come in. I'll do his shopping – actually, I'll *take* him shopping, because I expect he'd like to choose his own groceries. I'll do the things around the house he can't; I'll drive him to his doctor and hospital appointments; I'll—'

'Stop! Please, just stop. You can't.' She drew in a shaky breath, feeling like she'd been punched in the solar plexus. There wasn't enough air, despite the stiff breeze blowing across her face.

The whole thing was surreal. She must be hallucinating or dreaming.

But Mack didn't stop. 'I'm not suggesting you stay there forever. At some point, Vinnie will need more care than I'll be able to give him, but right now, he'll be fine. New York is only a flight away. You can come home for a couple of days whenever you want. Hell, I'll even bring him over to visit you.'

She shook her head. 'No, you can't. It's not right. Your boat, your...' She stopped, bewildered. 'You're offering to put *your* life on hold to care for *my* father, while I bugger off to the States?'

Mack hung his head and dropped his gaze. 'Yes.'

'I... I don't know what to say.' What *could* she say? The idea was preposterous. It was unthinkable. Her father was *her* responsibility, not Mack's.

He thought he'd got it all worked out and maybe he had, because he'd certainly done his research, but she couldn't possibly agree to it.

'No,' she said.

His head shot up. 'Please, you must.'

'Mack, if I were to go to the States, I'd want to give it my best shot. There'd be no half measures.'

'I understand.'

'It wouldn't be a short-term thing. I would be gone years, not months.'

'I expect nothing less.'

'You can't look after my father for that length of time. You're being ridiculous! What if you meet someone and fall in love?'

'I won't.'

'You can't possibly know that.'

'Believe me, Freya, I do. I'm in love with *you*. You're the only woman for me. If I can't have you, I don't want anyone else.'

Freya froze, her heart thudding. 'You *love* me?'

This was too much: finding out that her dad had a serious, debilitating disease and realising that she wouldn't go to New York, then now being told that she could go after all, if she wanted, and that the man who could make this happen was in love with her— She felt overwhelmed.

'I can't deal with this,' she said, backing away and shaking her head in disbelief. She turned on her heel, walking fast.

'Freya! Stop.'

She carried on walking.

He didn't try to follow. When he called after her, 'At least think about it,' she ignored him.

Hurrying home, she didn't want to think about it, but she thought about it anyway, because Mack was offering Freya her life back. He was giving her a way to escape this island for a second time. And the temptation to take it was so incredibly great.

'Freya, is that you?'

'Yes, Dad.' She hung her coat in the tiny cupboard under the stairs and kicked off her boots.

'I didn't expect you back so soon,' he called. He was in the sitting room, watching TV. 'Where did you go?'

'Not far, a walk down by the loch. Tea?' Hopefully, the time it took to make it would give her a few more minutes to compose herself, because she hadn't done a very good job of it on the way home.

She squeezed her eyelids shut, a pulse throbbing at her temple. Freya wished Mack hadn't said anything. But he had and now she couldn't stop thinking about it, her emotions swinging from hope to despair, from temptation to denial.

What should she do? What *could* she do? What was she brave enough to do?

It's too late, she told herself. She had already turned down the offer from the Black and White Art Academy. Jocasta Black wouldn't be amused if she sent another email telling her she'd changed her mind and would like the job after all.

But if Freya explained…?

Her dad appeared in the doorway, making her jump.

'I thought you were making a cup of tea?' he said, then he saw her face. 'Freya? What's wrong?'

'Mack is in love with me.' The words slipped out of her mouth before she could stop them.

'Is that all? I thought something awful had happened.'

'*You know?*' If Mack had spoken to her dad about this before—

She gasped. Had they cooked it up between them? She wouldn't put it past her dad to have talked Mack into this hare-brained scheme. No wonder her father had gone quiet lately; he'd been busy hatching this!

'I guessed,' Vinnie said. 'He looks at you the way you look at him.'

'What's that supposed to mean?'

'Me and your mother used to look at each other like that. You make a lovely couple.'

Freya slumped into a chair. 'He's got this idea.'

She worried at her lip, wondering if it was wise to tell her dad. If he hadn't been in on it before, he'd be all for it once he knew. She would hardly get an unbiased opinion. But she was so confused, she had to talk it over with someone, and this affected him too…

When she'd finished telling him, she waited for him to list all the reasons why she should agree to Mack's plan, but he didn't say a word.

Instead, he filled the kettle and took two mugs off the wooden tree. Today was one of his better days, the tremor in his hand barely noticeable and his gait less of a shuffle.

He waited until they had a cuppa in front of them before he spoke.

'Love is a funny thing,' he said. 'You can't make it happen, and you can't make it go away. It's just there. Sometimes it's the most beautiful thing in the world and it brings you more joy than you can ever imagine. And sometimes it brings you more pain than one person should ever have to bear.'

His eyes grew damp and Freya knew he was thinking about her mum. She reached across the table and clasped his hand, and he smiled tearily.

Clearing his throat, he carried on. 'Love is a precious gift; hold on to it as hard as you can. But holding on also means letting go. That's when you know it's true love. I love you with every fibre of my being, Freya. I want you to be happy. If that means letting you live the life you want to live, even if it is halfway across the world, so be it. It hurt to think of you so far away in London. It hurt not to see you every day. But that's nothing compared to the joy I feel knowing you're living your best life. If Mack loves you enough to let you go, then he loves you with all his heart. It's a rare thing, that kind of love.'

Freya sat there, tears trickling down her face.

Her father's words touched her soul; their truth was seared on her heart, and she knew what she had to do. There was only one option. Maybe there had only ever been one, but she'd had to leave Skye and come back to realise it.

Freya found Mack sitting on the lawn at the rear of his house. The reason she knew where he was, and the reason she didn't bother ringing the doorbell, was because he was playing The Rolling Stones at full volume again. The front door was unlocked, so she went inside. A bottle of whisky, half-full, sat on the worktop, and she grabbed it, along with a fresh tumbler, and took them outside.

Mack's eyes were closed, his head tilted back to rest on the same wooden lawn chair he'd sat in the last time she'd drunk whisky with him, and he was nursing another glass of pale amber.

After sitting down next to him, Freya poured herself a generous dram. There was no need to ration it: she wouldn't be driving anywhere and neither would she be walking.

Without opening his eyes, he turned the volume down.

'What are we drinking to?' he asked. His voice was gruff.

'The future.'

'And which future would that be?'

'The one where we spend the rest of our lives together.' She took a sip. It was seriously smooth whisky and she congratulated herself on her good taste.

Mack opened first one eye, then the other. A slow sexy smile spread across his face, his mouth quirking up on one side.

Without taking his gaze from her, he raised his glass. 'Before I drink this, I want to check a couple of details. One, are you or are you not going to America?'

'I'm not. I thought that was obvious.'

'Nothing is ever obvious when it comes to you, Freya, and I want to make sure of my facts. Second, would you like me to convert my byre into a pottery studio?'

She bit her lip. 'You know I would.'

'Good, that's settled.'

'Aren't you going to ask me anything else?'

'No, I don't think so. Should I?'

'You haven't asked me whether I love you.'

His eyes twinkled and he smiled that smile again, the one that warmed her from the inside out. 'Do you?'

'Yes. I love you with all my heart. I think I always have and I know I always will.'

Freya took the tumbler from his hand and placed it on the table. She was going to show Mack that she loved him with her heart, her body and her soul, and if it took all night…

Epilogue

January

Freya smoothed down the skirt of her dress, feeling self-conscious, despite every other person in the room (except for the serving staff) wearing tartan. The reason was twofold. Tonight was 25 January, Burns Night, and it was also the opening night of the first exhibition of her work in New York.

The exhibition was called *The Colours of Skye* (the title shamelessly stolen from Mhairi) and Freya's ceramics reflected the island's vibrant hues. Purple, salmon, pink, russet – the infinite shades of the sky, the loch, the mountains. She'd tried her best, but despite the accolades tonight, she knew she hadn't done them justice. Hers were muted in comparison. As she kept telling everyone, you had to see Skye for yourself to appreciate it.

A middle-aged couple blocked her view, and she smiled politely at them.

'Marvin and Patty Rokovitz,' the woman said, holding out a hand with a diamond ring the size of a cherry tomato on her middle finger. It couldn't possibly be real, could it? 'We're from Texas,' she added.

'Freya Sinclair, from Skye. Pleased to meet you.'

Mrs Rokovitz tinkled out a laugh. 'We know who you are, dear. Isn't this fabulous? You are so talented. I've already picked out the pieces I want.'

'That's very kind of you. And thank you so much for coming this evening,' Freya replied.

'Honey, I love your accent. I could listen to it all night. Marvin, we simply have to go to Scotland.' She turned back to Freya. 'I've got Scottish ancestors on my mother's side.'

'Then you should definitely come to Skye,' Freya urged.

'What month do you recommend?'

'Any time of the year is great, but I love summer best.'

'Summer it is, Marvin!' She giggled loudly again, and Freya guessed the woman had availed herself of the single malt that was being served instead of the usual champagne. There were also nibbles in the form of Scottish smoked salmon, haggis bites, Scotch eggs and shortbread, and bagpipe music played in the background. Thankfully, Jocasta had taken Freya's advice and hadn't hired a piper otherwise no one would have been able to hear themselves think.

Freya caught sight of Jocasta Black chatting with a group of men in suits, and Jocasta smiled at her and inclined her head. It was she who was responsible for Freya being here, and for the exhibition, and Freya was incredibly grateful. Mind you, Freya had been persuaded to give a series of guest lectures in return, so Jocasta wasn't hosting the exhibition entirely out of the goodness of her heart, and the Academy was also taking a generous commission on any sales.

'Gorgeous dress,' a woman in a short, red-checked skirt declared. 'Is it authentic?'

Freya hedged. 'It depends on what you mean by authentic.'

'Is it real tartan?'

'Yes, it is.' The material had been woven in a mill in the Scottish Borders. It was called 'Isle of Skye tartan', and although it wasn't associated with any clan, its soft purples and greens reflected the colours of the island. The fabric was heavy, and she was hot underneath its layers.

She searched the room again, looking for a tall man with golden hair. He, too, was wearing the Isle of Skye tartan, but considering his was a kilt, Freya assumed he wasn't in danger of overheating.

Spying him lurking in a corner, she made her way towards him, keeping her head down and hoping not to be waylaid.

His eyes lit up when he saw her, a broad smile illuminating his face. 'How are your tootsies? Hurting?'

She lifted the skirt of her long dress and showed him her boots. It had been his suggestion that she wore her Doc Martens tonight, since the length of the skirt meant they'd be hidden, and very grateful she was too.

'Where's Dad?' she asked.

Mack pointed.

Vinnie was sitting on one of the few chairs in the room, a crowd of people around him like courtiers around a throne.

'He's been telling stories of the selkie folk to anyone who'll listen,' Mack said. 'He's so proud of you. So am I. You make a decent pot.'

'Thanks,' she said wryly.

'I wouldn't want you to get too big-headed. You might get ideas.'

'Such as?'

'Refusing to take a walk with me in Times Square.' He held out his hand.

'*Now?*'

'Why not?'

'What about Jocasta? She won't be happy if I bugger off. And what about my dad? I can't abandon him.'

'I'm not suggesting we stay out all night – just for a minute, or two.'

'Why?'

'It's snowing. I've been told there's something magical about snow in Times Square.'

'Just for a few minutes?'

'A few minutes,' he confirmed.

When they stepped outside, fat white flakes were drifting in the air, and Freya lifted her face to the sky, letting them fall onto her heated cheeks. She would soon become chilled, but for now she was enjoying the moment.

Mack was right, it *was* magical. She found it hard to believe she was actually here. Far from Freya's career being over, it was flourishing. Not only that – her dad was doing OK, the progression of the disease slow (for now at least) and she was thrilled he was well enough to accompany her to New York. He was thrilled too, and the delight in his eyes had brought tears to her own.

Then there was Mack: her rock, her soulmate, her heart.

And at this moment her rock was behaving like one, because he was sitting on the ground and—

No, not *sitting*. He was on one knee, and he'd managed to gather quite a crowd while she'd been gazing up at the snowflakes and the bright lights.

'I was going to propose on Skye,' he said, 'but your dad told me I should do it here, in Times Square.'

'Do you always do what my dad tells you to do?'

'Only when it comes to you. He loves you. As do I. Freya Sinclair, will you do me the honour of being my wife?'

The ring he was offering her was purple, like the heather, an amethyst set in platinum, and to either side were small emeralds. Purple, green and white – the colours of Skye, the colours of the tartan she wore, and the colours of the very first bowl that she had made in the byre.

'Yes, a thousand times yes!' she cried, and when bagpipes began to play a familiar song, she joined in with the chorus, singing, '*Over the sea to Skye…*'

Skye was her home, her heart, her life. It was where she belonged – by the side of the man she loved.

Acknowledgements

When I write an acknowledgement, I feel a bit like I'm standing at the podium receiving an Oscar and wanting to thank anyone and everyone I've ever met. So I'm going to start with the usual suspects who deserve to be thanked at the end of every book, even if I do forget to do an acknowledgement page (which sometimes happens!).

I'll start with my family – you know who you are, so I'm not going to list you all, except for the dog, because she always shows an interest even if she doesn't have a clue what I'm saying. Then there's Catherine, Valerie and Simone – thanks, my lovelies, for your friendship and support. And Emily, of course, my wonderful editor at Canelo, for reading the book at least twenty-six times and making it better each time.

But this is where I need to thank someone else: Mr Nicklin, my art teacher when I was in school (so many years ago) for introducing me to clay and not laughing at the result, even if my vase looked weirdly like a bottom. My mother pointed that out when I proudly brought it home. She still has it, but I'm not sure whether that's because she likes abstract nude buttocks, or despite it looking like an abstract nude backside. She told me I can have it back any time I like. I'm not sure I want it…

So, back to Mr Nicklin. Huge thanks to him and all the other teachers and mentors who pass on their skill and knowledge, enabling the rest of us to become creators of our own masterpieces.